I0723597

CAN'T FIGHT IT

LESSONS LEARNED
BOOK 3

ALLIE WINTERS

WWW.SMARTYPANTSROMANCE.COM

COPYRIGHT

CONTENT WARNING

Please be aware this story contains mature themes including mentions of home invasions and assault.

CHAPTER ONE

TESSA

"YOU EXCITED ABOUT TODAY?"

I stare at my toaster, my reflection comically distorted in the dented stainless steel. How long do Pop-Tarts take to cook, anyway?

"Tessa?"

"Oh, yeah." I mentally shake my head, tuning back in to Mia on the phone. "Just trying not to psych myself out too much."

"You and Joel will do great," she assures me. "Dr. Price loves your study."

Easy for her to say. She already has a published one under her belt.

No, that's not fair. Mia's been nothing but helpful. She helped me design the experiment, for Christ's sake. I should be kissing her boots.

"You really think he likes it?" I ask as my Pop-Tarts finally pop up. I snatch them from the toaster and drop them onto a plate, sucking on my burned fingertips. How do I manage to do that every time?

"He wouldn't have approved it if he didn't. Besides, even Tyler said what you guys have is good. And you know he doesn't say things just to be nice."

Now that does make me feel better. Her boyfriend pulls no punches when it comes to the Stress Lab.

I shoulder my backpack and grab my keys off the kitchen counter, stuffing them in my back pocket before I pick up my water bottle and plate. Breakfast will have to be in the car if I'm going to make it to my Abnormal Psych class with enough time to review my notes before our quiz today. It's only the third week into the semester and the pace is already picking up.

As I near the front door, the distinctive jingle of keys has my steps slowing, though. "Ugh."

"What, Tyler?" Mia asks.

"No, no. My neighbor." I peek through the door's peephole. Yep, it's him. "I don't like being outside when he's around."

"What's wrong with him?"

I sigh, studying him through the warped lens. That's the thing. I can't pinpoint any one issue that sets off my internal alarm. "He's... intimidating."

Too tall. Ridiculously muscled. Shoulder-length blond hair and overgrown beard that reminds me of some Viking warlord ready to pillage. Plus, in the month since I've moved in, I've never once seen him smile.

Not that I've been looking.

"Did he threaten you?"

My lips twitch at the hardness in her tone, as if she's prepared to come over here and avenge me. "No. I can't explain it, but there's something about him that seems... dangerous. I'd just rather avoid him."

And after everything I've been through, danger is the one thing I'll never invite into my life. It's better to play it safe.

Through the peephole, he pauses before leaving, swiveling in the direction of my door.

My heart falters in its rhythm. He can't see through here, right? No, don't be ridiculous.

Everything in me freezes, though, as he knocks on my door, his broad shoulders encased in a scuffed leather jacket filling the peephole's view.

I cover my mouth to contain my gasp, forgetting that I'm holding my plate of Pop-Tarts in that hand, which promptly clatters to the floor. Wonderful.

"I know you're in there," he says, his deep voice making me jump.

Crap. Crap. Triple crap.

I push aside my ruined breakfast, my stomach rumbling in annoyance, and undo the chain lock, opening the door a crack. His gaze bores into me, the stormy gray of his eyes unexpected in their intensity.

"Just so you know, when you're in the hallway, you can hear everything inside. The doors aren't soundproof."

Heat washes over me, climbing up my neck and over my cheeks until my resemblance to a tomato is uncanny. So that means he heard me tell Mia I find him intimidating, dangerous, and purposely avoid him?

"I… um… okay." My voice is a faint breath of air, hardly qualifying as a response, but I'm in no mental state to reply. What would I even say that could make things better?

His gaze lingers over me for a moment, further intensifying the heat, then he walks away without a backward glance, his footfalls heavy on the concrete.

I can't move as I watch him stalk into the parking lot and straddle a black motorcycle, the rev of the engine as it kicks on finally startling me into slamming the door.

"Tessa?"

I clue back in, remembering Mia's still on the line, and race to my bedroom, shutting and locking the door behind me, as if that makes any difference when he's already gone.

"Did you hear that?" I ask, practically breathless with how hard my heart is beating.

"Yeah… I couldn't help it. That was your neighbor?"

I nod, then realize she can't see me. "Yep. Just my luck, right?"

Better to joke about it. Make light of the situation. It doesn't have to be serious. Just because he overheard me say that doesn't mean he's mad. Doesn't mean I've made an enemy. Doesn't mean he'll retaliate.

I'm safe here. This apartment is safe. Nothing bad will happen.

"Listen, I have to go," I tell her before she can say anything. "I'll talk to you in the Stress Lab later."

"Yeah, okay. Text me if you need to."

"Thanks," I whisper as I end the call, my eyes squeezing shut. Making friends with her last semester in one of our Psych classes had been a stroke of luck. God knows I have hardly anyone else to rely on.

I take deep breaths, consciously slowing down my heart rate, and progressively tense and relax my muscles, going through the familiar routine until I'm calmer. In a way, I guess it's helpful to go through the process myself before I guide others through it later today during the study.

Heading into the minuscule kitchen area, I rip open a new package of Pop-Tarts, not bothering to heat them this time before stuffing one in my mouth in an attempt to distract myself.

Why would I think it's a good idea to announce all that stuff right near the door? It's not like I could even use the excuse of saying I was talking about someone else. I outright said *my neighbor*, and there are only the two of us on the ground floor.

What the hell am I going to say the next time I run into him? Yeah, I've successfully avoided him so far, but it's bound to happen at some point.

No, what I need to focus on right now is getting to class and preparing for my quiz, not run-ins with my neighbor.

No matter how awkward they may be.

———

Chocolate melts on my tongue, creamy and sweet, and I quickly grab a second cube of fudge from the container Mia holds out to me, sampling another bite. "I don't understand what you do to make it so good," I mutter around a mouthful. "And how you just happened to have a tub of fudge on the day I need it most."

Her lips tip up at the corners. "Well, I made it to celebrate the first day of your study. It's a coincidence you need it for… other reasons, too."

I wave off her enigmatic statement, not wanting to relive my embarrassment for the trillionth time today. It was the only thing running through my mind during my two classes earlier. I probably bombed my quiz.

"Don't tell anyone. Please. If I don't talk about it, it's like it never happened."

"Right," she drawls. "Mum's the word, then."

I nod, licking the remaining chocolate off my fingers as my lab partner, Joel, arrives and slings his backpack on the floor. His plaid button-up is rumpled as usual, brown hair messy after he rakes a hand through it.

"Whatcha got there, Mia?" he asks, studying the container with curiosity.

"Fudge. Don't eat too much or you'll get sick."

"Me?" He holds a hand to his chest, faux affronted. "Never."

I bite my lip to hold back a smile, remembering how nauseated he'd made himself after eating too many desserts at our holiday party. "Seriously," I tell him. "We don't want a repeat of last month. Everything needs to go perfect today."

"Don't get your panties in a wad," he mutters, already chowing down on a piece. "Trust me. I'm completely prepared. How about you?"

I take a deep breath and recite my spiel. "Scalp, face, jaw, neck, shoulders, chest, arms, hands, stomach, back, butt, legs, feet."

He grins, chocolate all over his two front teeth. "Now say that three times fast."

Mia hands the container of fudge to me. "Be responsible with this," she says with mock seriousness. "And text me later to let me know how everything goes."

I can't tell if she means it as a friend or because as a senior, Dr. Price assigned her to be our point person to reach out to if there's any trouble with our study. Tyler is the point person for the two other juniors running their study this semester.

Either way, I nod, faking my confidence in front of her. "I've got this." I waggle my thumb between me and Joel. "We've got this," I amend.

She smiles. "I know you do. And I told you your last guy of the day is Tyler's gym buddy, right?"

I grab my roster off the desk. "Austin? I'll be extra nice to him."

"Do the Stress Lab proud," she says, exiting the room.

Without her, my faith wanes until Joel rests a steady hand on my shoulder, his gaze earnest. "You're sure you're okay?"

I let out a slow breath, releasing the tension lingering in my shoulders. "Yeah, of course."

"I'll be right next door if you need help."

I shrug off his hand, rolling my eyes as I adjust the participant's chair. "Like I'm going to interrupt your meditation session."

"I'm just saying you can if you have to."

"And mess up the study? Yeah, right. We've only got a fifteen-minute cushion before Noah and Chris need our rooms."

He blows out a breath, sticking his hands in his pockets. "Listen, I was thinking afterward we could—"

There's a knock on the door and then Kelly, the Stress Lab's receptionist, pokes her head in. "Your first participant is here, Joel."

He nods, but makes no motion to leave. "Great. Thanks."

I pick up my script for one last run-through before my own participant shows up. "Were you going to say something?" I ask, half my mind already on running through the applied relaxation sequence I'm teaching everyone today.

"Oh, um, no." He shuffles his feet long enough to have me glancing at him, nervousness crossing his features. "I'll catch you later."

He speeds past me and out the door. Must be more anxious than he let on.

I finish going over my notes and head into the lobby to wait by Kelly's desk, smoothing my palms down the front of my jeans.

I'll do fine. This is what I've been waiting for. Dr. Price picked two studies out of all the juniors who applied and mine is one of them. That has to count for something.

The nerves leave me as a girl I recognize from a class last semester walks in with a smile on her face. That's why the name looked familiar on the roster sheet.

I lead her down the hall and into the room, going over the informed consent form and then guiding her through the procedure of progressive muscle relaxation.

This is where I'm in my element. I don't know why I was so nervous earlier.

The time flies as I run through my first five participants, my mind relaxed as I head back down the hall to wait for my last one of the day. I hope Joel's sessions have gone as well as mine.

As I reach the waiting area, though, the loose, easy feeling inside me tightens as I spot a familiar head of dark blond hair turned away from me.

No. There's no way.

Lots of guys have artfully messy hair that exact shade. With the same broken-in leather jacket. And the same impossibly broad shoulders. It's a coincidence. Has to be.

"A-Austin," I croak out, my voice all high and squeaky.

It can't be him. Mia said it was Tyler's friend from the gym. Mia goes to that gym, too. That's another connection I can't afford if it turns out he's…

He stands, all six feet plus of him, steel-toed work boots heavy on the carpet as he pivots in my direction, that flinty gray gaze finally lifting to meet mine. Surprise flitters over his face for the briefest of seconds before he shuts it down, stoic again as he crosses the room toward me.

It's him. Definitely him. My neighbor. The one I unwittingly insulted this morning.

Crap. Crap. Triple crap.

CHAPTER TWO

AUSTIN

IS it wrong that I find the tiniest bit of satisfaction in her discomfort? She insulted me this morning, after all.

Intimidating. Dangerous. Some might take the words as a compliment, but it was clear she didn't intend them that way.

Then again, it's nothing I haven't heard before.

Her mouth gapes open awkwardly, pink spreading across her cheeks like wildfire until she turns, her dark hair falling over her shoulder to shield her features as she strides down the hall.

Am I supposed to follow her? She called my name, so it must be her I'm meeting with.

And I sure as hell won't be the one to speak first.

She stops in front of a door, her hand pausing on the knob before opening it, and waits until we're both in the room before she speaks.

"Look, I'm…" She releases a breath, peeking over at me through the curtain of her hair. "That was awful of me to say earlier. I'm sorry."

I shrug, appreciating her apology even if it's unnecessary. "You can think whatever. Doesn't affect me any."

Since she moved in a month ago, she's scurried away any time I've remotely come near, either racing into her apartment or the Kia in the parking lot with the rear fender that's about to fall off. I got the message pretty quickly.

"No, that's not fair to you. I don't even know you." She picks at her thumbnail, studying it. "I've been letting some… past experiences color my thinking."

I stay silent, sensing she has more to say.

"Sometimes big guys scare me," she mumbles, barely audible.

Well, shit. How am I supposed to respond to that?

Tugging at the ends of my beard, I'm reminded I need to trim it soon. "I didn't mean to make you uncomfortable." Taking a step back, I glance behind me at the door. "I can go if—"

"No." She reaches forward, her delicate fingers unable to completely encircle my wrist.

She snatches her hand back just as quickly, holding it to her chest as if I've hurt her.

"This is my issue, not yours. I'm only explaining why I haven't really been friendly as a neighbor. It has nothing to do with you personally."

I'm not sure how else to take it, but whatever she says. "Listen, I signed up for this study as a favor to Tyler, but if it's not going to work out—"

"No, it will," she interrupts. "You don't have to leave." She merely holds out a hand this time, not willing to risk touching me again.

Message received.

"Why don't we go over the informed consent form?" she says brightly, her smile forced.

I sigh, tugging off my jacket before sitting in the chair she indicates, ignoring the way her eyes widen as I push up the sleeves of my henley. It's getting ready to snow outside, but it's a lot warmer in this office.

She positions herself behind the desk, a clear division between us. "First, did you have any questions about the paperwork we emailed to you?"

"I didn't get to it." It had all been a bunch of legalese I couldn't fully decipher. Maybe she can explain it face-to-face better.

She blinks at me for a moment before jumping into a clearly rehearsed spiel. "Well, it's a six-week study looking at how different forms of non-physical stress management impact athletes. You'll get paid seventy-five dollars a week, made payable at the three-week and six-week mark, which is dependent upon your attendance in the Stress Lab weekly and completion of the exercises we'll go over."

Exercises? Tyler didn't say anything about that. At least the money part sounds good.

"The two main stress management techniques we're studying are applied relaxation and meditation," she continues. "We've randomly split the participants and you're in the applied relaxation group."

Sure. Whatever.

She picks up a handful of papers off the desk, shuffling through them. "What kind of, um, athlete are you?"

"Boxer."

Her gaze rakes me up and down, giving me a once-over. Based on her earlier admission, I shouldn't read into it at all, but something about it has a tingle racing down my spine, the baser part of me ready and at attention.

Down boy.

The girl made it clear she couldn't be less interested. And if she was the one that wrote that paperwork, she's obviously way out of my league in the smarts department.

She looks down at her papers. "I didn't realize the university offered that sport."

"I have no idea. I don't go here."

"Oh. I guess I assumed."

"Yeah, well…" I rub the back of my neck, not liking this turn in conversation. "I never went to college."

She's quiet for a moment. "That's not a big deal," she says softly. "Lots of people don't."

I nod, not having anything to say about it.

"Anyway, today I'm going to teach you progressive muscle relaxation. You'll practice it daily on your own throughout the week and next Tuesday when you come back, we'll go over a shorthand version of it."

Okay, that sounds more involved than what Tyler made it seem like. "What's, uh… muscle whatever you said?"

"Progressive muscle relaxation. We'll contract and relax different muscle groups of the body, with the goal being to reduce somatic anxiety symptoms."

I cross my arms over my chest. What the hell is she talking about?

She must notice my blank look because she immediately says, "Sorry, I got used to using all these technical terms when writing the IRB application. I forget they mean nothing in the real world. Basically, what we'll do is learn a tool you can use to lessen the physical effects of stress."

"Sure," I grunt. "Sounds good."

She goes over some form with me, spouting stuff about *methodologies* and *confidentiality*, but I can't keep track of it all, and sign my name at the bottom when she's finished. Pretty sure I'm not signing away my life's rights or anything.

She hands me two other pieces of paper. "Before I forget, here's the baseline questionnaire you'll need to fill out tonight. You can bring it back next Tuesday." She pauses. "Or I guess you could bring it to me next door." She gives a weak chuckle, then stops when she sees I'm not laughing. "And this has the instructions for the progressive muscle relaxation sequence you'll do at home twice a day."

I place the papers on the edge of the desk. What did I get myself involved with?

"So, if you're ready, we can start now."

"Uh, sure."

She dims the lights and tells me to sit back in my chair. "For each muscle group, you'll tense as you breathe in for five seconds, hard but not to the point of pain. Then as you exhale, you'll relax all at once, letting go of the tension."

I shake out my limbs, settling further into the seat.

"Close your eyes," she murmurs in a soft tone, "and be aware of any sensations you experience during today's session."

The hesitant girl from earlier is gone, something hypnotic about her voice as my eyelids drift shut, listening to her tell me to bring my eyebrows high and tense my forehead and scalp, hold, and relax.

I do as she says, the exaggerated motions ridiculous. "This feels kind of silly," I mutter.

"Don't worry how you look. It's only me in here."

Yeah, I know.

"I want you to notice how relaxed you are as you let go of those muscles. The way your body feels light and loose in the immediate moments afterward."

We repeat the movement, then move on to the face next.

"Here, you'll need to tense the middle of your face by squeezing your eyes tight and wrinkling your nose like this."

I open my eyes, finding her face adorably scrunched.

Whoa… adorable? Where'd that come from?

I quickly shut my eyes before she catches me staring at her and copy her expression, ignoring how stupid I must look.

We move on to the jaw and then the neck, the strangeness of the actions gradually fading the longer we go.

"Now bring your shoulders up," she says, "as if you're trying to touch your ears with the tops of them. Good."

I peek at her, not realizing she was doing the movements along with me.

"And exhale, relaxing. One more time now, tense up… and let all the tension drain away. Pay attention to how it feels when the muscles soften."

I focus on her words, conscious of doing what she says, noting the weightlessness of my shoulders. If I'm going to be here, I might as well go all in.

My chest is next, then my back as I squeeze my shoulder blades behind me.

"All right, now rest your arms on your thighs, bending them at the elbow, hands facing up. Tighten your biceps, making sure not to clench your fists."

This time, she doesn't perform the action along with me, staring instead at my upper arms.

I let go of the tension after five seconds, even though she doesn't instruct me to, and wait the normal ten seconds before doing it again like we've done for the other muscle groups.

"Am I doing it right?" I ask, unsure since her gaze is still transfixed on me.

She glances up. "What? Oh, yeah." She clears her throat. "Good job. Um, fists now." She holds her hands out in front of her to demonstrate. "Clench them as tightly as you can, taking note if there's any tingling in your palms. And then let the tension flow from your hands and out your fingertips, replaced with a sense of relaxation."

She's back to her calm, soothing voice as we continue to the stomach, where we draw our belly buttons tightly toward our spines, then our backs as we arch like there's a pillow behind us.

"Allow the relaxation to spread to all the muscles of your back, going deeper and deeper. Then we'll move on to the… the…"

Her words trail off and I look over, finding her cheeks as pink as they were when she discovered it was me in the waiting area.

"The…?" I ask, confused as to why she's flustered again.

"The butt," she whispers, more a breath than a sound.

Oh, that's why.

We can be adults about this, though. Right? "So, I should clench my butt?"

She nods, a strangled noise escaping her. She pounds on her chest twice before dropping into the chair behind the desk. "Let's move on to the thighs."

She doesn't join in on the exercises for the rest of the session, and I finish up my thighs, legs, and feet by myself, following her instructions.

Her cheeks return to a normal shade by the time she's finished, her professional mask in place again as she asks me how I'm feeling after completing the sequence.

I take stock of my body, not sure how to describe it aloud. "You said something earlier about the relaxation spreading throughout me. It's like that, I guess." A warm easiness in my joints, different from the warmth that runs through me after an intense session at the boxing gym. "I don't know, I've never been good with words."

Not like with her. Everything she'd said during the lesson today had been... soothing. Flowing. Peaceful.

Except when it comes to butts. Is she that put off by me?

"No, no. That's fine," she assures me. "You should feel relaxed. That's the goal." She runs a hand up and down her arm. "Thanks for being so cool about everything. After all the stuff I said."

"You don't have to keep bringing it up."

She bites at her bottom lip. "Right. Well, I'll see you here next week?"

I stand, putting on my jacket. "Or at home."

A sheepish expression crosses her face before she tilts her head down. "There, too."

Ah, shit. I didn't mean to rub it in.

I grab the papers she gave me earlier and leave before I can say another wrong thing, speeding past the woman at the front desk and down the stairs, slowing as I exit the glass doors. Picturesque snow covers the grounds, stately historic buildings within sight as far as the eye can see. What must it be like to go here? To be smart enough to attend a university like this?

A group of girls in wool pea coats and knee-high boots passes by ahead, looking over at me, then twitter among themselves, obnoxiously obvious. Two of them glance over their shoulders again, then one whispers loudly, "Do you think he goes here?"

Do they recognize how out of place I am? Wondering why I'd be in a psychology building when I can barely spell the word?

I shrug off the thought and make my way down the sidewalk toward the parking lot where my bike is. Undoing the lock around my helmet, I stuff it on my head, appreciating the meager warmth it provides, and throw the papers in the tail pack on the back.

Raising the kickstand, I climb on and rev the engine, letting it warm a bit before I go. At least the roads aren't icy. But that leaves me time to think again.

Is all this worth seventy-five a week? Having to come here on campus, knowing a place like this has never been an option for someone like me? Dad would laugh his ass off if he saw me here pretending to fit in.

Not that I pretended anything. I'd told that girl I wasn't a student. And she'd seemed surprised of all things. Does that mean everyone else in the study is? I'm the odd man out? She'd said it wasn't a big deal, but that could have been pity talking.

You know what? If she believes I'm good enough for her study, then that's all that matters. Any issue she has with me as a neighbor is just that—her issue. And if she wants to avoid me outside of the Stress Lab, that's fine.

Doesn't bother me any.

CHAPTER THREE

TESSA

AT WHAT POINT can I justify buying my own washer and dryer?

If I spend five dollars a week on doing laundry, annually that's… I do some quick mental math. Two-fifty? No, there are fifty-two weeks in a year, not fifty. Two-sixty a year. Now how much do machines cost?

I hitch my basket higher on my hip, careful not to let it tip as I walk the last few feet toward the apartment complex's laundry room. I punch in the code, freezing in the doorway as I recognize who's already seated in one of the room's two chairs, elbows braced on his knees.

Of course he'd be here.

A brisk wind blows from behind me, and I let the door slam shut, huddling into my fleece jacket. "Hi."

He glances up, doing that head nod thing guys do, his steel-gray gaze seeming to penetrate me.

No, what am I thinking? That's ridiculous.

The room's lone functioning dryer is already at work, but the washer is free. "Are you using that?" I ask, pointing to it.

He gives a single shake of his head, leaning back and crossing his arms over that massive chest.

Tough crowd.

Does he think I'm still avoiding him after apologizing on Tuesday? It's only been two days. It's not like our paths crossed a lot to begin with.

Or maybe he's simply not the chatty type. Fine. I can be like that, too.

I set my basket on top of the washer, the steady rumble of the dryer covering up the silence between us as I discreetly place my bras and undies into my mesh bag, my back to him. Why in the hell didn't I do that at home first?

I glance over my shoulder, finding his gaze still on me. Can't he at least pretend to look at his phone?

"Um, when will those be up and running again?" I point at the two sets of washers and dryers along the far wall. "They've been out of commission every time I've come in here."

His attention finally snaps away toward where I'm pointing. "Those have been out since I moved in."

"When was that?"

His forehead wrinkles. "About four and a half years ago."

Oh. "So top priority for management to fix them, huh?"

His mouth twitches for the briefest of moments as he looks back at me, and I glance away hastily, not wanting him to catch me looking.

I cross over to the change machine, pulling my tips out of my coin purse to feed into it for quarters. "Wish they had a card reader in here."

He gives a soft grunt, stretching out lower in his seat. "If they won't fix the rest of the washers and dryers, they're not going to add that."

Fair point. "At least I get plenty of singles at work." I hold up all the dollar bills in my hand, then shut my eyes, immediately realizing how that sounded. Heat washes over me, my tongue tripping over itself to explain. "I'm not a stripper." God, that was even worse.

His brows raise, but he stays otherwise quiet.

"I work at a diner," I clarify. "I'm a server there. These are tips from serving food. Not… other stuff."

I'm providing him with a minefield of joke material, aren't I? Begging him to say something about me twirling on a pole on stage. Why can't I keep my mouth shut around him?

"I thought you worked in the Stress Lab," he says, letting me off the hook easy.

I let out a breath, some of the warmth receding from my face and chest. "No, I don't get paid for that."

His brows shoot up even higher. "You do all that for free?"

"Yeah, for experience. I'll have a published study to my name when I apply for grad school next year. It's a huge leg up."

His gaze roams my face, studying me. Is it still pink? "You going to be a doctor or something? One of those PhDs?"

I shrug. "Hopefully. If I get accepted somewhere." And if I figure out how to pay for it.

I retrieve my quarters from the change machine, carefully placing them into the tiny slots on top of the washer.

"Did you write that email?" he asks.

I turn to him, cocking my head.

"The one that was sent before the study."

"Oh, yeah. My partner and I crafted it together. Our advisor looked it over but made minimal changes."

He nods. "You'll get in, then. I couldn't understand half of it."

He couldn't understand it? We tried to use layman's terms whenever possible. "That's not good."

"No, it is. That means it was smart."

My mouth opens and closes, not sure what to say, but the dryer's buzzer goes off, saving me from commenting.

I measure out my laundry detergent instead, dump everything into the washer, and crank the dial to start.

He pulls a basket out from under his chair and stands, seeming to take up so much more of the room now. Opening the dryer door, he tugs out a black shirt, folding it neatly before placing it in his basket.

I can't explain it, but there's something almost... intimate about watching him do such a personal task. Like I don't know him well enough to be here while he does this.

"I guess I'll come back later to switch this over," I say, putting my detergent away.

He pulls another black shirt out of the dryer that's identical to the first. "I'd be careful if I were you."

"Hmm?"

"I had clothes stolen out of here once. I stay the whole time now."

As if on cue, the door behind us opens, a frazzled middle-aged woman there with her basket perched on her hip. "How much longer will you be?" she demands without preamble.

"Um, I just put my stuff in."

"Typical," she huffs, slamming the door shut.

I glance over at Austin, who merely keeps folding his laundry.

"You think she would have taken my clothes out if I hadn't been here?"

He shrugs. "What do you think?"

"Right. So, paper-thin walls, only one washer and dryer for the whole complex, and neighbors that steal your clothes. Anything else I should know about this place?"

He strokes his beard, noticeably shorter and trimmed up compared to a couple of days ago. The style suits him.

"The front gate at the entrance is always out of order. I think they have it there so they can say it's a gated community. But the rent's cheaper here than anywhere else nearby, so there's that."

A shiver runs through me as a thought occurs. "Have there ever been any problems with break-ins?" Please say no.

He frowns. "Not that I know of."

Good.

I glance over to find him studying me. Crap.

"Can I help you fold?" I ask, pointing to the dryer. "I like to keep busy."

He gestures toward his clothes. "Have at it."

And of course the first thing I pull out is… his boxers.

Why is the universe hellbent on embarrassing me in front of this man? Did I do something in a past life to piss off one of the gods?

He takes them gently from me when all I do is stand there, unsure what to do. After how flustered I got the other day thinking about his butt in the lab, no wonder he doesn't trust me with his underwear.

I cross my arms tightly over my chest, abandoning my offer of help. Time to grasp at any shred of distracting conversation. "Did you move in here after high school?" If it was four and a half years ago, that puts him at about the right age.

"Yep."

See, I was right before. Not chatty.

"You didn't want to live at home anymore?"

The question comes out with an edge of bitterness I didn't intend. Hopefully, he doesn't pick up on it. But people don't realize how lucky they are to even have the option.

It takes him a moment to answer. "Me and my dad do better when we don't live under the same roof."

Interesting. "Does he live close by?"

"Listen," he says kindly. "You don't have to go out of your way to talk to me because I overheard you. I was just letting you know how crappy the construction is in these buildings."

Am I that obvious?

I scuff a toe along a crack in the linoleum. "It was silly of me not to try to get to know you. It could be a good thing. Like, I might need to borrow a cup of sugar one day."

A wrinkle forms between his brows. "You think I bake?"

"You know what I mean. Maybe I need to borrow some…" I throw my hands up, not sure what he'd have that I don't. "Tools or engine parts or something."

He cracks a smile. Oh, he really shouldn't do that. The action transforms his face, the gray of his eyes softening, the previous *leave me alone* vibe gone. Like someone who would protect rather than do damage.

I blink rapidly. What am I thinking?

"He lives about fifteen minutes away," he says, answering my earlier question.

So he will talk to me, then. "Any other family?"

He pulls a pair of faded jeans out next. "A sister. Two years younger, before you ask."

I cover my mouth to hide my smile.

"And what made you move in here?" he asks. "Thought a college girl like you would live on campus."

There's something about the way he says *college girl*. Not an insult, but not affectionately either. I can't quite place my finger on it.

"I did, actually. My first two years I had a scholarship that covered room and board, but it was too expensive to pay out of pocket after that." I was tired of sharing a room with someone else, anyway. Too many years of doing that with strangers growing up. "I rented a room with a group of girls in a house this past summer, but things didn't work out." Turns out I wasn't a party girl like they were expecting. Good thing it was only a six-month lease. "So I decided I'd try living on my own. I've never done it before."

"No boyfriend to move in with?"

"No." He's not asking because he's… interested, is he? No, no. That's ridiculous. Hunky motorcycle-riding boxers don't go for mousy nerds who constantly stick their feet in their mouth like me.

"And? You like it?"

"Living alone? It's… different. I like not having to worry about anyone else.

But…" I shake my head. "It's so stupid, but I keep getting freaked out by any noise I hear at night. Things I always attributed to another person."

He nods as if he understands.

"You do that, too?"

"Used to. Now I blame it on my cat."

"You have a cat?" I wouldn't have pegged him for a cat guy.

He shrugs. "Boots kind of invited herself in about a year ago."

Boots? "What does she look like?"

"She's all gray, except for her white feet." There's a softness in his tone I wasn't expecting.

"She sounds adorable. Do you have a picture?"

He sets down the socks he was pairing together and pulls his phone out of his front pocket, swiping a few times on it. He holds it out to me, my heart melting at the image of a tiny fluff ball with the aforementioned white feet sprawled out on his chest. His mouth is set in a crooked grin in the picture, a selfie on a couch from the looks of it, with one arm tucked behind his head, his bicep flexing enticingly.

No, don't look. It was bad enough watching him flex everything in the lab the other day. I don't need to see pictures of it, too.

I step back, giving him a brief smile. "She's precious."

His mouth crooks at the corner, almost the same as in that photo. "She's trouble, is what she is."

Okay, I really want to meet this cat now. It would be weird if I invited myself over, though. Right? "I'm sure she's a perfect angel baby."

He laughs, seeming surprised at himself, and his grin drops. What's that about?

He rushes through folding the last few items of his and grabs his basket, stepping forward suddenly.

I automatically retreat in response, bumping against the counter, hating my body's reaction even as I do it. "You're leaving?" I ask, my fingers finding a loose thread on the hem of my jacket to tug. There's no way he didn't notice what I just did.

"Yeah," he says neutrally, careful not to make any more sudden movements as he maneuvers toward the door. God, could I be any more obvious?

He pauses, his back to me as his hand hovers over the doorknob. "Why don't you like big guys?"

I grip the counter behind me. "W-what?" He remembers that from Tuesday?

"I would never try something with you. If you were worried."

Oh, he thinks… "No, it's nothing like that. Not like a sexual…" My face heats as I trail off. Why'd I have to use that word? "More like a safety thing." I wrinkle my nose, knowing I'm bungling this. "Don't worry about it. It's all good."

He nods, but I have no idea what he's thinking as he leaves, cold air blasting through the door before it shuts behind him.

I slump against the counter, my eyes squeezing shut as the conversation brings back flashes of that night.

The larger than life guy crawling through my window.

The scream caught in my throat as I lay paralyzed under the bed covers.

Mom's blood-curdling shriek less than a minute later.

No, no. I'm not thinking about that. I'm safe. I'm in control. Nothing like that is happening again.

I take a deep breath, calling to mind all the progressive muscle relaxation techniques I've learned. Warmth runs through me as my muscles eventually relax and my heartbeat returns to normal, logically knowing I have nothing to worry about despite my body's fight or flight response.

I'm safe.

CHAPTER FOUR

AUSTIN

I TOSS the laundry basket on my bed, reaching in for my pile of shirts to put away.

Why the hell did I have to ask her that? I should have pretended to not notice her reaction, not call it out.

And why am I even getting friendly with her to begin with? Answering all her questions, asking her things of my own. I'd outright asked her if she has a boyfriend, for Christ's sake. How fucking stupid. Her jumping away from me, eyes wide with fear as I approached, was all the answer I needed for that.

She'd obviously still felt bad for saying that stuff on Tuesday and was overcompensating by talking to me now. At least I'd come to my senses when I realized I was laughing at her comment about Boots.

The cat in question struts in, meowing loudly as she twines herself around my leg.

"I'll feed you in a minute. Let me finish this first."

Finish putting away the laundry? Or finish beating myself up for talking to that girl? I don't even know her name. She'd never introduced herself at the Stress Lab.

But still, despite her reaction to me, there's something about her that's... endearing.

I scrub a hand down my face, groaning. What the hell am I going on about?

I put everything away and head into the kitchen to open a can of Friskies for Boots, enjoying the way she chatters at me as she waits for her meal.

On the counter is that questionnaire for the study I still haven't filled out. I have to do that, don't I? The longer I look at it, the more weighed down I am by guilt.

After putting out the dish of wet food for Boots, I grab a pen out of the drawer, going through the first few questions about my daily stress levels, then a chart rating the frequency of my stress symptoms. Let's see, no headaches, insomnia, or depression. A bit of fatigue and tense muscles, but that's probably more because of my job and boxing than actual stress. Anxiety, worry, or phobias? No, not really. I pause at the box asking about irritability. Haven't I just spent the last ten minutes irritated? Yeah, but I was supposed to fill this out on Tuesday.

Even though I was irritated then, too.

But not because of me. Because of her. She was the one who said those things.

And why do I care? I told myself I didn't, but seeing her again today…

Fuck, I'm not some psychologist like her. I don't know the answer.

The words *Perceived Stress Scale* are in bold along the top of the next page. I skim through it, my brows narrowing at the questions. How often have I felt things were going my way? How often have I felt not in control? How often have I felt nervous? Upset? Angry?

Why are these so hard? I swear, before this week it would have been a breeze to answer them. But suddenly, it doesn't seem so simple.

I set the paper aside, scratching Boots above her tail as she jumps up next to me. "You're lucky you're a cat. You don't have to worry about stress, do you?"

She arches her lower back into my hand, telling me without words that she wants more pets. I comply, letting go of any anxiety about this stupid form. It's ironic that filling this out is what's stressing me out.

I bubble in some responses, not putting too much thought into it. What is she going to do? Argue with me about it? The thing is too hard, anyway. All that schooling and she couldn't come up with something easier?

Jesus Christ, get a grip. She said she's doing this whole study unpaid. Combined with going to school and having a serving job, she must work her ass off.

And what am I doing with my life? I work all day in a warehouse and then come home and sit on my ass or go to the gym and box. I'll go pro soon if Dad has anything to say about it, not that he ever actually asked me if that's what I wanted.

And why am I even comparing myself to this girl? We're nothing alike. She's smart enough to go to college and have some fancy psychology study. She even said she had a scholarship. They don't just hand those out.

Kind enough to apologize to me for what she said. Brave enough to keep talking to me, despite how she really feels. Beautiful with that long, dark hair and warm, brown eyes, the lightest dusting of freckles over the bridge of her nose...

Fuck. There I go again. I need to stop thinking about her. I'm no one to her.

Even if a part of me wishes... No. Best not to go there.

"You let him put you in the corner already," Lawrence shouts at Ethan. "You need to find a way out."

"Nobody puts baby in the corner," Ethan says, grinning, but it doesn't have the effect he wants it to with his mouthguard in, his words muffled.

I crowd him in, toying with him, and keep my fists at the ready, waiting for his strike.

He sends a jab toward my face, and I automatically step back to avoid it. He uses the opportunity to slip by me to the center of the ring.

"There you go," Lawrence says. "Don't let him get you back in."

I feel him out, feinting a few times, and eventually maneuver him to the corner again.

"Damn it," Ethan growls, knowing exactly what I've done. He has to learn, though. You can't let your opponent do what they want with you. You have to take control.

He swipes at me but I easily block it, and he returns his hands close to his face to guard. He's not aggressive enough.

I keep my stance loose, bobbing back and forth, and wait for him to take the bait. He finally does, coming at me, but I'm ready for him, evading, and he stumbles off balance. I manage to get two into his side.

Instead of retreating, he comes at me, the two of us going for the upper hand, ending up with us both missing, locked together in a clinch. He tries to escape, and I let him, going in immediately again, knocking him against the ropes. He holds his hands in front of his face, and when he pulls them away, there's a light in his eyes. He's ready for more.

"Go on the offensive, Ethan."

I dance around the ring, sidestepping his attempts, enjoying his growing frustration. When people get frustrated, they make mistakes.

After another minute, Lawrence calls time and I touch gloves with Ethan, both of us wiping sweat out of our eyes. The guy's improved a lot over the last few months, especially as he's cleaned up his diet and put on more lean muscle. Boxing in his first real fight helped open his eyes to what he needs to work on, too.

"I can't wait to get to your level," he says, holding his side gingerly as we leave the ring.

I spit out my mouthguard and undo the velcro on one of my gloves with my teeth. "You got some good licks in."

"Yeah, but not like yours."

With anyone else, I'd take his statement as either hero worship or whining, but I know he doesn't mean it like that. He sincerely wants to get better.

"You still haven't figured out my weakness yet, have you?"

He leans in with interest.

I pause for dramatic effect. "It's that I don't have one."

A grin splits his face as he punches my shoulder. "I'm going to the diner across the street later. You want to go with?"

"Yeah, sure." I could eat.

"Lexie works there. I'll see if she'll let you use her employee discount."

"Okay." It's a diner. How expensive can it be?

"Give me twenty minutes? I want to work on some of the things Lawrence mentioned on the speed bag, then hit the shower."

I nod, spotting Tyler and his girlfriend over by the heavy bags. "Catch you later."

I finish unwrapping my hands, flexing my fingers once they're free. My knuckles are red and I already know it's going to hurt moving boxes tomorrow at work.

And it's only Monday.

I cross the large, open space and wave a hand at Uncle Marty in his office, who gives me a brief acknowledgment back.

Near the heavy bags, Tyler tips his chin toward me and I approach. "Hey, man."

Next to him, Mia is a red-faced, sweaty mess, her curls wild around her head as she huffs and puffs while punching the bag. Though nowhere near boxing level, she's incrementally gotten better over the last year or so.

"You didn't tell me what this study would really be like," I say, cutting to the chase. "You made it sound easy."

He holds up a hand, stopping me from saying anything else. "Trust me, if I could go back in time, I wouldn't have asked any of you to be a part of it."

His girlfriend grins. "You brought this on yourself, you know. And Austin's not the problem. Ethan is."

I glance questioningly between the two of them. I expected Tyler to apologize, not act hassled. "What's wrong with Ethan?"

Tyler rolls his eyes. "He's taking this study way too seriously and is all into meditation now." He must be in that other group. "Does it twice a day, thirty minutes a pop, and can't have any noise during his meditation time. He's driving me crazy."

At least with me, there's no one else at home to interrupt my relaxing sequence.

Except Boots.

"So what's your problem with it?" he asks.

"Same as why you're annoyed, I guess. I have to do stuff twice a day for it."

"But you're getting paid. And it's helping you, right?"

"Well, yeah, but—"

He waves a hand to cut me off. "Go talk to Ethan about it. I'm done with pysch studies for the day." He stalks off toward the locker room.

Mia stops her punching and rips off one of her gloves, then grabs a towel off to the side to wipe her face on. "Ignore him. He got a bad grade on a test today and he's been in a pissy mood ever since." She gives a small smile. "Not that he's a ray of sunshine to begin with."

No, he's not. But he's at least gotten infinitely better since he started bringing her around more. "Maybe he needs some meditation."

She claps her hands together in front of her, grinning. "Oh, I have to tell him that later. He'll be so mad."

Right.

"Well, you're not dropping out of the study, are you?" she asks. "Tessa will be crushed."

So her name is Tessa? I was hoping I could find a roundabout way to ask that.

"No, I just wanted to give Tyler a hard time."

"Mission accomplished, then. Oh, and I was the one on the phone with Tessa during, um… When she said…"

"Yeah, I know." She doesn't need to say it aloud.

She gives me a sympathetic look. Great. Now I've got girls everywhere pitying me. Plus, if she knows, then she told Tyler, who probably told Ethan… which means the whole gym knows.

"She felt awful about it."

"She already apologized."

"I know, but I don't think it had anything to do with you personally."

"She said that, too."

She glances around and steps closer, lowering her voice. "Did she tell you why?"

Uh… "No. Just a comment about big guys scaring her."

She nods conspiratorially. "I won't say too much, but she had something traumatic happen to her as a kid. And maybe you remind her of it."

What the hell happened to her? And what do I have to do with it?

Her brows pinch together as she bites at her bottom lip. "I'm sorry. I shouldn't have said anything. Forget it."

Forget it? Yeah, right.

"I should go find Tyler," she mumbles, leaving me standing there, more confused than ever.

What was it Tessa said last week in the laundry room? She wasn't scared of big guys because of a sexual thing, but as a safety thing. Was she assaulted or something? By someone that looks like me? Is that it?

Now the question is, will I leave it alone… or try to find out?

CHAPTER FIVE

TESSA

"TESSA, YOUR TWO-TOP'S UP," Manuel calls, pointing to the club sandwich and burger in the window.

"Thanks. You made the fries extra crispy, right?" I grab a tray and start loading it up, inspecting the food.

"If you wrote it on the ticket, I did."

Ah, look at those golden brown fries. "And that's why you're my favorite cook."

"Because I read the instructions you write?"

"Exactly."

"Only you and Lexie do that. The rest assume I'm a mind reader."

Lexie rounds the corner, digging in her apron for something, and hands me three crumpled bills, followed by two quarters. "Your half of the tip from that group of guys. Thanks for taking them. If I'd had to keep going over there, I might've punched one of them."

"No problem." Since she started working here a few months ago, we make a pretty good team. Plus, we're the only servers under the age of forty-five. There's a certain amount of mutual bonding in that.

"Uh oh. Here comes trouble." She smirks, and I glance over my shoulder as I lift my tray.

Through the diner's front windows, I spot her boyfriend, Ethan, who's made himself a regular here since she started working. There's someone else behind him, but I can't make out…

What's he doing here? And how does he know Lexie's boyfriend?

"Looks like he brought Austin with him," she says, heading to the door to greet them. "That's new."

She knows him, too?

Crap. Crap. Triple crap.

How is it that within a week, he's invaded all these parts of my life? After our conversation in the laundry room last Thursday, where I made such stupid comments as *I'm not a stripper* and backed away from him like I thought he was going to attack me, I've been keeping my distance. And by that, I mean avoiding leaving the apartment if I heard the faintest noise outside that might be him.

How does he make me say and do the dumbest things? Why do I get so flustered around him?

I head for my table before he and Ethan enter, angling my body away from the door as I deliver the food.

Does he know I work here? Is that why he came? Or is it a coincidence?

I should go over to greet him and get it over with. I should also refill the drinks of my three-top in the corner. But instead, I scurry in the opposite direction toward the bathrooms and grip the edge of the sink as I take a deep breath.

What's the big deal? I'll see him tomorrow in the Stress Lab, anyway. But there, I'm in control. And here…

I glance down at my baby blue 1950s style uniform, the white half-apron dingy with stains. Turning on the tap, I wet my fingers and rub at the spots, hoping at least some of them come out. After that, I rewet my hands and tame the flyaway hairs around my head, wishing I'd done more than the simple ponytail to keep my hair out of my face.

Good enough, I guess.

I swing open the door, colliding with a brick wall that steadies me before I fall, two big hands gripping my shoulders before they let go.

"Tessa?"

I crane my neck up at Austin, something in my belly going warm and gooey hearing my name in that low, rumbly voice.

Oh my God, what is wrong with me? I just ran into him.

I open my mouth to apologize, but he beats me to the punch.

"Are you following me? First the laundry room, now here?"

"No," I sputter, then recognize too late the smile lurking around his mouth.

"I was kidding." He sticks his hands in his pockets, calling attention to the way his black shirt clings to his torso. "My buddy invited me. I didn't know you work here."

How does he… Oh, right. My uniform. Can't imagine I'd be wearing this otherwise.

I clear my throat, hating the frog stuck in it. "Is that Ethan? He comes in to visit Lexie all the time."

He nods. "You know him?"

"Only really from what Lexie mentions. How do you know him?"

He points across the street. "I box with him. Lexie does the accounting there, too."

Okay, that makes sense. She mentioned being a bookkeeper somewhere once. "You just came from there? From boxing?"

He nods again.

"I'm guessing you're sitting in Lexie's section?"

"Yeah, she took our drink orders already."

"Okay, great." I tuck my hands in my apron pocket, then realize I'm mimicking his pose and cross my arms instead. "Um, I should get back to work."

"I'll see you tomorrow, then?"

His gaze is steady on me, fully focused, and I get caught up in studying him for a moment. The straight nose and light brown slash of his brows. The trimmed beard that frames his face, a square jaw lurking underneath. The surprisingly full lips that are quirked up at one corner.

Oh, God. I'm staring, aren't I?

I dash off, muttering under my breath about how I should mind my own business, and refill my table's drinks, keeping myself busy for the next thirty minutes so I don't spend any time gawking at him.

Silverware needs rolling? I'm on it.

The salt and pepper shakers need refilling? Yep, I can do that.

Fountain machine needs unclogging? Got you covered.

That doesn't mean I'm unaware of what's happening at his table, though. I mean, do I hand Lexie a bottle of ketchup when I notice the one he's using is low? Sure. Do I give her the water pitcher when I see his drink is half empty? Of course.

But that's just helping my coworker out. I wouldn't want her to get a bad tip.

I nearly snort to myself. As if that would happen. Ethan overtips her every time he comes in.

When they get up to leave, I pause from cleaning out the ice machine, watching as Austin looks around the restaurant. What's he looking for?

He holds a hand up as he spots me, and I tentatively raise mine in return.

Then he's gone, a motorcycle engine starting up a few moments later outside. My pulse slowly returns to normal, not that I'm sure why it was high to begin with. What's the big deal about seeing him? I could see him any time I want. He lives across the hall.

And what's this ache in my chest about? Like I'm… disappointed or something. Like I wanted him to come over and actually tell me goodbye. Even though I spent his whole visit avoiding him.

I must be mental.

I go back to scrubbing the interior stainless steel wall of the machine, wiping it down until it's sparkling.

"You know Kate won't give you a raise for doing that, right?" Lexie asks, behind the counter again now that her boyfriend's gone.

"I know."

"Were you cleaning to avoid Austin?"

The rag in my hand drops, and I hastily pick it up, throwing it into the bucket to wash later. "What are you talking about?"

She rolls her eyes, reaching up to tighten her auburn ponytail. "You did everything but look at him the whole time he was here. Like he was a black hole you were afraid you'd fall into."

That's… actually a good analogy.

I shrug instead of acknowledging how right she is. "I barely know him. We met last week."

She leans against the counter, settling in. It's forty minutes to close and we each only have one table. Monday nights are usually pretty dead. "Austin keeps to himself for the most part, although Ethan's drawn him out some. How'd you meet Mister Boxer?"

I grab a fresh rag along with the cleaning spray and start wiping down the counter. "When did you get so chatty?" When she first started working here, it was like pulling teeth trying to get any info out of her. She's loosened up a lot since then, though.

"I'm bored. At my last job, there was at least a TV we could watch if it wasn't busy. This place has nothing." And God forbid if Kate catches us on our phones. That's a write-up for sure.

I sigh, knowing I have to say something eventually. I can't distract myself with cleaning much longer when I've already cleaned practically everything in here. "He's in a psych study I'm running on campus."

"Oh, right. The meditation thing." She blows a raspberry. "I'll be glad when the six weeks is over. No offense."

I hold up my hands, unoffended. Ethan's in Joel's cohort. What happens in his group is his deal. "And I found out he's my neighbor. But we hadn't talked before the study."

"Small world, then."

Tell me about it.

"So, um, he and Ethan box together?" I ask, shifting topics.

"Yeah." She holds a hand out, examining her nails, then picks at her thumbnail. "He's freakishly good. I think his record's twenty-zero. In official tournaments and everything."

"Twenty wins and no losses?" That seems impressive.

She nods. "He could go pro any time he wants, but he hasn't yet."

"Is going pro a big deal?"

"Yeah. You can make real money from it, then."

"So why hasn't he?"

She shrugs. "Beats me. But he's been helping Ethan a lot so I'm not complaining. They usually get together Monday and Wednesday nights over there." She points across the street.

I peer through the windows, but it's too dark to make anything out. Who knew his boxing gym was so close to my work this whole time?

I wonder what Austin's job is. Maybe he makes more doing that than whatever a pro boxer makes.

"So, if him and Ethan aren't pro, what are they? You said something about tournaments?"

"They're amateurs. It sounds bad but it really only means they don't earn money from it. There are plenty of amateurs who are better than these guys that declare themselves pro for the hell of it."

"Why would you want to be an amateur if you make nothing from it?"

"Some people, like Ethan, do it as a hobby but don't intend for it to be a career. Some guys train to compete in the Olympics, though I don't know of anyone at Marty's gym that does that. And some want to hone their skills without it affecting their professional record. Once you go pro, you can't go back. And the better your record, the better fights you can get."

Wow, that's a lot to take in. "Did Ethan teach you all this?"

She makes a *pfft* noise. "More like I taught him. My dad's been boxing forever. He's a trainer at their gym."

"Oh, is that how you and Ethan met?"

She leans away from the counter, glancing toward her table on the far side of the restaurant. "Sort of. But that's a longer story. I think my table's ready to cash out."

I nod, going back to scrubbing as she leaves. I'll see Austin tomorrow in the Stress Lab and it won't be a big deal at all. Just because we've run into each other a few times doesn't mean he wants to be friends or anything. He's my participant for my study and I'll be neighborly if I see him at the apartment.

That's all we need to be.

CHAPTER SIX

TESSA

"KNOCK, KNOCK."

I glance up from my spot at the desk to find Joel in the doorway of my room in the Stress Lab, holding two cups from the campus library's coffee shop. "Got you a coffee," he says, placing one on my desk.

At three forty-five in the afternoon? "You didn't have to do that." I swear I've told him before I don't drink coffee.

"Need to make sure you're good to go for today. How'd the applied relaxation go last week?"

"Great. Everyone seemed to understand the exercises we went through. I'm interested to see how they've been doing on their own. And how was your meditation?"

"Great. No complications." He takes a long sip of his coffee. "I booked one of the study rooms at the library for tomorrow night. Want to look at the data we have so far?"

What data? The participants haven't even turned in their questionnaires from last week yet. "Sorry, I have to work." Didn't we go over our weekly availability when we came up with times to hold the training sessions with participants? I told him a million times I work every Monday and Wednesday night, plus all weekend. "How about Thursday night after we finish our second sessions for the week?"

"Yeah, sure."

He's free all the time since he doesn't work and his parents pay for all his expenses.

Okay, not being fair again. It's not his fault his family is well-off.

"Hey, I've got a paper for Somatic Psych coming up," he says, perching on the edge of my desk. I quickly pull papers out of the way before he crumples them. "You took that last semester, right? Would you mind helping me with it?"

I shuffle the papers in my hand, now all disorganized from my quick grab. "No, I had Social Psych. I'm pretty sure Mia took Somatic, though. You should ask her."

"Right," he murmurs, taking another long draw of coffee. "You going to drink that?" He points to the still full cup on my desk, smiling. "Don't tell me I wasted my money."

You mean the drink I don't like and didn't ask him to buy?

Ugh, why am I in such a bad mood? He did something nice for me. "Maybe later. I wanted to go over the sequence for today in my head one more time. We've only got ten minutes left."

"Yeah, okay." He stands, knocking one of my folders to the ground. "I'll get out of your hair, then."

I get up and grab the folder, smiling at him as he exits. He really is a good friend. Without him, I wouldn't even be doing a study.

I run through the shortened version of the progressive muscle relaxation sequence I have planned for today one last time, then go out in the lobby area to wait for Tamara, my first participant of the day.

An hour and a half later, I'm ahead of schedule as my fifth participant finishes. That only leaves one more.

Austin.

And as I decided last night, it's not a big deal at all. Just because he makes me sort of… flustered… doesn't have to mean anything.

I head out into the lobby, my stomach jumping around a bit as the main door opens, but it's not my guy.

Not that he's *my* guy.

Half a minute later, it *is* him, though.

He runs a hand through his dark blond hair, natural streaks of lighter blond sprinkled throughout, and searches the lobby, looking for…

Me.

Our gazes lock, my belly dipping low for a moment at the way he seems to take me in all at once, his movements slowing, then speeding up as his heavy footfalls sound on the carpeted floor, getting closer, closer…

"Hey, Tessa."

I bite my lip, containing the unintelligible noise that itches to escape, and hold up a hand instead, waving.

God, why can't I be normal?

I spin around, silently berating myself as I lead us down the hall. Every time, I forget how much of the room he seems to take up, how my brain goes a little fuzzy, how my lips seem to get looser. I just need a minute to acclimate to him. To remember how to be myself.

"Lexie was telling me last night about the boxing you and Ethan do. She said you're really good."

There, that was totally normal. I breathe a sigh of relief, glad that my mouth is at least temporarily in working order.

He tilts his head in acknowledgment, taking off his worn leather jacket to hang on the back of his chair. He's got a different henley on this week, this time a charcoal color that complements the gray of his eyes. "I do all right."

"She said you're undefeated. Twenty wins or something?"

He shrugs, taking a seat. "Yeah, I guess."

I don't know why, but the way he says it has me smiling as I sit behind the desk. "You're awfully humble." Other guys would brag if they had that kind of skill.

Rubbing at the back of his neck, he says, "I mean, it's punching people. It's not important or anything. Not like what you do."

I stare at him for a moment. "You think my study's important?" I didn't get the impression he even thought all that much of it last week.

His mouth opens and closes, then he leans forward, resting his elbows on his knees. "Everything that goes on in this building must be, right?"

"Yeah, you could view it like that. But you shouldn't sell yourself short. It would be cool if I knew how to do what you can."

What would it be like to watch him box? To see him in action?

He looks over at me, a small smile on his lips. "You want to box?"

I can't help the laugh that escapes me. "Can you imagine me in a ring? I'd get pounded flat in about a second."

His smile grows. "We have some girls that come to the gym and train. Even Mia comes in and punches the heavy bags."

I shake my head. "No, I'd be ridiculous. Although, I've always wanted to learn some self-defense moves." Maybe it would help me feel better prepared if something were to ever happen again. Maybe if my mom had known…

No. Best not to go down that path.

"I could teach you."

It takes me a moment to process his words. "You'd teach me self-defense?"

He shrugs. "Yeah, sure."

Have I completely misinterpreted all our previous interactions? I thought he was barely tolerating me. "That would be amazing, but I can't really pay you. I'm kind of tight on money." I don't have the luxury of splitting costs with room-mates anymore, plus my moving expenses last month had been more than I expected.

"I don't want any money. I—" He pauses, shaking his head. "Never mind."

"No, I'd like you to," I blurt out. What, I could barely look at him yesterday in the diner and now I'm volunteering to spend extra time with him? What am I doing to myself? "I mean, if you're willing. But I don't want to take up a lot of your time."

"It's no trouble."

Really?

I can't help the wide grin that crosses my face before I quickly shut it down. "Is there something I can do for you in return?"

He shifts in his seat, the natural pause in a conversation stretching out longer than it should, and I run my words back through my head. Oh no, it sounded like… Does he think I'm propositioning him? Offering sexual favors in exchange?

"Actually, maybe there is."

Oh my God, is he taking me up on my unintended offer?

"I… Could you show me what it would take to get into a place like this?"

I blink at him, his comment not what I was expecting. "The Stress Lab?"

"The university," he clarifies, his left leg bouncing. "If you had to take a test or something."

He runs a hand through his hair, pushing it back, and it falls forward in waves again before he tucks it behind his ears.

"Are you thinking of applying?"

"No," he replies almost immediately. "But, you know, if someone was inter-ested?" He ends the word on an upward note, like it was a question.

Is he… nervous?

I thought I had the monopoly on that.

"Yeah, of course. Let me do some research and see what the current requirements are. I applied three years ago, so they might have changed since then."

He nods, crossing his arms over his chest. "It was just a thought. I know you have to be smart."

Something in my brain clicks, remembering how last week he'd been a mix of angry and ashamed when saying he'd never gone to college. How he'd said he's never been good with words, how the email I'd written was smart. Calling me *college girl* in that weird way.

Is he jealous?

"Austin." I wait until he looks at me, a pang echoing in my chest at how unsure he seems. "If you wanted to go to college, you absolutely could. We can look at your high school transcripts, your financial aid options, any upcoming course offerings. This could be a real thing."

His eyes widen. "Okay." He clears his throat, looking away again. "Cool."

"Maybe we could get together this Friday? I'm free, then." Wait. What am I thinking? It's a weekend night. He probably goes out and parties and dates and does actual social things.

"Sounds good. I get off of work at five-thirty."

Oh, wow. This is happening.

That's good, though. It'll be nice to have someone I know across the hall. What if there's an emergency or something?

"Okay, how about seven? So you have time to drive home and eat dinner and all that."

He nods. "I'll be over then."

Oh, so it's at my place? Nothing like having guests over to motivate me to actually clean the apartment.

"How about we get started?"

"Sure."

He settles into a comfortable position in his chair.

"So, we're learning a shorthand version of the progressive muscle relaxation sequence today. How's it been going on your own for the last week?"

"Fine." He rolls his shoulders back, then shakes out his arms, loosening up. "It's actually helped on the nights I box. And it's a good way to unwind at night."

A smile tugs at my lips. "Great. That's exactly what I hoped to hear." Who knew today would be such a breeze compared to the disastrous vision I had in my head? "We'll focus on four main areas—face, arms, torso, and legs. We'll tense and relax these larger muscle groups at once instead of separating them out, which will shorten the overall time of the sequence by about two-thirds."

As we begin, any lingering nerves from earlier fade until he's like any other participant. Tense and relax, tense and relax.

And luckily, I don't have to say the word *butt* today.

At the end, I hand him the new shorthand instructions. "I forgot to get your questionnaire from last week."

"Ah, shit," he mutters as he puts on his jacket. "Can I give it to you Friday?"

Right. Friday. When he's coming over to my apartment. "Yeah. Sure. Of course." Okay, I'm babbling now.

I cross over to the door, holding it open for him. "Make sure to practice the new sequence twice a day like last week."

The door next to mine opens, and Joel peeks his head out. "You finished?"

I hold up a finger. "Almost," I whisper.

Austin steps out of the room, zipping his jacket. He glances behind me at Joel, expression unchanging, then back to me. "See you Friday."

"See you."

He strides down the hall, Joel coming up beside me a moment later. "Jesus, how tall is that guy?"

"I know, right?"

I return inside, gathering all my papers off the desk to bring with me before the next study needs the room. Noah and Chris were early last week.

"Wait, did he say he was seeing you Friday?"

"Oh, it turns out we're neighbors. Isn't that crazy?" I unzip my backpack, stuffing everything in there. I'll sort through it later.

"So why are you seeing him?"

I pause, looking over at him in the doorway. Is it my imagination, or did he sound... accusatory?

"He's helping me with something." I finish zipping up my bag and swing it on my back, wishing my textbook for Abnormal Psych wasn't so heavy. Maybe I could use that for self-defense.

"He's also a participant in our study. Are you sure you should fraternize with him outside the Stress Lab?"

I laugh at his mock serious tone, then realize he isn't joking. "Oh my God, it's not that big a deal."

"Yeah, but..." He trails off, gaze darting back and forth. "It could influence the study."

I'm tempted to ask him how, but I don't want to argue. "We won't talk about the study," I promise. "There. No influencing."

The corners of his mouth turn down. "Do you know what you're doing? Who you're getting involved with?"

I move past him, adjusting my backpack so it sits higher on my back. "What are you talking about?"

He steps out into the hall beside me, glancing toward the lobby, but there's no one there. "That guy looks like he belongs in prison or something."

"Wow. Judgmental much?" But didn't I feel there was something dangerous about Austin initially, too? Not that I would have gone as far as *prison*. "He offered to show me some self-defense moves."

He makes a noise of disbelief. "Is that code for some kind of weird sex thing?"

I shove his shoulder. "No, you weirdo." Seriously, what's with him? He's never acted like this.

"Why would you even want to learn that?"

Um, what woman wouldn't? "Well, I told you about what happened when I was younger. With my mom."

He nods, sobering.

"This could help me. And he's a boxer. I mean, who better to teach me how to defend myself?"

"Yeah, you're right. Sorry."

There. That's more the Joel I know.

"Are we still on for Thursday night to go over the study?" he asks.

"Yep. Now I've got to crank out a paper for Behavioral Genetics."

He doesn't follow me as I trek down the hallway, but calls my name a moment later, standing in the open doorway of my room.

"You didn't drink your coffee," he calls out, holding the untouched cup.

Crap. I forgot about that.

I smack my forehead lightly, heading back toward him. "Sorry. Forgot all about it."

I move to take it from him, but he holds it out of reach. "And thank you Joel for getting it for me?" he says, a playful note in his voice.

Seriously? After that weird interrogation, he's going to act like this?

Better not make a big deal of it, though.

"Thanks," I mutter, forcing a smile.

He hands it to me and I speed walk down the hall, dumping the cup in the trash can right outside the Psychology building. What was with him today?

I put Joel out of my mind as I hike over to the campus library, ready to spend a few hours on research. This paper on epigenesis won't write itself.

But even as I should be focusing on school, I can't help the bubble of nervousness and excitement that runs through me thinking about what the end of the week holds.

Only three more days till Friday.

CHAPTER SEVEN

AUSTIN

I CHECK that my wallet's in my pocket for the third time, confirming it's there, and let out a sigh. It doesn't even matter if I have it. I'm only going across the hall.

To Tessa's.

Why the hell did I blurt out that I would teach her self-defense? What do I know about teaching someone? After doing some looking around online, it isn't anything like boxing.

But Tessa saying she wanted to learn it combined with what Mia had said earlier in the week made me feel like… I don't know. I should help her out.

The clock over the stove reads five till seven, but fuck it. I'm wearing the carpet down with my pacing.

I grab my keys and lock up, taking the three steps over to her door and knocking twice. Sticking my hands in the pockets of my basketball shorts, I have a split-second of doubt, wondering if I should have dressed up more.

No, no. It makes sense to wear something comfortable. We'll be moving around.

I breathe a sigh of relief as she opens the door wearing yoga pants and a long-sleeved tee.

"Come in." She waves me forward, quickly shutting the door behind me. "You must be freezing."

I honestly hadn't noticed the cold, my mind too focused elsewhere.

"Thanks again for offering to do this."

"Yeah, of course."

I wipe my palms on my shorts, glancing around her place. There are colorful throw pillows on the couch, plants on the shelves along one wall, framed art, and a ton of books on her bookshelves.

I point over in that direction. "You read a lot?"

She shrugs. "Yeah, I guess."

Do I even own a single book? I can't remember at the moment. What would she think if she came over to my place? That she entered a barren wasteland? This looks like an actual adult's house.

"To be fair, some of them I only bought for school." She crosses the room to pick up one of the books. "I don't read Shakespeare for fun."

I let out a weak chuckle, coming over to join her. On the way, I pass a cozy throw blanket laid across the back of the couch and an artfully arranged trio of candles on the coffee table. Is she a part-time interior designer, too?

"Your home is nice." Seriously, other than a mirrored layout, you wouldn't think our two apartments were even in the same complex.

She beams. "Thanks. I've spent a lot of time decorating over the last month. It's my first place that's all my own, so I wanted to go all out."

My gaze passes over the titles on her bookshelf, only recognizing a few, and lands on a picture frame with what looks like a young Tessa and a woman in her late twenties. "This is you and your mom?" The resemblance is too strong to be anyone else.

"Yeah." There's a wistful note in her voice, too faint to notice if I wasn't paying attention.

"You look a lot alike."

She nods, giving a brief smile.

There's a pause and I can hear my sister in my head, urging me to keep the conversation going.

You have to actually talk to people, Austin. Stop standing there like a bump on a log.

"Are you two close?"

She bites at her bottom lip, not answering for a few moments. "She died when I was eight," she finally says.

Ah, shit. Why am I even asking questions about mothers, anyway? I know better than that. "I'm sorry, I didn't know."

She waves away my statement. "Why would you?"

Picking up the photo frame, she gently strokes the glass, then sets it down. "You mentioned a dad and sister the other day, but what about your mom? Are you close to her?"

I rub at the back of my neck, feeling foolish for even bringing up the topic to begin with. "She died when I was four."

Her eyes widen. "We're quite a pair, aren't we?"

"Guess so."

She turns away, moving to the center of the living room. "Well, this got depressing, didn't it?"

Fuck. This was a bad idea. "I—"

"I'm joking," she interrupts. "Humor as a defense mechanism and all that. Except, I'm not funny, so it doesn't work."

I stare at her for a moment, thrown off. What's she talking about? She's funny.

"I'm sorry about your mom, too. I know how difficult it is."

I shrug. "I barely remember her." I'm not sure either which memories are real or pictures I've seen.

She nods, crossing her arms over her chest. "Sometimes I worry I'll forget my mom. I do what I can to keep her memory alive, even when it's hard to think about her." She chews on her bottom lip, seeming lost for a moment, then focuses back in, giving me a small smile. "Should we get started?"

"Yeah." I don't know why I brought up anything personal to begin with. "Do you mind if I move some of this furniture out of the way?"

"Sure, but it's heav—"

She cuts off as I pick up the coffee table and place it near the bookcase, then scoot the couch back to give us more room to practice. That should be enough space.

She points a finger between where the furniture was and where it is now. "You just moved that stuff."

Uh... "I thought you said I could."

She shakes her head. "No, I mean you moved it with no problem. I can barely budge it." Her gaze sweeps over me, lingering over my arms and chest. "I guess your muscles aren't only for show?"

Warmth pools in the pit of my stomach until she turns away, holding her hands to her temples. "Oh my God, I can't believe I said that," she mutters. "Ignore me, please."

From what I know of her already, there doesn't seem to be much of a filter on her mouth. Maybe it's best to do as she asks.

"You ready to get started?"

She glances over one shoulder and nods.

I approach her slowly, careful not to cause another reaction like in the laundry room. "I want to start out by saying I don't know what the hell I'm doing. I'm no teacher."

Some of the tension in her eases as she turns to face me. "Me either."

"I help some of the guys out at the gym with their technique, but I've never officially done anything. In case you're expecting a lot."

"No. This was all kind of spur of the moment."

I nod, wiping my palms on my shorts again. Why are they so sweaty? "So I was coming up with what we should do, and I thought of that scene from *Miss Congeniality*—"

"Wait." She holds up a hand to stop me. "You've seen *Miss Congeniality*?"

I shrug. "Yeah…"

She brings her hand to her chest. "I love that movie. It doesn't seem like something you'd watch, though."

"I mean, I'm not watching it at home by myself with a tub of popcorn. I'm pretty sure I saw it with my sister."

The corner of her mouth lifts on one side. "Fair enough. So you're talking about the scene where she beats her partner up on stage? And she's wearing the Bavarian outfit?"

"Right."

"I can't do that. Doesn't she flip him over her back? You think I could do that?"

There's no chance in hell she could do that. "Well, the other stuff. Thrusting the heel of your hand into their nose is a good move."

"Like this?"

She drives her palm up, and I barely swerve out of the way in time to avoid it. Girl's got fast reflexes.

"I didn't mean do it now."

She snatches her hand back to her side. "Sorry."

"No, I wasn't clear. I don't want you to try anything on me yet. Especially not the next one."

She winces, her gaze flicking down briefly. "Hitting a guy in the balls?"

I nod. "Or kicking, depending on the situation. It's a classic for a reason."

She gives a nervous laugh. "Does it really hurt that much?"

"It feels like…" I run a hand over my beard, considering how I can describe it. "Like you're going to throw up and shit yourself and die all at the same time."

The alarm on her face nearly has me grinning.

"So only do it in an emergency. Not if you're just arguing or something."

She nods, wide-eyed.

I show her a few more moves like hammer and elbow strikes, and she practices them a few times.

"Be more decisive," I tell her. "Strike when they're not expecting it."

"Right." She adjusts her speed, determination on her face.

"Good. Give them everything you've got. Attack them quickly so you can get them off-balance and make your escape."

She nods, keeping at it. "We need one of those training dummies. Then I could get really good."

"You'd probably hurt yourself, to be honest. You haven't built up to that."

"What would I need to do?"

"Toughen up your hands, for one. It'll hurt if you don't have calluses."

"So how do I get them?"

"By punching things."

"But you said it'll hurt if I do that."

I rub at the back of my neck. "Yeah, it's kind of a catch twenty-two."

She holds the backs of her hands out to me. "Do I have any?"

I lean in, inspecting her knuckles, and sweep a thumb over them, silently reveling in how soft they are. Is she that soft everywhere?

I stumble back, thrown off by that unexpected thought. This isn't the time to think about stuff like that.

She quirks her head at me, confused.

"You'd probably split your knuckles if you punched anything remotely hard," I say, not acknowledging my weird movement. "How about you practice the movements until they feel more natural?"

Nodding, she thrusts her palm upward into the air, and I watch from a distance, occasionally correcting her form or giving pointers.

She pauses when her breathing becomes labored. "This is like an actual workout." She fans her shirt away from her body, then pushes her sleeves up past her elbows. "I might actually turn the heat off soon."

I grin at her. "I take it you don't do much cardio?"

She shakes her head. "I'm blessed with a fast metabolism. You probably have to do stuff for boxing, though, right?"

"I do interval running a few times a week. More often if I have a match coming up."

Stretching her arms out, she asks, "What's interval running?"

"Basically switching off running fast and slow. It prepares you better for your bouts in the ring."

"I'd like to see you box sometime." She pauses, then blinks. "I mean, all the participants in the study. You know, whatever their sport is." She twists her hands together in front of her. "Speaking of, do you have your questionnaire filled out?"

That's right. I never gave it to her.

I hitch a thumb toward my apartment. "I'll give it to you after this."

She fans her face, her cheeks still flushed. "I'm done for the night. That kind of took it out of me."

Maybe if she's serious about this we should work on her endurance next. She wouldn't last one round in the ring.

"Okay, I'll go get the paper, then."

"Um, could I come with you?"

I frown, mentally calculating how messy my apartment is. I wasn't expecting her to come over.

"I wanted to meet Boots," she explains, smoothing her palms down the sides of her shirt.

She wants to meet my cat?

"But I don't have to," she rushes to say. "I'm sorry, I shouldn't have invited myself. You can give me the questionnaire on Tuesday."

"No, it's fine. As long as you don't mind a little mess. I don't normally have visitors, but Boots will love having someone new around."

Her eyes light up in response.

Really? That's all it takes to make her happy? Visiting a cat?

"Come on."

I grab my keys out of my pocket and lead her across the hall, holding open the door for her.

"Will she hide if I come in?" She cautiously walks in, glancing around the main area.

I do a quick visual sweep myself, finding nothing too embarrassing laying out. If the worst thing out is a mostly empty beer bottle on the coffee table from dinner, then I'm okay.

"Probably not. She doesn't hide when Danielle stops by."

She turns to look over at me. "Is that your girlfriend?"

"No." I clear my throat, hating how fast that came out. "My sister."

"Right. The one who's two years younger."

She remembers that?

There's a thud from the direction of my bedroom, and then Boots saunters out, opening her jaws wide in a yawn.

Tessa gives a quiet squeal, holding her fists to her mouth. "She's even cuter in person."

She bends down and holds out a hand, making soft kissing sounds to attract her.

Boots approaches with no issue, rubbing her cheek on Tessa's outstretched fingers.

Tessa looks up at me, her dark eyes shining with excitement. "She likes me."

I stick my hands in my pockets, unable to help the smile that overtakes my face. "Yeah, looks like it."

She sits on the floor cross-legged, giving under the chin scratches and base of the tail pets to my cat who looks like Christmas came twice.

"Have you ever had a cat?"

Boots circles her, coming back for another round of petting.

"No, but a family I lived with did." She strokes Boots from head to tail. "Whiskers."

A family she lived with? What does that mean?

"You said you've had her for a year?" she asks.

"Yeah, she used to hang around outside. I felt bad for her and started leaving out food." I kneel, reaching out a hand, and Boots comes to me, rubbing her cheek against my index finger once before returning to Tessa for more pets. "One day, I came home and opened the door, and she waltzed right in alongside me and curled up on the couch like she owned the place."

"That was sweet of you to let her stay."

I glance over at her, the expression on her face almost like… admiration. For taking in a cat? That's a pretty low bar.

The back of my neck burns hot. "I wasn't going to kick her out," I mumble, standing and leaning against the arm of the couch so I'm not so close.

Boots curls up in Tessa's lap, her head tipped to the side for easier access to her chin, purring all the while.

Tessa obliges her, running a gentle hand over the silky fur. "I'm in love."

My chest tightens at the soft curve of her smile, the murmured words of affection she gives to Boots, the contentment she radiates.

"Anytime you want to come over—you know, to visit her—you can."

She looks up at me, her smile growing wider. "I'd like that."

I nod, absent-mindedly rubbing at my chest.

"Could I come over tomorrow night to practice some more?"

How can I say no? "Yes... I mean, no. I have plans." How mad would Danielle be if I backed out of dinner? No, I won't do that to her.

"Right." She waves a hand in my direction. "Obviously you have plans."

My brows narrow. "What do you mean *obviously*?" Does she think I'm lying?

She gives me a look like I'm simple. "Because tomorrow's Saturday night. You probably do cool things every weekend. I'm lucky enough you were free tonight."

She thinks I'm... cool?

"What do you think I do on the weekend?"

She shrugs. "I don't know. Parties. Dates. Bars. Other generally social things."

I bring a hand up to cover my grin. Is that how she sees me? What would she say if I told her I pretty much never do those things?

"I'm having dinner with my family. But I'm free Sunday."

Her cheeks pinken the slightest bit. "Okay, Sunday. How about seven again? And I'll bring my notes about applying to the university. I'm still researching a few things."

I forgot I made that stupid request. What was I thinking?

"Yeah, great." Now I can sit through a reminder that college isn't in the cards for me, despite her assurances the other day that it's a possibility.

Even so, her words rekindle that strange sense of hope from talking to her about it on Tuesday. The thought that maybe I could...

No. Better not start thinking I can do stuff out of my league.

The same way I need to stop looking at her.

CHAPTER EIGHT

TESSA

"CHEAPSKATES," Lexie mutters once the couple she was serving walks out the door. "They left me a dollar-fifty on a thirty-dollar check. That's five fucking percent."

I finish wiping down the counter by the register and throw the rag into the bucket behind me. "Sorry. They did the same thing to me last time they came in."

She huffs a sigh of disgust. "Don't people realize we make practically nothing per hour? This is criminal."

"They probably know and don't care. You've been here, what? Almost four months? Welcome to the world of serving."

"Yeah, yeah," she grumbles, stuffing the money in her coin purse with the rest of her tips.

I glance over to check on my one table, but they're doing fine. Now that the lunch rush is over, we're in that afternoon slump where hardly anyone comes in. Only thirty minutes left of my shift, at least.

"What have you got planned for tonight?" I ask her. On a Saturday night, she and Ethan must have somewhere cool to go.

She rests her elbows on the counter, blowing out a sigh. "Nothing much. I'll probably work on this presentation I have for one of my classes next week."

"You don't go out on the weekends?"

"Nah, I'm more of a homebody."

"Oh." I assumed they went out all the time. Ethan's so outgoing.

"I do have to stop by the gym before I go home, though. I left my flash drive there."

I perk up. "You mean the boxing gym?"

"Yeah." She flicks a balled-up straw wrapper across the counter.

"What's it like there?"

She looks over at me, raising her brows. "Don't tell me you're interested in boxing."

"No, no." Last night proved I'm incredibly out of shape exercise-wise. "I just have no idea what to picture."

"Okay, imagine a giant room full of sweaty guys who've never heard of showering… and that's it."

"Doesn't your boyfriend go there?"

She waves a hand in front of her in dismissal. "Besides him."

"And your dad works there?"

She grins. "Including him."

She straightens as a car parks outside and heads over to the hostess stand to grab menus. "It's not some mystery place. You can come with me if you want."

I can? "Yeah, sure."

A swirl of excitement runs through my belly. Will Austin be there? Will I get to see him in action?

No, what am I thinking? He has that family dinner tonight.

Still, I'd like to see where he trains.

When our shifts end at four, I follow her across the street and down the steps to the basement level entrance.

"Whoa," I mutter under my breath as I take everything in. Exposed beams run the length of the room, with punching bags hanging down over in the far corner, and two rings on the opposite side. Guys mill around the place, some of them sparring with each other, some solo at the bags, and others by the edges of the rings. There must be a fitness requirement to get in or something because all of them are buff.

Lexie motions me to the right toward an enclosed office with glass windows, and I trail her closely, not wanting to get separated. Any one of these guys could eat me alive.

I take a breath of fresh air as we enter the office. Lexie wasn't kidding about the smell.

A grizzled man looks up from his desk, glancing between us. "You recruiting people now?" he asks Lexie gruffly.

"No. I need to pick up a flash drive I left."

"Like I know what the hell you're talking about," he mutters.

She points toward his computer. "That. Sticking out there. No, don't pull it out. You'll corrupt it."

"Corrupt it? What are you—"

"You have to eject it first. The arrow on the lower right-hand part of the screen. Here, let me do it."

She rounds the desk, shooing him out of the way, and he comes over to stand beside me, muttering under his breath something about how bossy she is.

"You interested in boxing?" he asks me when he catches me peering out the windows onto the main floor.

I press a hand to my chest. "Me? Oh, I just wanted to see what it's like in here."

"Want a tour?"

Is he for real?

"Marty, she's not a prospective client," Lexie says from the desk. "Tessa works with me at Kate's Kitchen. We only stopped in for a second to get this." She holds up her retrieved flash drive.

His mouth crooks up on one side. "Let me at least try to squeeze a membership out of her."

Me? A member here? He must be kidding. Those guys out there could bench press me. "Oh, I was just curious about this place because I know someone who trains here."

"Her boyfriend?"

"No, um, Austin Langford."

His brows narrow as he folds his arms across his barrel chest. He has to be at least in his fifties, but he's still in incredible shape. "How do you know my nephew?"

His nephew?

I study him, searching for any similarities. Definitely the size. He's got the same height and broad shoulders. Other than that, it's hard to pinpoint anything in particular.

Oh, wait. He's expecting an answer, isn't he?

"He's my neighbor," I rush to say. "He was actually showing me some self-defense moves last night."

His grin from earlier returns. "Is that what they're calling it nowadays?"

I blink, my cheeks reddening as his meaning washes over me. "No, we're not—"

"I'm kidding," he says. "Come on, let me give you the tour."

I glance over at Lexie, who rolls her eyes as she gets up from the desk and follows us out.

"Marty Farrell, by the way. I'm the owner here." He holds out a hand for me to shake, nearly crushing my fingers with his grip.

"Tessa Hooper." I stick my hand in my coat pocket when he lets go, hoping he didn't notice me wincing.

"Equipment racks are along this wall here." He points to shelving units full of gloves, mitts, gauze wraps, and jump ropes. "Aerobic area for practicing with speed ropes and any partner work." He gestures further down past the office. "Just put up some reflex and double end bags last month. Guys seem to like them."

I ignore the curious glances I receive as we make our way past a row of punching bags suspended from the ceiling, trying not to flinch at the hard pound of fists striking leather. At least it's not other people.

"Heavy bags and speed bags on this side. Lockers and showers through that door there. And our two rings take up the rest. One on the left is a twenty by twenty, the other's sixteen by sixteen."

"That was your tour?" Lexie asks as we stop in front of the larger ring. There are people in there fighting, but I can't see over the group of guys. "Where's the pizzazz? Where's the upsell? All you did was point things out around the room."

I glimpse a guy with a large, muscled back in the ring, with dark blond hair tied out of the way. Could that be…

"What are you talking about?" Marty counters. "What's wrong with my spiel?"

"Listen, I do your books. I know how many new memberships you get a month. Maybe we need to work on your selling technique."

I move to the right as they bicker, past the group of guys until I have a clear view of the ring. The guy with blond hair is turned away from me, his gray y-back tank dark with sweat in spots. His opponent wipes at his forehead with his arm, face weary as he brings his gloves up to defend himself against the incoming attacks.

"You can block better than that, Johnson," a third guy in the corner of the rings calls out. A trainer, maybe? "Don't let him intimidate you."

The blond rains down blows on this Johnson guy, each one brutally fast. Tension rises within me at the carnal display, a sick fascination growing as I continue to watch. The precision of each punch, the physicality of it, the way the muscles in his upper back flex and release.

He turns slightly, enough to see his profile, and my breath hitches, my brain finally catching up with what my body already knew.

It's Austin.

He's methodical as he circles Johnson, waiting for the right moment to strike. Powerful as he lunges in for a hit, connecting with his mid-section with a soft thud as glove meets flesh. Agile as he rears back when the guy swings at him in response.

The entire event occurs within a five second span, but it's like time seems to slow as it happens. There's beauty in his movements, as barbaric as they are. A predator playing with his prey as he comes in close, taunting him with quick punches the guy can't react to in time, dancing away afterward, light on his feet even with as big as he is.

I'm mesmerized watching him for untold minutes, masterfully commanding the ring, untouchable as he leads his opponent to do exactly what he wants. Austin's at another level, even as Johnson tries his hardest to keep up. No wonder Lexie said he could go pro.

Previously, he alluded to not being smart, but it's apparent this takes a different kind of intelligence. Balancing speed and strength. Power and agility. Employing focus, discipline, tactics, and control. And all while facing dangerous consequences if you miscalculate.

What he's doing isn't blindly swinging at people. There's strategy there, with a keen, sharp mind behind it. The amount of skill it must take to get to his level is unfathomable, his body and mind working together to create something breathtaking.

I could watch him all day.

"Tessa, you ready to go?" Lexie asks with a light tap on my shoulder, startling me. How long have I been out of it?

At her first word, Austin comes out of his stance, turning to face the room, his gaze flicking over the crowd until it lands on me with a flare of recognition. I swear something passes between us, and a sizzle runs down my spine unexpectedly, but not unpleasantly.

"Tessa?" he says, barely audible from this far away, and takes a step toward me.

Too late, I realize Johnson didn't get the memo that Austin's stopped for the moment, watching with horror as he clocks him in the temple.

Austin lurches to the side and there's a collective groan from the group of guys to my left, one commenting that he's never seen anyone make contact with Austin like that.

He shakes his head dazedly, holding a glove to the area as he continues to stare at me.

My hands are over my mouth, heart somewhere in my throat as I stare back. Is he okay? Should I help him?

"You good?" the guy in the corner of the ring calls out.

Austin gives one last shake of his head. "Give me a minute."

He slips through the ropes by me and nudges me over to the wall, away from the others.

I glance behind me, holding a finger up to Lexie, who's watching us with brows raised.

"I am so sorry," I whisper to him when we're out of earshot. "I didn't mean to distract you."

"What are you doing here?" His gaze sweeps over me, bewilderment still on his face.

"Lexie came by to pick something up and I was with her. And I…" I pull my coat tighter around me, glad he can't see my stupid waitress uniform again. "I wanted to see where you box, too," I admit. "But I didn't know you'd be here. I thought you had that dinner."

"It's not till six," he mumbles, still holding the side of his head.

"Are you okay?" I motion to his glove. "Can I see?"

He moves his hand, nodding slowly, and I step in closer, moving light fingers over his temple.

"Nothing's cut or split," I murmur, sifting through the strands of hair, damp with sweat.

He shudders, letting out a shaky breath, and I falter.

"Sorry, did I hurt you?" It must be tender.

It takes him a moment to answer. "Just caught me off guard."

"I don't know how you're even standing right now." I continue searching for any lumps or bruises on his scalp, coming up with nothing. "I'd be out for the count."

"I've had plenty worse."

How can he say that so nonchalantly?

"I think you'll be okay," I declare, stopping my inspection. "Maybe some ice on it tonight, though?"

He nods, turning to face me. This close, he seems even bigger, especially with that shirt he has on. There's no leaving to the imagination the breadth of his shoulders or thickness of his upper arms.

But where a week and a half ago I would have been intimidated by someone his size, it doesn't feel that way now. And despite what I witnessed him do in the ring, that once-dangerous air I perceived about him doesn't seem the same. Or that I'm safe from it, at least.

"You were incredible in there," I find myself telling him. "I'm really impressed."

He tilts his head down, rubbing at the nape of his neck. "It's nothing."

"You finished playing doctor?" Lexie calls out, and I step back, realizing now I'm too close.

Oh God, I was manhandling him, wasn't I? Just took it upon myself to touch him, as if I have any right to. What's wrong with me?

"I should go." I stick my hands in my coat pockets again so I'm not tempted to do anything else stupid. "Have fun at your dinner later."

I turn around, discovering the group of guys watching us, blatant curiosity all over their faces. They're probably wondering why their boxing god is allowing some mousy girl to check him for injury. I didn't ruin his man cred, did I?

Letting my hair fall forward to curtain my face, I join a smirking Lexie, following her toward the entrance.

"So you wouldn't look at him a week ago and now you're all over him?" she asks as we walk back up the steps to the parking lot.

I groan at her too-accurate comment. I didn't mean to do all that, it was just kind of… instinctual.

"He got hit because he was distracted by me, so I wanted to make sure he was all right." Is that a crime?

She makes a *hmm* sound, clearly not buying what I'm trying to sell, but I don't know what else to say. How to explain the sensations coursing through me as I watched him box. How alive I felt. How visceral everything seemed. How I didn't think twice about checking him out as he came over to me, only wanting to make sure he was okay.

She waves bye to me as she gets in her rusted car, and I head to my own, not that it's much better. The rear fender has been hanging on for dear life for a while now.

I rest my head on the steering wheel when I get in, breathing in and out slowly. It wasn't a big thing. He would've said something if it was, not stood there and let me do it. I'm overthinking things as usual. Everything is fine.

We'll practice more self-defense tomorrow, I'll show him the college info I found, and I'll get to pet Boots some more. Just because I liked watching him box, because I got close to him, because I touched him... it doesn't mean anything.

We're neighbors. Sort of even friends now.

And I'm happy with that.

I am.

CHAPTER NINE

AUSTIN

I HEAD STRAIGHT into the locker area, ignoring the guys' questions.

Who was that?

You okay?

Is that your girl?

No, she's not my girl. Far from it.

But that doesn't keep me from reliving her gentle touch, how soft her fingers were, the concern in her voice. The way my heart had stopped as she'd caressed the side of my face, unable to do anything but stand there, barely breathing. Wanting her to continue touching me, to slide her hand through my hair, breaths warm against my skin, lips whispering across my neck...

Fuck. No. What am I thinking? She was completely innocent doing that. She was trying to help me, for God's sake. If she knew what was going on in my head, she'd be horrified.

It's only recently she's become more comfortable around me, talking to me, getting closer. But I have no delusions she thinks of me in a sexual way at all.

I can't say I feel the same, though. Even knowing we're nothing alike. That she's way too good for me. That she previously avoided me, flinched if I moved too fast.

What must she have thought watching me in the ring? Did it confirm all her initial impressions?

Intimidating. Dangerous.

But today, she'd cared that I was hurt. Touched me without a second thought. Said my boxing was impressive.

And why am I still arguing with myself about this? There's nothing to argue about. Nothing between us.

I strip off my clothes and stride into the showers, turning the water to cold. The icy spray shocks me out of my warped daydreams, calming me, and I finish cleaning up and dress, once again avoiding everyone's eyes as I exit and walk straight out the doors, jogging up the steps to ground level.

I'm sure word will get around to Uncle Marty at some point about the incident, but I can put that off until another time. For now, I have to get over to Dad's place for dinner.

I'm way earlier than expected, arriving right behind Danielle, who's struggling with an armful of groceries as she gets out of her car.

"You actually showed up early? That's a first."

I roll my eyes. "I was going to help you with those." I motion toward her full arms. "But not anymore."

"These are yours, asshole," she says without heat. "Or do you want me to keep your food hostage?"

Oh, that's right. I did ask her to pick up some stuff for me.

"When are you buying an actual car so you can shop for yourself?" she asks as I take the bags from her.

"You were at the store, anyway. What do I owe you?"

"Thirty." She walks ahead of me, careful to sidestep the clump of snow in the driveway that always refuses to melt after it snows. "And they were out of cat litter. I'll have to stop somewhere else."

"That's fine. I'll Venmo the money to you."

"So why are you early?"

I shrug, not wanting to admit how stupid I'd been to get distracted by Tessa in the first place. "I finished at the gym ahead of schedule."

"You ready for Dad's weekly interrogation?"

"Sure," I mutter, bracing myself as she slides her key in the lock.

"Danielle?" Dad calls out as the front door squeaks open. "That you?"

"Yeah. Austin's here with me, too."

"You're not training?"

And it's started already.

He's in the kitchen stirring an oversized pot of chili on the stove, the smell of ancho peppers thick in the air, and I pass by him to stick my bags in the fridge until it's time to leave. "I just came from the gym."

"How's Marty?"

"Fine." Not that I talked to him today.

"I asked him about getting you another fight soon."

Of course he did. "He didn't mention anything to me about it."

"Why aren't you being proactive? You need to go after more opportunities."

I sigh, making eye contact with Danielle in the doorway to the kitchen. She narrows her eyes, shaking her head slightly.

Got it. *Don't piss him off.*

"I'll talk to him." Not about more fights, but he doesn't have to know that.

"Good. Grab some bowls."

I move over to the cabinet that houses the dishes and pull out three bowls, then to the drawer with silverware.

"He said you're ready to go pro, too."

I still, my hand hovering over the spoons. How many times will we have this conversation?

"I'd like to get some more fights in first." Anything to get him off my back.

"Why? You've been training for years. This is what you've been working toward."

No, what he's been pushing me toward.

I make a noncommittal noise, bringing everything over to the kitchen table.

"I came down there last week and watched you in the ring," he continues.

He did? When was this?

"You were dominating in there. As good as Marty in his heyday."

I glance over my shoulder, finding him smiling to himself.

"I remember one match of his that me and your mother went to. Marty was obliterating this guy. It was like I was looking at him thirty years ago when I saw you."

Danielle walks further into the kitchen, leaning against the counter. "Did Mom like going to his matches?"

Dad lifts the pot of chili, bringing it over to the table to set on the trivet in the center. "Well, it was her brother. That's what you do for family. You show up for them." He ladles out a portion into his bowl and sits down, then picks up his spoon. "Enough about that, though. When are you getting your pro license?"

I release a breath, sitting across from him at the table. "I'll talk to Uncle Marty."

Danielle pats me on the shoulder as she passes by. "So, my roommate got a new dog," she says, thankfully changing the subject. "Dad, you'd love him. He's a lab mix and the sweetest thing."

I let their conversation wash over me, answering direct questions but otherwise staying silent, mulling over Dad's routine demands. What started as a way for me to stay close to Mom's brother after her death has morphed into something entirely different. Boxing was supposed to be a fun thing I learned from my uncle, not become my whole life.

When Dad discovered I had natural talent at it, that I was better than anyone had expected, it's the only thing he wanted me to focus on, to the exclusion of all else. Why bother doing well in school when I was going to be a pro fighter, anyway?

It's not that I don't love boxing, I just don't want it to be… everything. To be decided for me, no question about it. When do I get a say?

Tessa's coming over tomorrow to talk about going to college. What am I supposed to say to her? Nod along politely and throw away anything she gives me later?

Or maybe take her seriously, imagining a different future…

"Austin."

I jerk my head up, finding them both looking at me expectantly. I need to stop daydreaming about things that'll never happen.

No matter how appealing they may be.

I look over the apartment for the hundredth time, not that anything has changed since I last looked it over, and sit down on the couch, knowing there's nothing else to do. The place is clean.

I stand after another few seconds, pacing the length of the room, unsure what to do with this restlessness coursing through me. It was the same on Friday night before going to Tessa's, like my skin is too small for my body, like there's not enough space to function.

Like my heart is beating faster than it should in anticipation for… I'm not sure what.

I'm just showing her some more self-defense moves. Listening to her tell me about what it takes to get into college. That's all it is.

At the knock at the door, I'm practically sprinting there, opening it way too fast to seem normal, immediately cursing myself for the unintentional eagerness.

She blinks up at me, startled, then smiles, the sprinkling of freckles over the bridge of her nose more pronounced in the fluorescent light of the outdoor hallway's lamp.

My breath hitches for a moment staring at her, then I remember myself, opening the door wider to let her in. "Hey."

"Hi."

She's clutching a folder to her chest, along with something else that makes a shaking sound with each step as she passes by.

"I got some cat treats for Boots. Is that okay? Is she allowed to have them?"

"Yeah, sure." I take them from her, looking at the smiling cat on the front of the package. "You didn't have to do that."

"I wanted to. She's so sweet."

I shake the bag and Boots comes running out of my bedroom, curious as to what I have.

Ripping it open, I hand it back to Tessa. "You should be the one to give them to her."

She pours a few out in her palm and places them on the ground, petting Boots as the cat sniffs at them and chows down.

"You didn't want to practice self-defense at all, did you? It was a cover to see her."

She grins widely. "I would never."

After giving a few more under the chin scratches, she stands, placing her folder on the coffee table. "Okay, I'm ready. What are we learning today?"

"You've been practicing the moves from Friday?"

"Was I supposed to?"

"Well, it's a good idea. You want it to come second nature to you when you're in an actual situation."

She nods seriously. "Right. That makes sense. Do you have to do that for boxing?"

"Yep. When you're getting pounded, you need to instinctively react. To have that muscle memory."

"Okay, so heel thrust." She does the accompanying movement. "Groin kick. Elbow strike. Hammer strike." She runs through each of them a few times, her face set in concentration.

"Feel like you got those down?"

"I think so. Could we work on getting out of holds next? Or is that too advanced? It's not like I could flip you over and pin you."

Pinning me? Like straddling me on the ground, her hips atop mine, pressing me down…

Fuck. I've got to stop thinking like this.

I shake my head, clearing it. "We're not doing any jiu jitsu style stuff."

"Okay. Do you think I could actually get out of a guy's hold? I'm pretty small."

Yeah, she is. She only reaches my shoulder, with a petite build that doesn't inspire any kind of confidence in her gaining an edge on a guy like me.

"Chances are someone that's assaulting you will be bigger and stronger, right?"

She nods warily.

"So what you want to focus on is being faster and ruthless."

She swallows heavily. "Ruthless?"

"Yep. Stomp on their feet. Elbow them in the gut. If your hand is free, bring it as hard as you can into their face, into their groin. Scratch them. Bite them. Yell and scream. Attract attention. Whatever you can do to get away."

She blinks at me a few times. Did I shock her?

"Why don't we try it out? But don't really hit me. Just tell me what you'd do."

She nods and I move in, stopping when her eyes go wide, panic on her face. The same as that day in the laundry room.

She holds her hands up to her face, covering it. "Sorry, I did it again, didn't I? I thought I was over this."

Over what?

"Come at me." She motions toward herself, seeming to brace for impact, like I'm going to tackle her.

"I don't want to scare you."

"You don't," she insists.

I raise a brow, the evidence suggesting otherwise.

"Only when you move quickly," she explains. "It doesn't seem like you'd be able to move that fast with how big you are." Her cheeks pinken almost immediately. "Not that you're fat. Obviously you're not. You're in amazing shape." She wipes her hands on her pants, glancing around. "Just broad. Like your shoulders and back and arms…"

I stare at her, unsure if she's finished.

"Let's just do it." She spins so her back is to me. "Now I can't see you. It'll be like a real attack."

"Tessa, I'm not attacking you."

"Fake attacking me."

I walk over to her slowly. "Did I scare you yesterday in the ring?"

Her shoulders raise and lower, as if she's taking a deep breath. "No."

I was moving faster then. Hitting another guy. Shouldn't that have been the place she was scared?

"So why do I scare you now?"

CHAPTER TEN

TESSA

I PLACE a hand on my chest, willing myself to breathe slower.

"Can we talk about something else?" I mumble, heat washing over me. Why can't I get myself under control?

He steps even closer, unnaturally silent for his size, but there's a primal awareness that alerts me to his nearness. "If someone came up to you like this," he murmurs, "would you be able to act? Or would you freeze?"

"I… I don't know," I admit.

My eyes squeeze shut as memories from that awful night engulf me. Frozen stiff lying in my bed, helpless to do anything as that giant climbed through my window, somehow not noticing me in the darkness of the room. Mind racing with worry, wondering what I should do. Shout for Mom? Lock my bedroom door? Follow him to see what he's doing? Crawl out the open window and head for the neighbor's house?

In the end, I couldn't do anything, too terrified to move, even after hearing Mom's scream, the deafening bang of the gun, the front door opening and closing a few moments later. Lying motionless for who knows how long, eventually gathering the courage to rise from my bed once I was sure he was gone. Padding down the hallway, my feet the only noise in the house, that sickening drop in my stomach as I'd discovered Mom, glassy-eyed in her bed, red all over her chest.

Is that destined to be me forever? The girl too paralyzed with fear to act? If

I'd screamed for Mom, she would have had the forewarning that someone was there. If I'd gone straight to her after he'd left, maybe I could have saved her somehow. Called 911 and they would have told me what to do.

A light hand settles on my shoulder, bringing me back to the present.

I blink, realizing there are tears in my eyes, that I'm shaking, that it's difficult to take a breath.

"Tessa?"

It's the gentleness in his voice that undoes me, the tears flowing faster. I wipe at my face frantically, not wanting him to see me like this.

"I'm sorry if I did anything," he says quietly. "I didn't mean to upset you."

"No, you didn't."

He's silent, probably because I'm clearly lying.

I step away from him and over to his couch, tucking my feet under me as I sit down. "What would you do if someone broke into your house while you were sleeping? How would you defend yourself, then?" That's what it all boils down to, right?

He studies me, that sharp, gray gaze flicking over me, face impassive. How red is my nose after crying? How puffy are my eyes? How pathetic must he think I am?

"What I'd do is different than what you should do," he finally says.

I find a loose hangnail on my thumb, pulling it off. "So, what should I do?"

"Do you sleep with your bedroom door locked?"

I nod, picking at my thumbnail now.

"Do you have a window in there? Mine doesn't have one."

"There's no window." That was my only requirement when looking for a place of my own.

"You have your phone right by you?"

I shake my head. "I charge it on my dresser overnight. It's on the opposite wall."

"You should move it next to you. In case you need to call or text the police and want to limit the amount of noise you make. I can give you my number, too. If you ever feel unsafe or like something's not right, you can call me."

He'd do that for me?

A shaky smile crosses my lips. "That actually makes me feel better."

He nods, pausing before he asks his next question. "Is this scenario something you're seriously worried about or a hypothetical situation?"

My smile drops. "It's serious."

"Have you thought about getting a gun?"

"No gun."

He recoils slightly, my hard tone probably over the top, but I can't help it. How could I ever own one after what happened to Mom?

"They scare me," I murmur, staring at my lap.

He takes a seat on the other side of the couch, a whole cushion between us, but for some reason, it feels closer than that.

"What about something like an air horn? To throw the person off balance and distract them?"

"And what if I throw them off so much that they fire the gun at me?" That's what the police said likely happened with Mom. She startled the robber so much with her scream, that he accidentally shot her. A break-in gone terribly wrong.

I press the heels of my palms to my eyes, not letting any more tears come out. "This was a bad idea. I'm sorry."

"I… okay."

I glance over at him, the confusion on his face sending a stab of guilt through me. He offers to help me with self-defense and then I flake out on him with a bunch of cryptic remarks? Some friend I am.

I should just say it. Get it out of the way so I stop looking like such a weirdo.

"Can I tell you something?"

He nods, his brows narrowing a bit.

"When I was eight…" I clear my throat, rubbing my suddenly sweaty palms on my pants. "I woke in the middle of the night from my bedroom window sliding open. It was a man."

"A big man?" he asks, voice barely above a whisper.

I nod. "Your body type, yes. Although, he seemed like a giant to me at the time."

I rub the bridge of my nose, not wanting to go through the whole explanation. To relive those memories again. Better keep it short and sweet. "He shot and killed my mother."

He inhales sharply. "I'm so sorry."

I wave away his concern. "I don't want pity. I just want you to understand where I'm coming from. Why this is… hard for me. Harder than expected. I thought I'd moved past this."

"Is that something you ever fully move past?"

I cross my arms, hunching into myself. "I saw the therapist the state provided, okay?"

"No, no." He shifts on the couch, facing more toward me. "I meant you shouldn't beat yourself up about it still affecting you. It's okay for this to be, I don't know, triggering."

I take a deep breath and let it out slowly. He's right. Haven't I gone over this kind of stuff in my psychology classes before?

"I'd like to work on this. To not freeze up if something were to happen."

"Yeah, of course."

"I'm sorry to waste your time like this."

"It's not a waste. I…" His knee bounces for a moment before he places a hand on it to stop it. "I like hanging out with you."

I sit up straighter. What? Why? All I do is continually embarrass myself in front of him. "I don't think anyone's ever outright said that to me before."

"Really?"

"Yeah, I…" Now it's my turn to pause. But if I told him about my mom, I can tell him this, too. "I had trouble getting close to people after, you know, everything that happened. I only really started opening up again when I got into college. I wanted to reinvent myself. To be a different person."

He nods. "I understand that. Wanting to be different."

He feels the same way? "What do you wish was different?"

He shrugs, scratching at his elbow. "Just… expectations, I guess."

What kind of expectations does he have?

"Does this have anything to do with you asking about college info?" I ask as the thought occurs to me.

His gaze cuts to me. "I knew you were smart, but damn."

My cheeks flush with a mixture of embarrassment and pleasure. "Is your dad pressuring you to go to college but you want to box instead?"

He gives the slightest shake of his head. "The opposite, actually."

Interesting. "He doesn't want you to go to college? But you do?"

He folds his hands in his lap, clenching his fingers together. "I want… the chance, at least. Dad kind of mapped out what he wanted for me a long time ago."

"What does he want you to do?"

"Pro boxing."

"And you don't want that?" He was so amazing in the ring, though. And Lexie said he's good enough to go pro.

His lips purse. "Don't get me wrong—I love boxing. But it's not something you can do long-term. I would have maybe fifteen years tops before my body's run into the ground. You see it all the time. Punch-drunk syndrome's a real thing." He shakes his head sadly. "And then what would I have? No other skills. I've put my whole life into fighting and have nothing left. I don't want that."

"It's smart to take your future into account. Have you explained it to your dad?"

He grimaces. "He doesn't listen. He just points to my uncle. As if everyone can open their own boxing gym when they retire."

"Would you want to do that?"

He shrugs. "That'd be cool as shit. But who in their right mind would give me a loan to do something like that? I… Damn." He slumps down, shoulders curling forward. "I didn't mean to rant about this."

"I don't mind listening."

"No, I'm supposed to be helping you out with self-defense stuff."

"And I said I'd help you figure out college stuff. This is part of that."

I grab the folder I brought with me and open it up. Thank God I have something else to focus on now. Something where I'm in my element.

"The biggest question is—do you actually want to go to college? Is it for you? Or because your dad doesn't want you to?"

He rubs his hands along the front of his athletic shorts. "Didn't know I'd be going to a therapy session," he mumbles.

I grin at him. "I'm a psychology major. What'd you expect?"

He bites his lip, staring at the papers in the folder. "I don't know. I haven't let myself consider it before."

"Well, what might you be interested in doing career-wise?"

Crossing his arms over his chest, he says, "Fuck if I know."

"You don't have to make any decisions now." I pull the first page out, laying it on the couch cushion between us. "These are the requirements for my university if you want to look it over, though."

He takes it, looking it over, then glances at me with wide eyes. "You need this kind of GPA? Mine was… not that."

"Well, it's a prestigious school. There was a senator's daughter who went there a few years ago. Kaitlyn Parker. Senator Worthington's son goes there, too, but I don't know him well. He's a frat guy."

"Not your crowd?"

I tuck a loose strand of hair behind my ear. "Um, no."

"How do you know all this?"

I shrug. "I like researching things. Oh, and you know Denver Sandeke? The billionaire? His son Martin went there, too."

"Must be expensive, then."

"Yeah, the tuition is insane if you pay out of pocket. I was incredibly lucky to get the scholarships I did."

His head falls back against the couch, and he blows out a breath as he stares up at the ceiling.

Oh, crap. I'm supposed to be hyping college up, not bringing it down.

"But I also pulled info on the local community college. That'd be a more realistic goal for you, considering you're not sure what you want to do."

I sort through the papers until I find the one I'm searching for.

"The cost per credit hour is a lot lower here. Plus, there are no GPA requirements."

"What about the SAT?" He's still not looking at me, choosing to look upward instead. "I never took it."

"It's not required for community college. But they'll probably have you take a placement test to figure out what level of classes you should start at."

"Probably boom boom level," he mutters.

"Level… what?"

"That's what we called the lowest level classes at my high school." He finally glances over, a small smile playing over his lips. "You definitely wouldn't have been a boom boom kid."

"Um, thanks?"

His smile grows, the frustration on his face from earlier gone. "Sorry for not seeming appreciative. I am. But it's a lot to take in."

"I understand."

The urge to reach over and stroke his arm in comfort is so strong, I nearly do it before I catch myself. What am I thinking?

"Can I show you more?" I ask, directing my mind away from anything I shouldn't be doing.

He nods and I pull out the paper with the list of the most popular majors at the community college, going over them with him. Then there are the financial aid options that are best for him as a non-traditional student since he's not fresh out of high school. After that are some good test prep sites I found online that will help him with placement tests.

An hour later when we're going through sample classes he'd likely have his first semester, he finally calls for a break.

"I don't think I can take much more tonight."

I gather all the papers I printed out at the campus computer lab and stuff them back in the folder, placing it on his coffee table. "How are you feeling about the idea now?"

He leans forward, resting his elbows on his knees, hands clasped together. "It seems more real. Like it's something I could actually do. Although, once I take a look at those test prep sites... Well, that'll be the real test, won't it? I wasn't the best student in high school."

"Did you apply yourself?"

"No," he admits with a sheepish grin. "But this time around it'd be different. I'm only worried—"

He cuts himself off abruptly, looking down at his shoes.

I scoot nearer to him. "What is it?"

"What if... What if I try and I'm still not any good?"

I reach out, the tips of my fingers barely making contact with the dusting of dark blond hair on his forearm. After the last hour of him patiently listening to me babble about school, silently absorbing all the facts and figures I threw his way, we're a little closer than we were before. "That's a chance we all take any time we try something new. I mean, look at me and this self-defense stuff. I'm a huge failure so far. But I'm going to keep working on it."

"You're not a failure."

I raise my brows. "What would you call my freak out earlier, then?"

"You're a beginner. You're learning. You're—" He swallows hard. "Yeah, okay. I see the similarities."

"Do you think you could help me out some more? With self-defense? I know it's asking a lot—"

"Of course I'll help. I said I would."

"Because you like hanging out with me?" I tease.

His eyes widen slightly, mouth unsmiling, and my stomach drops. Is it too soon for teasing?

"You said it earlier," I remind him, and his expression softens.

He runs a hand through his hair, scraping it back. "Right. I forgot I said that. I don't... Well, I don't usually talk this much. But there's something about you that makes me want to, I don't know... open up."

The lead ball in my stomach from earlier disappears as a warm, fuzzy lightness spreads throughout me. He likes hanging out *and* talking to me? Today's been some kind of breakthrough.

"Well, I seem to talk too much around you, so it only makes sense."

The corner of his mouth lifts in acknowledgment. "So, you want to get together sometime this week? Practice your stuff some more?"

"Yeah. I need to work on not freezing up. How about Tuesday night? I'm free after the study."

"Sounds good."

I stand, sensing the night has come to an end, and he stands too, walking me over to the door. I glance around for Boots, but she's nowhere to be found, probably back in Austin's bedroom. That'd be too weird if I invited myself into his private space to look for the cat.

"Thanks for everything," I tell him. "I mean, putting up with my ridiculousness and all."

"There's nothing about you that's ridiculous," he murmurs, kindness in his voice.

That warm fuzziness permeates me again, lifting me enough to impulsively hug him, his body heat warming me in the chilliness of the early February air. He's so tall, it's all I can do to wrap my arms over his broad shoulders, muscles like granite under my hands.

Oh God, what am I doing? We're not on hugging terms yet.

"Sorry." I release him and step back, tilting my head down so he can't see my hot cheeks. "I'll see you Tuesday."

Opening the door myself, I slip through and grab my keys out of my pocket, fumbling at the lock. When I finally get it open, I can't help glancing over my shoulder one last time.

He's standing in his doorway, gazing at me soberly, but it's impossible to tell what he's thinking. That I was way too forward? That I shouldn't have done it?

Or is it possible… he might have liked it, too?

CHAPTER ELEVEN

TESSA

"HOW'S THE MEDITATION GROUP DOING?" I ask Joel, adjusting my backpack so it sits higher on my back. This Abnormal Psych textbook is so damn heavy.

He glances over at me as we make our way down the hallway toward Dr. Price's office. Today we're officially halfway through the study, so it's time to meet with him for a status report. "Good. They're all getting the hang of it."

"And you know what you'll say to Dr. Price?"

He gives me an exaggerated squint. "Isn't it usually me checking up on you like this?"

My lips press together in a sheepish grin. "Sorry. I just want to make sure all our bases are covered."

"Hmm." He pretends to stroke a nonexistent beard. "You're not projecting, are you? How is *your* group doing?"

"Projecting?" I hold a hand to my chest, mock scandalized. "I'll have you know my progressive muscle relaxation group is the cream of the crop. They're on their A game."

He holds his hands up, grinning. "If you say so."

We turn the corner and stop in front of Dr. Price's office. After knocking, I open the door at the call of greeting from inside.

"Tessa. Joel." Our professor runs a hand through his salt and pepper hair, seeming frazzled as he stands and motions toward the chairs on the other side of his desk, full of piles of paper. "You can move those out of the way."

I set the stacks on the floor, wondering if he ever cleans this office. It's been like this every time I've visited.

"How's the study going? Mia's told me good things."

So she's been updating him?

I open my mouth to answer, but Joel beats me to the punch, going on about the progress of his group. I sit back in my seat, folding my hands in my lap, waiting for a question, but Joel keeps taking them all. It's not until almost the end of our meeting that Dr. Price specifically asks about my group and I'm finally able to get a word in.

After we exit and head out, I pause at the top of the stairwell. "You could have saved a question for me."

Joel stops a few steps ahead, turning around to look up at me. "What?"

"You dominated the conversation." Normally, I wouldn't say anything, but that was ridiculous.

He shakes his head, hair getting in his eyes before he pushes it away. "You answered some."

"Only when he asked about my group. You took all the rest."

He squints, but it's not like last time when he was joking. Now it's like he doesn't believe me. "What's the big deal?"

"I want him to know we're splitting everything equally. That I'm doing just as much work as you. You might not realize it, but it's harder for girls to be taken seriously by their professors compared to guys."

He blinks at me for a moment. "I don't remember taking all the questions, but I'm sorry if I did."

That's… not really an apology. That's like one of those *I'm sorry you feel that way* answers.

"I guess I got caught up in the excitement of our study," he continues. "Here, let me make it up to you. How about dinner tonight?"

Seems like that's all the acknowledgement I'll get about it, then.

"I have plans." And honestly, I'm too annoyed to have dinner with him.

I move past him on the stairs, but he stops me with a hand on my shoulder. "But you're always free Thursday nights. You didn't pick up another shift at the diner, did you?"

"No."

I leave it at that, not wanting to bring up that my plans are with Austin. On

Tuesday, we worked on me getting more comfortable with a potential attacker approaching, to the point where I barely flinch. It's not much, but it's progress. Thank goodness he's so patient with me.

Joel's grip on my shoulder tightens. "You're seeing that guy, aren't you? The one from your Tuesday group."

And this is why I didn't mention it. He got all weird about it before. "He's teaching me self-defense."

"Didn't you do that last week?"

I move my arm so I'm no longer within his reach. "It's an ongoing process. Why do you keep bringing it up?"

"Because I'm worried about you."

I can't help the laugh that escapes me. What in the world could he possibly be worried about? "Why?"

He purses his lips, moving closer. "He's not good for you."

My brows narrow. "You literally don't know him. He's a friend. My neighbor. Ask Tyler to vouch for him if you're so concerned. They box together."

He scoffs. "Tyler's not exactly the best judge of character."

What's he got against Tyler? "Well, what about me? You don't trust me?"

"Of course I do. But you can also be kind of… naive at times."

I tilt my head, clamping my mouth shut so the first thing that comes to mind doesn't fly out. He wants to talk about naive? He's never had a job in his life, relying on his parents' generous monthly allowance along with everything else they pay for him. He literally has nothing to stress about.

"Can you give me an example?" I ask through clenched teeth. Seriously, where is this coming from?

"Listen, I don't want to fight. I'm sorry I said anything."

Sorry I called him out on it, he means?

"I'll bring you a venti coffee next week," he says enticingly. As if I'd sweep this all under the rug because of that?

"I don't like coffee," I mutter as I head down the stairs.

"Tessa—"

"Make it a chai tea," I shout from halfway down the next landing. Continuing this conversation won't go anywhere. Better to cool down some.

Forty-five minutes later there's a rhythmic knock at the door, reminiscent of the "Shave and a Haircut" tune. That's weird. I didn't take Austin for that kind of knocker. That's something more like… No, I'm being silly.

But the thought won't leave me as I head to answer it. Joel knows I have plans. He wouldn't interrupt me at home. Especially not after how he acted earlier.

Each footstep seems harder to take, though, the simple distance between the couch and front door multiplying, something deep in my gut knowing it's not Austin on the other side.

He could just be early. He could be that kind of knocker.

And my spidey senses could be right.

Peering through the peephole, a familiar head of floppy brown hair fills my vision, my stomach sinking. It's not like I can pretend I'm not home, though. My car's right outside.

I open the door, a bouquet of flowers greeting me. Well, that's a surprise.

I take the arrangement of carnations, daisies, and baby's breath from him, unsure what to say. I'm guessing this is his way of apologizing?

"Can I come in?" he asks.

"Uh, sure."

I hold the door open wider and Joel walks in, his head swiveling as he searches the apartment. He could at least be a little more circumspect.

"Austin's not here," I tell him, getting it out of the way.

He spins around, guilt flashing over his face. "I wasn't… I came here to make sure we're good. I don't like fighting with you."

I let out a sigh. "You basically said today you don't trust my judgment. That obviously upset me."

"I'm sorry. I shouldn't have said that."

I mull over his response for a moment. "You're sorry you said it out loud? Or you're sorry and don't really mean it?"

"The second one," he stutters. "And you can hang out with anyone you want. You're right that I don't know this guy."

I nod. "Thanks for saying that."

"So I'm forgiven?"

God, I hate being put on the spot like this. If I say no, I'm a bitch, aren't I?

"Sure." I move past him to grab a vase from beneath the kitchen sink and fill it with water before sticking the flowers in.

"I was thinking I should get to know him, too. I could join you for your self-defense lesson."

My lips part, but no sound escapes. He wants to join us? Is it wrong that I don't want him to? "I, um, I haven't cleared it with Austin. If he'd be comfortable with that."

He takes a seat on my couch, propping his feet on the coffee table. "I'm sure it'll be fine. What's one more person? I mean, all you're doing is self-defense, right? Not anything else?"

Irritation flares within me before I tamp it down. Why does he keep implying I'm guilty of something? "No, just self-defense."

"Great. Can't wait to learn some moves."

I stare at him, my fingers flexing at my sides. Joel's my friend. I shouldn't be this annoyed. But that doesn't change that I am.

There's a knock at the door and I whirl around and open it, stepping outside before Austin sees Joel. "Hi."

He steps back to give me room and hitches a thumb over his shoulder, glancing at my closed door. "Hey. Did you want to go to my place instead or something?"

"No, my friend stopped by unexpectedly."

"Oh." He sticks his hands in his pockets. "Did you need to cancel?"

"He was actually hoping to join us." I cross my arms, unprepared for the cold out here. "It's my study partner, Joel. You might have seen him at the Stress Lab?"

He scratches at the back of his neck, forehead wrinkled. "Uh…"

"I understand if you say no. It's super last minute."

"No, no. It's fine."

A pang of disappointment blooms in my chest. I should be happy he's being so accepting, though, shouldn't I?

"Great. Let's get started."

My mouth won't quite form the smile I intend, so I head inside instead.

"You're in luck," I tell Joel. "He can teach both of us."

"Cool. Do you have something to drink, Tess? I'm parched."

"Sure. Is water okay?"

"You have any soda?"

I keep my sigh contained. "Let me see."

I rummage around in my fridge, not expecting anything to magically appear, but you never know. "Nope. I've cut back on extras after all those moving expenses wiped me clean in December. I've got water, tea, and milk."

"Hmm." I glance behind me to catch Joel's disappointed face. "Never mind."

Didn't he say he was parched?

"You want anything, Austin?" I ask.

He shakes his head, still standing by the front door.

Oh, right. I should formally introduce them. "Austin, this is Joel." I motion between them. "And Joel, this is Austin."

Austin raises a hand in welcome. "Nice to meet you, man."

Joel gives him a head nod. "Heard a lot about you."

Austin's gaze cuts to me and I quickly turn back to the fridge, hiding my face. I grab the Brita pitcher and pour a glass of water, using the time to let my cheeks cool.

It's going to be a long night.

CHAPTER TWELVE

AUSTIN

"THERE, YOU'RE GETTING IT." I study Tessa's form as she practices a hammer strike, her arm arcing gracefully in front of her. "Think of the movement as an extension of your body. You want all your power behind it."

She nods, that familiar concentration on her face as she does it again, more forcefully this time. She's set her mind to the task this week of practicing the moves I've taught her.

I glance up, catching Joel scowling at me before he wipes his expression clear. I'm not sure what his agenda is here, but it's clearly not to learn self-defense. After a few half-hearted attempts at learning the techniques I've been going through with Tessa, he settled on the couch, offering unsolicited critiques instead.

"You should do it harder, Tess," Joel says. "What you're doing won't hurt a real attacker."

I bite my tongue, my patience pushed to the limit.

You're not moving fast enough.

They'd laugh at you for doing that.

Are you sure you should be doing this at all?

If he says one more negative thing, I swear to God…

"I need a break," I mutter. "Can I get some water?"

Tessa nods. "Let me get you a glass."

I follow her the few steps over to the kitchen and lean against the far wall as she pours me a drink.

Joel gets off his lazy ass and disappears into what I assume is the bathroom, based on the layout of my own apartment.

I motion toward the closed door with my glass. "He knows his way around here."

She grabs her glass from earlier and refills hers, too. "He helped me move in." She takes a small sip. "Well, more like directed the movers. I don't think he actually carried anything."

Yeah, that seems about right from what I've seen so far.

"He's, uh…" I search for the best way to say this, nothing tactful coming to mind. "He's kind of annoying."

Her lips press together tightly.

"I wouldn't normally shit on anyone's friends," I continue, "but I'm almost at my limit here. He hasn't said a single nice thing to you all night."

Her head tilts down, her silence speaking volumes.

"Is he always like this?"

"I've been noticing it more lately," she murmurs.

"So why are you friends with him?"

"I…" She glances behind her, the bathroom door still closed. "Maybe he's stressed. He's only been acting like this for the last couple of weeks. I'm sure he'll be back to normal soon."

I shrug, but there's a nagging feeling I can't let go of. "Is there anything going on between you two?" Maybe he thinks I'm encroaching on his territory or something. Not that that explains why he keeps insulting Tessa.

She blinks at me, brows narrowing. "Like romantically? No."

There's clear dismissal in her tone, something easing within me at her response.

Not that it should matter, I remind myself.

"Why would you think that?" she asks, still seeming perplexed.

"I'm just trying to put a motive to his behavior. Sorry for suggesting it."

The bathroom door finally opens and Joel takes his seat on the couch again, looking at us expectantly. "You done practicing?"

"I still wanted to do some more," Tessa replies, heading back to the living room.

"How about elbow strikes next?" I suggest.

She grins at me. "I was working on those last night after work."

She does the movement a few times, but it's not long before Mister Criticism has something to say.

"You've been practicing? Doesn't look like it."

"Can you be positive at all?" I ask him, keeping my voice as even as I can. "She's trying really hard."

He recoils, as if I shouted at him, when I most definitely did not. Trust me, I wanted to.

"I'm helping Tessa."

"Well, nothing you're saying is constructive. So maybe you should keep it to yourself."

His lips thin, nostrils flaring. "She knows I'm helping. I've known her way longer than you have."

"I'm actually finished after all," Tessa says, stepping between us to block our line of sight. "Maybe we could pick this up another night?" she asks me.

I draw in a steady breath, willing myself to cool off. "Sure."

"I'll walk you out."

I follow her the few steps across the hall to my apartment door, shutting her front door behind us.

"Sorry about that," she whispers. "About him."

I tilt my neck toward my left shoulder, then my right, enjoying the crack and accompanying release of tension. I'll definitely be going through the long version of the applied relaxation sequence she taught me tonight.

"I didn't like hearing him say that stuff to you," I admit. "It didn't serve any purpose."

She shrugs lightly. "Maybe in his mind he thought he was helping."

"Do you always see the good in people?"

She gives me a soft smile. "Not always. But I try to give people the benefit of the doubt. With all my time living with different foster families, I found it was better to do that, for my own sanity. To be thankful for the things I did have rather than focusing on what I didn't. I would have driven myself crazy otherwise."

"There was no other family to take you in?"

She shakes her head. "My grandparents died before I was born and Mom was an only child. I have no idea who my dad is."

I look down at my feet, not knowing what to say. How hard did she have it growing up?

"Maybe we could get together tomorrow night again?" she asks, changing the subject. "Without Joel."

"Yeah. How about eight?" That way I have time to stop by the gym first. I already wish it wasn't too late to go tonight.

"Okay. I, um, have to get back in."

"Right. See you."

She returns to her apartment, but I don't head inside yet, walking in the direction of the parking lot instead. The night air is blisteringly cold against my skin, but it does little to focus my mind elsewhere. Should I have not said anything to Joel about his comments? Should I have spoken up sooner?

Maybe their friendship is different than what I'm used to, but this wasn't the boxing gym where it's a trainer's job to point out what you're doing wrong. She was learning the basics. She needed praise and reassurance, not unending criticism. Couldn't he see that?

At the very least, he won't be with us tomorrow night. And she's made progress, regardless of what he said. I think it's time we kick it up a level.

As long as she's on board.

I roll my shoulders back, the ache gratifying despite the pain. I shouldn't have gone so hard in the ring earlier, but it barely felt like anything at the time. And if I'm being honest, I may have pictured Joel as my opponent once or twice.

Or maybe the whole time.

I still don't get what Tessa sees in him as a friend. At least she said she wasn't interested in him.

I push that thought away, knowing it doesn't matter. She's not interested in *me*. She made that clear from the beginning.

Even though she's a hell of a lot more comfortable around me now. And no longer flinches after us working on it earlier in the week. And even hugged me goodbye on Sunday…

What the hell am I thinking? We're becoming friends. It doesn't mean anything more.

My phone buzzes, saving me from this ridiculous line of thought, but it only brings up a different kind of frustration.

Dad: *Any word on a tournament coming up?*

Is that the only thing on his mind? The only thing he can talk to me about?

There's a knock on my door and I tuck my phone back in my pocket, happy to ignore it. Tessa's here.

Her eyes are wide as I open the door, her gaze zeroed in on my left brow.

"What happened? Are you okay?"

"What?" What is she talking about?

"You're bleeding. Right here." She points at her eyebrow and that's when I remember Ethan's lucky shot from earlier. He must have split the skin. I didn't notice it with how sore everything else is.

"I'm sure it's fine. It'll heal on its own."

"You should at least put some antibacterial ointment on it. Do you need some?" She gestures behind her toward her apartment. "I can get mine."

"Uh, sure." If she's that concerned about it.

She's back in a minute with a shoebox full of supplies tucked under one arm. "I keep all my medicine stuff in here," she explains, setting it down on the coffee table. "Sit here."

She points to the couch and I sit down, amused when she props a pillow behind me as if I'm an invalid.

Rummaging through her box, she finds what she needs and kneels next to me, closer than I expected. Her delicate fingers brush my hair away from my temple and I nearly groan aloud at her touch, not knowing it would affect me like that. That the only thing I want to feel again is the featherlight stroke of those fingers down the side of my face and jaw, down my neck to my chest, heading further south…

I inhale, trying to get my thoughts under control, only to have a tantalizing hint of vanilla hit my nose. Is that what she smells like this close?

This is so much worse than her touching me at the gym. There, we had an audience. I was dazed from being hit.

But here, we're alone. My mind isn't addled. All I can focus on is her.

My chest constricts, trying not to breathe in her fragrance. I shut my eyes so I can't see the way she's leaning over me, so fucking close to my face. I need to desensitize myself, to ignore how gentle she is as she applies cream to my brow, her breaths soft and sweet.

"Shouldn't need stitches," she murmurs, pressing a bandage carefully over the area.

Good. I wasn't going to get them, anyway.

I reach up, gingerly touching the bandage, and she exclaims again.

"What happened to your knuckles?"

I hold my hand out in front of me, examining it. Yeah, the knuckles are red and cracked, but not especially bad. Between the cold weather and boxing, it's bound to happen.

"Good thing I brought the whole box," she says, rummaging through it. She pulls out a jar and holds it up. "This stuff has lanolin in it. It's great for your skin. I can put some on you."

I nod, afraid of what I'll say if I open my mouth.

Please God, touch me. Anything you want to do to me you can.

It's like her touch flipped a switch within me. Yes, I admit I was attracted to her before, but she's never willingly got this close in private. Never touched me without reserve. Never gave me a reason to wonder…

"My hands get so dry in the winter," she comments as she scoops out a dollop of cream and rubs it over my knuckles. "I call it my iguana skin."

Her touch is light and purposeful, nothing sexual about it, but I still can't help but imagine how her hands would feel on different parts of my body, rubbing in that same way, with the same level of care and attention…

Shit. I can't get aroused now. And if she called her own skin rough, what must she think of mine?

"You should take care of yourself more," she says softly.

I look up, her gaze meeting mine, and I make a noise of agreement, caught up for a moment in the warmth of her brown eyes, the curve of her smile. Does she have any idea how beautiful she is?

I swallow hard, breaking eye contact with her, and stand. "I think that's good."

"But I didn't get your left hand."

"I'll get it later." If her hands are on me for one second longer, I'm afraid of what I might do.

She puts away her jar in the shoebox. "Sorry I bombarded you with all this."

"No, you're fine. Thanks for doing it. I… I guess I don't have anyone else that would care about stuff like this."

"What about your sister?"

A huff of laughter escapes me. "She'd probably call me a dumbass for getting hit in the first place."

Her mouth quirks up on one side. "Well, any time you need help with something, let me know."

I nod, unsure how to respond. I'm not used to people offering to help me.

She stands and moves out from between the coffee table and couch to the other side of the living room where there's more space. "So, what are we working on tonight?"

The plan I had last night to take her training to the next level suddenly seems like a bad idea. It would involve… touching.

"I…" I falter, unsure what to say. "What else do you want to learn?" Better to leave it to her.

She scuffs a toe in front of her, looking down at the pattern she makes in the carpet. "Actually, as much as you disagreed with Joel's comments yesterday, he brought up a good point."

I raise my brows, now wanting to think about him.

"He said something about an attacker—I don't remember exactly what—and it got me thinking that everything we've gone over assumes they're coming at me from the front. But what if they get me in a hold from behind?" She gives a self-deprecating smile. "Not that I can do some over the shoulder flips, but how could I get out? At least enough to run away?"

Damn. That's a valid concern. And unfortunately, will likely involve… touching.

God, I have to get a grip.

"So you want to practice how to get out of holds from behind?"

She nods. "And for the record, Joel apologized to me after you left last night. He said he didn't realize he was being so negative."

Yeah, right. Not my problem, though.

I move over to where she's standing. "Since we don't have defensive gear, some of this will have to be theoretical. I don't want you hitting me in the balls."

"Duly noted."

"Are you ready?"

She nods, some of her earlier surety gone in the wake of what we're doing.

I slip behind her, placing my hands on her shoulders. "I'm going to put my arm around you now, okay?"

"Okay."

Is it my imagination, or is her voice breathier than normal?

There's no way to do this without being awkward, but I shift my arm forward, bringing it around her neck in a loose imitation of a chokehold. I'm not applying any pressure, but her breathing still picks up anyway, her hands coming up to grip me.

"How would you get out of a hold like this?"

I focus only on making sure she doesn't panic, ignoring how much more intense the scent of vanilla is this close to her, how petite she is, how all I want to do is press into her from behind.

No, I'm here to help her. Not hit on her.

"I…" She swallows hard, her fingers gripping my arm tighter for a moment before relaxing her hold. "The only place I'm trapped is around my neck. My arms are free so I could elbow you in the gut. If there was enough space between us, I could also swing a fist behind me and hit you in the balls."

"Good." I let go of her neck and take hold of her arms, bringing them behind her, then encircle a hand around her crossed wrists. "What if your hands were bound behind your back?"

I can't resist the impulse to sweep a thumb across the delicate skin of her inner wrists, the hitch in her breath making my belly dip low for a moment. What the fuck is wrong with me?

"My legs are free, so I could stomp on your feet." She mimes picking up a foot and lightly presses down on the top of my shoe. "That might distract you enough that you would loosen your hold on me and I could slip out."

"Yeah, great." It takes me a moment to let go of her, not wanting to lose that connection.

"What if my arms and legs weren't free?" she asks, turning to face me. "What could I do, then?"

"What kind of hold would that be?"

"Maybe pressed against a wall or something?"

Or a bed.

Fuck. Stop thinking like that.

"Did you want me to…"

Her cheeks flush. "No. Like you said, it's theoretical."

"If they're close enough, you could slam your head back. Catch their nose and hurt them."

"That's a good plan."

We keep going through practice holds, but it doesn't get any easier as we continue. I show her different ways she could strike me, but all I can think of is her gentle touch from earlier. How soft her fingers had been. I don't know what she was talking about having rough skin. It felt like velvet to me.

How she could keep touching me, her delicate fingers traveling down, down…

God, it's going to be a long fucking night.

CHAPTER THIRTEEN

TESSA

I COUNT out the dollar bills on the table and stuff them in my apron pocket, silently thanking the couple that just left for leaving a twenty percent tip. Combined with everything else, it was actually a decent Monday night.

"You ready to tackle the dishes?" Lexie asks, locking the front door.

"Yeah, let me wipe this table first."

If the dishwasher calls out one more time, Lexie and I should revolt. Why should we have to cover his job?

Then again, the cook still has to clean the grill and mop the whole restaurant. I guess what Lexie and I have to do isn't so bad.

She's already spraying down the glassware from tonight in the sink when I bring the last of the dirty dishes into the back.

"Did Kate ask you about covering Irene's shift Friday night?" she asks me, now loading the first tray of glasses into the dishwasher.

"No." I only get one day off a week between school and work. And even that's taken up with studying, catching up on housework, and all the errands I have to run. "Why does Irene need off?"

"Kate's got it covered," Manuel calls out from the other side of the kitchen as he scrapes the food and grease buildup off the flat top grill.

Well, that solves that.

"Guess she's got a hot date," Lexie whispers, waggling her eyebrows.

That's right. It's Valentine's Day on Friday.

"Who would go out with Irene?" I whisper. At best, she wouldn't even be called a handsome woman.

Lexie grimaces. "I don't want to know."

I pull the previously finished tray of glasses closer to me, finding a clean dishcloth to wipe them free of water spots. "Are you and Ethan doing anything for Valentine's Day?"

"Tyler and Mia are going to this Anti-Valentine's Day party at Element. We said we'd go, too."

"The club you used to bartend at?"

"Yeah. I left on good terms, though. There's only one girl there I can't stand, and now I can tell her to fuck off if she gives me an attitude."

I smile, wishing I had the nerve to say something like that to someone's face. "You have plans?"

I glance over at her. "Me?" A half laugh-half snort escapes me. "No."

"You holding out for a date with Austin?"

The previous sound I was making turns into a sputter. "What?"

She rolls her eyes. "You're so easy to rile."

"Hey." I throw the dishcloth at her. "Not cool."

She smirks. "Sorry."

The industrial-sized dishwasher beeps, signaling it's done, and I pull it open, swatting away the heavy cloud of steam. Lexie loads the next tray in and I go back to wiping off the glasses.

"What's Element like?"

"Never been?"

"No." Who would I go to clubs with?

"Why don't you come with us? Mia said her roommate and a bunch of her friends are going, too."

"Okay." That could be fun.

"And I could have Ethan invite Austin..." She doesn't even try to hide her sly grin.

"I never said I was interested in him." Said the girl whose heart is beating faster at the thought of going to a club with him... dancing together... on Valentine's Day of all days.

She gives me a look like I've got about two working brain cells and one just gave out. "I've seen you with him twice. That's it. Two times. You didn't need to say anything out loud."

I tilt my head down to hide my heated cheeks. What I did at the boxing gym may have been a bit much.

"He's not interested in me like that," I mumble. "I mean, he's... Well, look at him. And then there's me."

"You try to do a nice thing," she mutters, shaking her head. "Do you want me to have Ethan invite him or not? They're training across the street right now."

I bite my lip, not sure what to say. I guess it couldn't hurt if Ethan extends the invitation. Austin doesn't know it's coming from me. And he might decline anyway...

"Yes," I blurt out, not letting myself overanalyze things too much.

"Keep washing for me," she says, turning off the sprayer. "I'll text Ethan."

***

"Ready for week four?"

I glance up at Joel in the doorway of my room at the Stress Lab. "Hey."

I return to going over my notes for today's sessions, still a little miffed at him. Yeah, he apologized, but the more I thought about how negative he was being, the more it unsettled me. Would I even have noticed it as much if Austin hadn't said something? And then the way Austin had defended me, pointed out how hard I'd been trying... It was nice to be recognized.

Especially when half the time I have to remind myself to focus when I'm with him. Friday night when he had first put his arm around me, I should have been scared. I should have been imagining him as an attacker.

But all I could think of was how much I liked Austin being that close. How instead of feeling threatened, I felt safe. That when I'm with him now, I don't need to keep any kind of guard up. In the few weeks I've known him, he's already shown me how patient he is, how understanding. It's a complete reversal of my first impression of him.

"I had a good time Thursday night," Joel says, interrupting me from my train of thought. "We should do it again sometime."

"But you didn't do any of the self-defense moves." He sat on the couch nearly the whole time.

His smile falters for a moment. "I was soaking it in. You know, like auditing a class before I take it for real."

Right.

"And I'm sorry again for saying anything negative. Didn't even realize I was doing it."

I nod to acknowledge him. He apologized, so I should take him at his word. "No problem."

"How about we get together this Friday? You don't work that day, right?"

"I have plans."

There's that falter again in his smile, but it's not quite the same. More like he's… composing himself.

"Who with?"

"Some friends."

"On Valentine's Day?"

"Yeah."

Why does it matter if it's on Valentine's Day if he wanted to hang out with me then?

He grips the straps of his backpack, his mouth compressing. "Are you going out with Austin?"

Why is he so hung up on that idea? "My friend Lexie from work invited me to a party." Technically, not a lie. It's just not a private party. And it doesn't seem wise to mention that Austin may go, too. Ethan hadn't texted her back by the time our shift was over last night.

"Where's it at?"

"I don't know the address." Also, technically not a lie. I don't know Element's exact address.

"So you'd rather hang out with your work friend than me?"

Though he says it jokingly, there's something serious underlying in his tone. Why is he trying to guilt trip me? He already crashed my self-defense lesson.

I put my script for today away in its folder, any chance of rehearsing it before my first participant shows up long gone now. "I told her I'd go. I don't want to seem flaky."

"Well, I'm sure you won't be out the whole night. I can stop by after."

"I can't make any promises. I have no idea how long we'll be."

One side of his mouth crooks up in a smirk. "You're not a party girl. You won't be out long."

Something about how he says it rubs me the wrong way. Not quite condescending, but…

I mentally shake my head. I'm just in a bad mood. Seeing and hearing things that aren't really there.

"I'm going to wait in the lobby for my first person," I tell him, hugging my folder to my chest.

"Sure."

He doesn't move out of the doorway, though, forcing me to brush past him on my way out.

Why have things been so weird with him lately? What's going on?

I don't have long to ponder it because my first participant is already in the lobby. I greet her, the next hour and forty minutes flying by until it's Austin's turn, the sight of his blond hair brushed back from his face bringing a smile to my lips.

I wave at him from my spot at the entrance to the hallway, and as he spots me, he smiles too, something electric flashing through me I can't explain.

A sudden flutter of nerves passes over me, even after thinking earlier I can act normal around him now, and I'm quiet as we walk toward the room.

God, I'm being stupid.

"We're doing cue-controlled relaxation today," I blurt out in the middle of him removing his jacket.

"Okay." He looks down at me, that same smile lingering on his lips. Have I ever noticed how good they look? Usually, the beard distracts me, but now that I study them, they're actually kind of… sexy.

Oh God, I'm staring at his lips, aren't I?

I turn away and open the door once we reach it, holding it for him.

He settles his jacket on the back of the chair he always sits in. "So what exactly is cue-controlled relaxation? You know you have to explain everything to me like I'm dumb."

"You're not dumb."

He blinks at me. "I…"

Okay, maybe I said that a little forcefully. "You keep referring to yourself as not smart, but that's not true at all. There are different types of intelligence. It's not all about having a high GPA or test scores."

He's silent for a moment. "What other kinds are there?"

Of course he'd ask that when I don't have access to a computer. "Off the top of my head, the ones that people think of the most are logical and linguistic. But there are others like being musical or how you relate to others. Two you'd probably score high in are kinesthetic and spatial."

His brows narrow slightly. "Those are real things?"

"Yeah. And they're important. Our society couldn't function if we didn't have people that think in different ways."

He nods. "Thanks. That…" He blows out a breath, raking a hand through his hair. "That's nice of you to say."

"It's the truth."

He smirks. "If someone as smart as you says I'm smart too, I guess I have to believe it."

I bite my lip to hide my smile as a warm fuzziness fills my stomach.

"You probably score high in that one about relating to others," he tells me.

I guffaw at his remark. "Oh my God, no. I'm always saying the wrong thing. Do you not remember how we met?"

His nose wrinkles. "Fair point. But after that… You bandaged me up the other night. And told me I could go to college if I want. You're really…" He sticks his hands in his pockets, head tilting down. "You're really caring."

Is that pink I spy on his cheeks?

"You are, too."

He looks up at that, confusion lurking in his eyes.

"You offered to help me with learning self-defense. You stood up for me with Joel. Those were both kind things to do."

He shrugs. "It's no big deal," he mumbles.

To him, maybe not. But to me it is.

More than he knows.

CHAPTER FOURTEEN

TESSA

I GLANCE at the clock on the opposite wall, remembering we need to get a move on so I can turn the room over in time.

"Are you ready to start?"

He nods, taking a seat in the guest chair.

"So we went pretty off tangent, but cue-controlled relaxation is all about using a keyword, or cue, to trigger a deeper state of relaxation. For this study, we'll use the word *relax*."

"Easy enough," he comments.

"Right. So when you hear *relax*, you'll think about the progressive muscle relaxation sequence you've been practicing for the last few weeks. Focus on the lightness and ease that comes in the moment after you release the tension from your muscles. The aim is to get into that relaxed state quicker by associating the word with the feeling."

"Like a Pavlovian response."

"Exactly. And you said you weren't smart."

He chuckles and we start a shortened version of the original sequence, this time adding the word *relax* when he's at rest. I give him instructions to continue the shorter sequence at home once a day using the cue, while also consciously thinking about relaxing his muscles randomly throughout the day when he has a free moment.

By the time we're finished, it's past six o'clock, but Nathan and Chris thankfully aren't waiting to use the room yet. Looking at the darkened room next door, it also appears Joel has already left, too. Thank God. It doesn't seem like a good idea to have him and Austin in the same room together again.

"You all finished?" Austin asks as we walk down the hallway.

"Yeah, you were my last participant for the day, and I don't have meetings with anyone else."

There's a comfortable silence as we descend the stairs, and I tighten my coat around me as we head outside, the cold nipping at my nose.

"You headed home now?" he asks.

"No, I'm walking over to the campus library. I've got an exam to study for."

"What class?"

"Advanced Statistics for Behavioral Scientists."

He shakes his head slightly. "Sounds like a breeze."

The corners of my lips tug up in a smile at his gentle sarcasm as we continue toward the parking lot. His motorcycle is parked right up front, but I don't want our time together to be done yet. "How was boxing last night?"

"How'd you know I was there?"

Oh God, I'm a stalker, aren't I? "Lexie mentioned at work that you and Ethan were training."

He nods. "It went fine. I got Ethan back for this." He lightly touches the area above his brow that's now scabbed over. "If you see him anytime soon, he should have a big, purple bruise on his cheekbone."

We reach his bike and I get ready to say goodbye, but he stops me instead. "I heard you'll be at Element with their group Friday night."

Oh, so Lexie spilled the beans to Ethan that I was going? Hopefully, she didn't say why Austin was specifically invited.

"Uh, yeah. It sounds like fun." My fingers flex inside my coat pockets, nervous about my next question. "Are you going?"

His gaze sweeps over me for the briefest moment, but it still sends a wave of warmth over me. Did I imagine that, or did it really happen?

"Yeah, I'll go. We could ride together, if you want."

My heartbeat picks up. He wants to go together?

No, *ride* together. There's a big difference.

"Sure. That makes sense. Since we live right next to each other and all." I force my mouth shut to stop babbling.

He nods as if the matter is resolved and messes with a combination lock on his bike to free his helmet.

"Wait," I blurt out. "Did you mean we'll ride on that?"

I point at the motorcycle, equally terrified and excited. I've never ridden on one of those before.

He grins, holding his helmet at his side. "Your car would make more sense, but we can take this if you want."

Should I take him up on his offer? The idea is kind of thrilling.

"I'll have to check the forecast, though," he adds. "If there's any chance of snow, I won't risk you on the bike."

And there he is looking out for me again.

"How about we just plan on taking my car?" It'll probably be too cold to be on that thing, anyway.

"Sounds good."

Is it wrong that I'm a little disappointed?

"You want to ride, don't you?"

I bite my lip to hide my smile. "Maybe."

"Here."

He hands me his helmet, but I'm not sure what to do with it. "Don't you need this?"

"It's the only way you're getting on. You'll need this, too."

Wait, is he taking me on his bike now?

He moves to unzip his leather jacket and I stop him. "No, you'll freeze."

"I'd rather you be protected in case something happens."

I stare at him for a moment, my heart melting into a pile of goo in my chest before I gather it back together. "I have a coat on," I tell him. "I'd rather *you* be protected."

He frowns, but I don't let him get a word in. "Especially if I'm already stealing your helmet. Now how do I put this thing on, anyway?"

He relents, zipping his jacket back up, and moves in closer, reaching out to tuck my hair behind my ears.

I shiver, though it has nothing to do with the cold weather, as he takes the helmet back from me and slips it over my head. Wow, that's more claustrophobic than I was expecting, but it also blocks out the elements, my nose and ears not as chilly anymore.

I flip up the front plastic piece so I can listen to him explain what to do.

"When you're behind me on the bike, the key is to keep your movements in alignment with mine. During corners you lean in, so let how I'm moving guide you. If I move, you move. If you shift unexpectedly, it could affect my balance."

I nod, all of this seeming a lot more serious than I was expecting.

"When you get on, your left foot goes on the peg, and you can hold on to my shoulders for balance as you step up and swing your right leg over. Once you're on, keep your feet on the pegs, even if we come to a stop. When I brake, brace yourself by squeezing your knees against my hips."

My thighs clench in response. God, I hope he didn't notice.

"Am I overwhelming you?" he asks, concern in his voice.

I shake my head.

"We won't be able to talk once we get going, but if you need me to pull over, tap on my shoulder twice. Any questions?"

I wipe my palms on the edge of my coat. "You won't go too fast, will you?"

"No." His surety sets me at ease. "Should be about a three-minute drive over to the library from here. I pass it on my way in. I'll go slow, I promise."

"Okay, I'm ready."

He straddles the bike and lifts the kickstand. "Hop on."

I carefully place a foot on the peg he indicated earlier and swing up behind him, unsure how to hold on once I'm seated.

"Grip my waist for balance," he says, as if he can read my mind.

He revs the engine and I startle in my seat, grabbing for him, then flip down the helmet lid.

I feel his chuckle more than hear it and tighten my thighs on the sides of the bike as he backs out of the space and takes off.

Logically, I know he's not going that fast because cars are passing us, but everything rushes past quicker than I was expecting, the wind buffeting me. How does he do this all the time?

I'm careful not to wiggle around, leaning with him as he makes the turn onto the main campus road that will take us to the library.

The ride I've taken a hundred times before in a car seems different with the rumble of the bike under me, exposed to the elements like this. Everything is slightly muted through the helmet, but that doesn't change how the campus is more alive, my senses attuned to the winter landscape.

I savor the feeling of holding onto Austin, my knees gripping his hips as we come to a stop in the no parking zone in the lot behind the library.

He shuts off the engine and puts down the kickstand. "You get off first," he says.

I bring my hands up to his shoulders, using them for leverage to swing my leg over, and remove the helmet, running a hand over my hair to straighten it. "That was… crazy."

He grins. "Crazy good or crazy bad?"

"Good. Exhilarating." The vibration from the engine still seems to reverberate through me, like it's flowing through my veins.

"Yeah? I'll take you on a longer ride sometime, if you like. I've got an old helmet at home you can use."

He'd do that? "That sounds amazing. When can we go?"

He chuckles. "How about when you don't have an exam to study for?"

Right. I'm getting ahead of myself, aren't I? "Okay, I'll let you know when I'm free. See you Friday night?"

"See you."

I turn toward the library, finally letting the goofy smile I didn't want him to see overtake my face. A few steps further, I catch sight of a group of girls whispering to themselves, all eyes on something behind me, interest on their faces.

I glance over my shoulder, finding Austin putting his helmet on, then he starts his bike and speeds away. Facing back toward the girls, one of them looks at me, sneering, then says something to the group. They all stare at me, my stomach dropping at the expressions I can't quite interpret. Jealousy? Disbelief?

I hurry past them, my buoyant mood gone. They're probably wondering why this plain, nobody girl would be getting a ride from him. I mean, he practically oozed sex appeal astride his bike like that. Like that guy from *Sons of Anarchy*.

Hair all sexily wind tousled. That broken-in leather jacket fitting him just right. And the way he had smiled at me when I said the ride was crazy, his eyes lighting up with amusement… Of course they'd be looking at him. He's the sort of man your gaze gravitates to.

What'll it be like at Element on Friday? Will he be snatched up by some girl as soon as we walk in the door? It's not like we're going together. We're part of a group. He's free to do whatever he wants. Dance with whomever he wants.

Go home with whomever he wants.

This was a terrible idea. Why'd I let Lexie talk me into inviting him? I don't want to see girls hitting on him. It's Valentine's Day. Presumably, it'll be a bunch of single girls looking to hook up with someone. And he more than fits the bill.

I drop my backpack at the first empty table inside the library and unload my textbook and notes, taking deep breaths to calm myself. I probably look like a crazy person to anyone passing by, but what's new?

Why am I getting worked up about this, anyway? Austin has become my friend. He's never hinted at feeling anything more than that toward me. He's been respectful. Kind. A gentleman, despite my initial impression of him.

I'm lucky he's spent so much time with me already. He could be spending his nights a million other ways than watching me make a fool of myself practicing these self-defense moves. I probably wouldn't even be able to use them in a real-life situation, anyway.

I'll make my first time at a club as fun as I can and test drive a new experience, but I'll ultimately be on my own. Lexie will be with Ethan, Mia with Tyler, Austin will get picked up by some beautiful girl, and I'll… dance, I guess. Even though I don't have a clue about that, either.

Yeah, this is going to be real fun.

CHAPTER FIFTEEN

AUSTIN

A WAVE of disgust crawls over me as the third person of the night knocks into me and disappears back into the crowd. All we've done is check our coats so far, but there are too many damn people in here. This is why I don't go out.

"Can you believe this place?" Tessa shouts over the pounding music. "It's crazy."

And not like our motorcycle ride earlier in the week. This is crazy bad. But where else will I get the chance to spend a night with her like this? I have a ready-made excuse to dance with her, to get close, to touch her again.

If she'll dance with me, that is. For all I know, she could meet someone else tonight. Despite the Anti-Valentine's Day party theme, there's an electric vibe in the atmosphere, people searching for others to connect with.

But if a guy were solely looking for a girl to hookup with, his gaze would probably pass over her, to be honest. She's dressed for warmth in a long-sleeve tee and jeans, no different from what she wears at the Stress Lab. It's a far cry from the minidresses and abundance of cleavage that grace the dance floor.

But those guys would miss the real Tessa. Not overtly sexy, but beautiful. A little nervous when she first meets you, but incredibly giving and kind once you get to know her. And so fucking smart. I wouldn't have a clue about whatever exam she was studying for the other day.

"Do you see them?" she shouts again, standing on her tiptoes to look around. She's too short to see over the mass of dancers, though.

Right. We're supposed to meet up with everyone.

Scanning the room, I spot Ethan and Tyler over in a booth along the wall. "Over there."

I point, not that she can see, and lead the way, skirting the edge of the dance floor to avoid the worst of the crowd.

"You want a drink?" I ask as we pass by the bar.

"Sure."

Over here, I can hear myself think, the music not as loud. "What's your poison?"

"Ooh." She motions to a pink drink in a martini glass that a bartender's handing to a girl. "What's that?"

A handmade signboard behind the counter labels it as a Love Bites cocktail. "It's got vodka, pomegranate liqueur, and pink grapefruit juice. You want it?"

"Yeah, why not?"

She reaches in her pocket and pulls out cash, but I stop her. "I'll get it."

Her eyes widen. "Really? You don't have to."

"I want to."

I turn to the bartender. "Can I get a Love Bites and a Stella Artois?"

"Tessa!"

I glance back, finding a head of wild, curly brown hair hugging Tessa, a smile on Mia's face. "I didn't know you'd be here."

"Lexie invited me," Tessa says.

"Right. I keep forgetting you work with her. Come sit with us, okay?"

"Yeah, we're just grabbing drinks now."

Mia finally seems to notice me. "Austin? Did Tyler invite you?"

"Ethan did."

"Yeah, that sounds more like him."

"Are you going to introduce me?" a blonde says from behind Mia.

"Sorry. Guys, this is Kelsey, my roommate. Tessa does research at the Stress Lab, too. And Austin goes to Tyler's boxing gym."

Kelsey points a finger between me and Tessa. "So you aren't together?"

Tessa looks up at me and quickly away, but it's Mia who answers. "No, they're not."

Kelsey smiles flirtatiously at me, giving me a once-over. "Dance with me later, okay?" She turns to Mia. "I'm going to find my friends."

I glance down at Tessa, her lips in a thin line as she watches the girl saunter away.

"Don't mind her," Mia says. "She's a big flirt."

I turn back to the counter, unsure how to respond, and wait for the bartender to finish making Tessa's cocktail. That was weird.

"What are you getting to drink?" Mia asks. "I got this cool pink cocktail when I came here last year."

"Yeah, that's what I got." Is it my imagination or does Tessa sound noticeably less enthused about it now?

I pay for the drinks and hand her hers. She smiles up at me gratefully and takes a long gulp, emptying half the glass.

"You might want to pace yourself." She weighs practically nothing. If she chugs it all in one go, how soon will it affect her?

She nods. "This is my only one of the night. I'm driving, remember?"

Tyler approaches us, startling Mia from behind as he wraps his arms around her waist.

"How'd you know I was here?" she asks him.

He smirks. "I could see your hair."

She rolls her eyes in response, but still smiles.

"Ethan and Lexie are at a booth over there," Tyler says to me, hitching a thumb over his shoulder.

I nod, bending down to whisper in Tessa's ear, "Come on." Pressing light fingertips to her lower back, I guide her over to where her friend is sitting, the two of us squeezing into the booth opposite them.

"How'd you manage to get this table?" I ask. "They're all full."

"I've got connections," Lexie says. "I used to work here."

Ethan removes his arm from around her shoulders and slides out of the booth. "But perfect timing. I didn't want to lose our spot, but I'm ready to dance."

He holds a hand out to Lexie, who takes it and joins him. "Have fun," she says to Tessa, a grin on her lips.

Tessa stares at her, something wordless passing between them, and Lexie laughs before she and Ethan disappear to the dance floor.

What was that about?

Tessa slumps in her seat, taking another sip of her cocktail.

"You seem annoyed."

She looks over at me, then away, setting her drink down. "Sorry."

"I thought you were excited about tonight." She was in the car on the way over, at least.

"I was. I mean, I am. I just…" She runs a hand through her long hair, playing with the ends. "I guess I'm waiting for Kelsey to come claim you for her dance."

What? "I never said I was dancing with her."

She blinks up at me. "You're not?"

"No." From our brief meeting, that girl had seemed way too high maintenance. And besides, she's not the one I'm interested in.

"Why?"

I take a swallow of my beer, not sure how much I should say. "I'd rather hang out with you."

"You would?"

Is she going to ask questions in response to everything I say? "Yeah. Unless you wanted to meet someone else tonight," I force myself to add. That's kind of the point of coming to a place like this, isn't it?

"No," she insists, so loudly it surprises me for a moment. "I mean, I just wanted to be with friends. Not meet anyone."

I nod, something in my gut easing.

She smiles shyly at me. "I bet you're an amazing dancer, though."

I nearly choke on my sip of beer. "What? I don't dance."

"I don't believe that for one second." She turns to me, more animated now. "I saw you in the ring. The way you move."

She was watching how I move? "Is this where you call me smart again?"

She laughs, her dark eyes sparkling. "I still maintain it's true."

"I looked it up, you know." I pick at the label of my beer bottle, peeling back the edge. "Took this online quiz and you were spot on. I hit all the marks for kinesthetic intelligence."

She lightly taps my shoulder. "Look at you, Mister Genius."

Yeah, right. I'll admit, it was interesting to read about, though.

"Now, me?" She points to herself. "I would have scored low. I'd be hopeless out there." She motions to the sea of dancers.

I glimpse Lexie and Ethan on the dance floor before someone moves in front of them, her hands wrapped around his shoulders, their bodies pressed tightly together, moving as one unit.

A yearning to do the same with Tessa races through me, frustration following soon after knowing it's not like that between us.

"You'd be fine," I tell her before taking another swallow of beer. "You got all those moves I taught you down pat. I bet you're better than you think."

She makes a noncommittal noise, but smiles at me all the same. "I've never danced in my life."

"You didn't go to prom?"

She shakes her head. "The foster family I lived with then wouldn't pay for things like that."

Well, that fucking sucks. "I'll take you out there."

Though the words are casual, I can't help the desire that leaks into my voice. I want more than anything to get close to her again.

She bites at her lip, glancing out at the other dancers. "I've embarrassed myself in front of you enough times by now. What's one more?"

I grin and slide out of the booth. Holding my hand out to her, my pulse picks up as she lays her hand in mine and scoots out next to me.

"Keep in mind, you're the one that has to be seen with me."

She acts like that's a bad thing. But I'm anticipating it.

She stands awkwardly at the edge of the dance floor looking at the others, then up at me, a wrinkle between her brows. "Everyone else knows what they're doing. I don't."

"Come here." I position her in front of me. "Don't worry about anyone else. It's just you and me."

She nods, releasing a breath.

She's right that it's like being in the ring, getting into the groove of the match, playing off of what your opponent does. But here, I want us moving together, not at odds. "Get comfortable with the music. Bob your head to the beat. Bounce. Get into the rhythm."

I let the flow of the song surround me and move to it, relishing her gaze on me.

She starts to dance, then stops and covers her eyes. "I feel silly."

I nudge her hand out of the way. "Can I help you?"

She nods, staring up at me as I step closer and place her hands on my shoulders.

"Remember us on my bike together? The way you moved when I moved? It's like that. We need to be in sync. Watch my hips and match my tempo."

She tilts her head down and moves after a moment, copying me. "Like this?"

I grip her waist, setting her to the right cadence. "There you go. Keep yourself loose and relaxed."

She smiles up at me. "You sound like me giving my spiel at the Stress Lab."

"If you can do that, you can do this, right?"

"Yeah, I—" She lets go of me and pulls her phone out of her back pocket, then shakes her head at the screen.

"Everything okay?"

"Yeah, fine." She stuffs the phone away. "So, you're sure you don't go out dancing on the weekends? Because you seem experienced."

"It's my kinesthetic intelligence."

She chuckles. "Well, thanks for teaching me. This is all new. I've never been to a club."

"Doesn't really seem like your kind of hangout. Mine either."

"Then why'd you come?"

Because she would be here.

I'm unsure if I should say that, though, and shrug instead. "Thought I'd give it a try. But I'm more of a homebody."

"Me, too."

"But that doesn't mean we can't enjoy ourselves tonight." I step closer. "You can put your hands on my shoulders again, if you want."

She nods, silent as she loops her arms around my neck, and I slip my hands high on her waist, moving our lower bodies in tandem. I can't help but imagine what it would be like to move with her in a different way. Both of us a lot sweatier, her gasping my name, clutching at me.

When she's in researcher mode in the Stress Lab, she seems so out of reach, this brainy girl I can never quite match. But here on the dance floor, nothing but our bodies between us, things seem easier, like maybe she might go for a guy like me…

I take a chance and bend down to brush my lips against hers, testing the waters. Leaning back, though, I don't get the response I want.

Her eyes are wide with shock, body no longer swaying to the music, frozen in place.

Shit. I read her wrong. It was just me feeling a connection.

"Sorry," I fumble to say. "I shouldn't have done that."

Her mouth opens and closes, but she doesn't say anything.

I wince, removing my palms from her waist, and her hands slip off my shoulders, returning to her sides.

"I guess the atmosphere got to me," I comment lamely, needing to fill the growing silence. "Valentine's Day and all."

She nods, dipping her chin down so I can't see her face.

Fuck, this is awkward. "I hope I didn't ruin things."

"No, you didn't."

I can barely hear her over the music, but it's something, at least.

She pulls her phone out of her pocket again, and I catch Joel's name on the screen. What does he want?

"I should take this. He keeps calling."

I nod, standing there like an idiot as she walks away to answer the call.

Returning to our table, I slam back the rest of my beer, wishing I could rewind the last few minutes. What the fuck was I thinking? She made it clear from the beginning she wasn't interested in me.

What, I thought because she no longer flinches from me that she'd magically be attracted to me now? That she'd forget that she's way too good for a schlub like me? I'm good at punching people. I don't exactly fit in with her over there getting research papers published and applying for grad school. I barely passed high school.

I rake a hand through my hair, debating whether I should get another beer, and decide against it. Getting drunk won't solve anything, especially not if I'm riding home with her later. Then I might do something really stupid like tell her how much I wanted her to kiss me back. To find a darkened corner we could be alone in. How amazing she is, how I wish I could deserve her. How I look forward to every time I see her, how I've been racking my brain thinking of more excuses for us to spend time together. How I love the way she gets tongue-tied sometimes, how she keeps me on my toes, how I didn't realize how much of my life was just going through the motions until she showed up.

I rub at my breastbone, these feelings too much to take. Even if she doesn't think of me in a romantic way, I hope to God she'll still want to be around me. That I didn't completely fuck everything up kissing her like that.

Glancing up, I find Tessa pushing through the crowd to me in a hurry, panic in her eyes.

My pity party is over in an instant as I meet her halfway, visually making sure she's physically okay. "What is it?"

Her lower lip trembles for a moment before she firms it. "Someone broke into my apartment."

CHAPTER SIXTEEN

TESSA

THE TIGHTNESS in my chest won't go away, growing stronger with each passing second.

Someone broke in. I could have been home. I could have been sleeping. They could have had a gun.

"Tessa."

I blink, Austin coming into focus, his brows drawing together in concern.

"We need to go."

I reach for his hand, unthinking, needing some of his strength. "You'll come with me?"

"Of course."

Some of the constriction in my chest loosens at the assurance in his voice.

"Come on." He keeps hold of me, leading us through the throng of dancers, people making way for him now that he's on a mission.

Retrieving our jackets from the coat check is a blur, Austin thankfully handling it. When we get to my car in the parking lot, he pulls my keys out of his pocket. It seems so long ago that I asked if he could hold on to them since my pockets are so small.

"Do you want me to drive?"

I nod, hiding my shaking hands by crossing my arms.

He opens the passenger door and gently guides me inside, then crouches so he's at eye level. "Everything will be okay, I promise."

I press my lips as tightly together as I can, willing myself not to cry. I'm afraid if I start, I'll never stop.

"What did Joel say?" he asks.

I swallow, once, twice, getting myself under control. "He stopped by my place and saw my door was ajar. It was damaged, like someone had forced it open. He called to make sure I was okay."

"Is he still there now? Did he call the police?"

"He said he'd wait for me, but didn't say anything about the police."

"Can I call them for you? They should check it out."

"Yes, please." Thank God he's here. I can't think straight, can't remember what I should be doing.

He drives us home, talking to a dispatcher on the way, but I can barely focus on what he's saying, dread rising within me as he makes the last turn toward our apartment complex.

Once he hangs up, he reaches for my hand, and I squeeze it tightly, not wanting to let go. Not wanting any of this to be real.

"Someone came into my home," I whisper. "They violated my space."

"I know."

"I can't go in there." My head shakes, unable to stop. "What if they're still in there? What if they get me when I'm sleeping?"

It's not logical, but it's all I can think of.

"The police will search your apartment. They'll make sure it's empty. And you can stay at my place tonight. If your front door is busted, I don't want you there alone."

I wipe at my eyes with my free hand, his generosity cracking more of the worry tangled up in my chest. How is he so good to me? Especially after I blew it out on the dance floor earlier.

I should have kissed him back when I had the chance, before he came to his senses. Instead, I froze up, unable to believe what was happening. And then the moment was gone.

"Thank you." My voice cracks, but at least I'm able to get it out, my throat clogged with emotion.

I take a second to center myself as he parks the car, focusing on Joel leaning against the side of the building, doing something on his phone.

He looks up as I shut the passenger door and does a double take at Austin getting out of the driver's side.

"Have the police arrived?" Austin asks as we join him. I can't see my door from this angle, and I turn so I'm not tempted to look. It's hard enough to be this close as it is.

Joel glances between us, blinking rapidly. "Police?"

"Austin called them," I explain. "In case someone's still in there."

"No, no. I already checked it out. It's clear. We don't need to involve the police."

"You went in there?" Austin asks, brows raised.

"Yeah. I wanted to make sure Tessa was okay."

Austin folds his arms over his chest. "Why are you here? Tessa wasn't home."

Joel makes a scoffing sound. "We had plans for later. I was just seeing if she was home yet. I think the real question is why were you in her car?"

"We were out."

Joel turns to me. "So you lied to me."

I press a hand firmly to my temple, still caught up in the weird power struggle going on between the two of them. "First of all, I didn't lie. Second of all, you and I didn't have plans. And third of all, who fucking cares?" I'm yelling by the last point, but I can't seem to control myself. "Someone broke into my home. You know that's my worst fear."

A cop car pulls in, its red and blue lights flashing, painting us all in an eerie light. Thank goodness.

"I'll go," Joel says, passing by me, and I stop him, tugging at his jacket.

"No, you have to stay and give a statement. You're the one that found the door."

His lips thin, but he doesn't go any further.

I answer the cop's questions as best I can, surprised that Joel stays silent. Now would be the time for him to be his usually verbose self, but it's Austin that helps me out when I'm too choked up to go on, the fear thickening in my chest again.

When the police officer leaves us to inspect my apartment, I stay outside, unable to follow him.

"You okay?" Austin asks.

I nod, hoping that if I pretend like I am, it'll be true.

"I'm going to check on Boots real quick. I'll be right back."

Joel waits until he's gone to ask, "He's checking on his boots?"

I cross my arms over my middle, keeping my unsettled stomach at bay. "His cat's name is Boots."

What's the police officer finding in there? Yeah, Joel said he checked it out, but he could have missed something.

"I can't believe you called the police," he mutters. "Why didn't you wait till you got here to ask me about it? Didn't you trust me to take care of things?"

I stare at him, unbelieving. "It has nothing to do with you. I'm glad Austin suggested calling them."

He sneers. "So it was his idea? You said you were out with a friend from work. Not him."

Why is he being like this? He sounds like a petulant child. "I was. Austin is friends with her boyfriend, so he was there, too."

"But you rode together."

"Yeah, when we realized we were going to the same group event we decided to carpool. Do you have any more questions? Interrogations? This is getting ridiculous."

He has the grace to at least look ashamed. "Sorry. I'm a little shaken, too. Not thinking right. I was so worried when I found your door like that."

He pulls me into a hug, my annoyance melting some. I get that he's stressed. I am, too.

"You shouldn't stay here with the door unsecured. Let's pack you a bag and I'll take you to my place."

I pull away, awkwardness settling over me. "Actually, I'm going to stay with Austin."

"What?"

"He offered. And it makes more sense to be right across the hall. That way, I'm here if I need anything from my apartment."

"Is he expecting you to sleep with him?"

All right, I'm done. "I don't have time for any more of your weird questions. I'm tired of defending myself over something that isn't anything. And even if it was, it doesn't concern you at all."

His brows narrow. "You said you wouldn't compromise the study."

I throw my hands up. "I'm not. My friendship with him has literally nothing to do with the study. It doesn't affect it at all. Besides, in less than two weeks, it'll be over."

"Tessa." His mouth is a white slash across his face, jaw set. "You barely know this guy. You shouldn't be staying over at his house."

"Right now, I'd say I know him a hell of a lot better than I know you. You're acting crazy."

"I'm acting *concerned*. Like a friend is supposed to. *I'm* the one who told you about your apartment." He jabs a finger at his chest. "You're supposed to come home with *me*."

I step back, my scalp prickling at the vehemence in his voice.

Austin's door opens, the sudden tension in my body releasing as I go to his side. Not that Joel was going to do anything, but I just feel... safer next to Austin.

"Everything okay out here?"

"We're fine," Joel says, then turns to me. "Are you coming with me or not?"

I shake my head.

He scoffs, lips twisting. "Fine. I'll see you on Tuesday."

He stalks off toward his car, door slamming after he gets in.

I cross my arms, the cold getting to me despite my coat. "I'm guessing you heard all that?"

"I was feeding the cat, so I don't know if I caught everything." He rubs at the back of his neck, looking down at his feet. "Listen, if you want to stay with someone else, I understand. I was only offering—"

"No, I want to stay with you." I reach for his arm, curling my hand around his bicep. "You make me feel... safe."

Relief crosses his face as he glances down at me. "I thought I was intimidating and dangerous."

I let out a weak chuckle. "No. Not anymore. Not to me." I take a shuddering breath, then another, the reality of the night catching up with me. "I don't know what I would have done without you tonight."

I lean against him, finally losing it as his hand slips over my back to rub soothing circles. No one's done that for me since my mom.

Tears leak down my cheeks and I wrap my arms around his middle, burrowing into his hard chest.

He murmurs soft words of comfort, stroking a hand down my hair, and it's all I can do not to melt in his arms. It feels so good to simply be touched, to connect with someone, warmth gradually replacing the worry.

This is what friendship should be. Someone to help you in times of crisis, not yell at you and accuse you of God knows what. And even if Austin had that accidental moment in the club when the dancing and the atmosphere got to him, I have no illusions he's actually attracted to me.

Despite Joel's insinuations otherwise.

CHAPTER SEVENTEEN

TESSA

MY FRONT DOOR OPENS, the police officer joining us in the hallway again, and I let go of Austin, scrubbing at my eyes.

"No sign of anyone inside," he says. "Doesn't appear they took anything of high value, either. TV and laptop are untouched in the living room."

I breathe a sigh of relief. Thank God. "Why would a robber leave those?" Especially the laptop. That's easy enough to grab.

"Could be they heard a noise and got spooked. Or they didn't plan on taking anything at all."

"What do you mean?" Austin asks.

"Two scenarios come to mind—someone might have been looking for you specifically or they could have been trying to scare you. Anyone you can think of who fits the bill?"

Like an enemy? "No."

The man shrugs. "It's probably a run-of-the-mill break-in gone wrong. But there's no real way for us to know with no surveillance or obvious motive. Anything else someone might have been looking for?"

"No, I don't own anything valuable." The TV and laptop would have been it since my phone has been on me all night.

"Keep an eye out for any suspicious activity, then. No reason to get forensics out here if nothing was stolen. Here's my card if you need anything."

I take the card from him and pocket it.

"You staying with your boyfriend until your landlord can fix this door?"

I glance up at Austin and back at the cop, my mouth opening and shutting, but nothing comes out. He thinks Austin is my boyfriend? Yeah, he caught us hugging, but do we really look like a couple?

"She's staying with me, yes," Austin answers when I take too long to respond.

"Good. Check out the place tomorrow with fresh eyes and give me a call if you find anything missing. Same if you notice anyone hanging around that shouldn't be here."

"Thank you, Officer."

He returns to his patrol car and Austin leads me into his apartment, holding the door open for me. I settle on the couch next to Boots, a wave of emotion washing over me when she crawls on my lap and purrs.

Petting her gently, I glance over toward Austin, finding him watching me, an unreadable expression on his face. "What is it?"

"Nothing." He shakes his head, breaking eye contact. "I'm glad you're here, is all."

He is? I'm inconveniencing him so much, though. "Thank you again."

"Of course. Anything you need."

"I—" I swallow hard, shutting my eyes. "I need to get some stuff from my apartment. Toothbrush, pajamas, that kind of thing. But I… I don't think I can…"

"I'll grab whatever you need. Make a list."

Tears well in the corners of my eyes at the kindness in his voice. "Thank you," I whisper. "I swear, I'm not normally this emotional."

"You have good reason to be. If you want to cry or yell or rant or anything, you can. You don't have to hold back in front of me."

The pressure behind my eyes grows stronger, the emotion I was suppressing before at the forefront again. "I'm sorry. You didn't sign up for this."

I look over at him, the genuine concern on his face unraveling the tightly wound knot within me.

"You're acting like you're a burden," he murmurs. "But you're not. Not at all."

A whimper escapes me, scaring Boots off. Doesn't he realize that's all I've ever been? Through every foster family I lived with, that was always clear.

I wipe under my eyes and stand, shaking off this emotion. I need to get myself under control. "Do you have a pen and paper? I'll make a quick list of what I need next door."

He nods after a moment and points to the fridge where a magnetic notepad hangs on the front, a mini pen on a string attached.

I fill it out with a few essentials and hand it to him, unsure what to do with myself once he leaves. There are no knickknacks in the apartment to inspect, no bookcases, no photos, no art to distract myself with. If he hadn't told me he moved in four and a half years ago, I would have thought it was last month.

Pulling my phone out, I text my boss to tell her I'm coming in late tomorrow. There's no way I'll make it in time to open the diner. How will I even sleep tonight?

I'll have to contact the apartment complex's management in the morning to let them know about the door, too. Hopefully, they fix things on weekends.

Stopping mid-pace as Austin returns, I give him a grateful smile as he hands me a bag loaded with my belongings.

"I wasn't sure about some of it, so I grabbed everything."

"Thank you. This is perfect."

"Bathroom is right there," he says, pointing to my left. "Well, you know. It's a mirror of your place."

I nod, excusing myself to change, and set my bag on the closed toilet seat lid, rummaging through it for what I need. He was serious when he said he grabbed everything.

Setting my stuff on the counter, I take a moment to look over his things, all lined up neatly to the right of the sink. Toothbrush, toothpaste, deodorant, hairbrush. Is that all he uses?

I glance toward the locked door, wondering if he can hear me in here, and quietly open the cabinet drawer, finding a lot of odds and ends. Floss, scissors, bandages—even a hair tie. Does he ever wear his hair up? Maybe in the summer when it's hotter? I only saw him do it that time at the gym.

I shut the drawer, guilt running through me at my invasion of his privacy, but I'm not finished yet. I uncap his deodorant, wondering if—yep, that's what makes him smell so good. I inhale the deliciously masculine scent, not caring that I'm being a total weirdo. I would only ever do this in private.

The cap slips from my fingers, bouncing loudly on the linoleum floor, and I grab it as quickly as I can, stuffing it back on. Shit. He can't tell what that was from out there, right?

I hurry and get ready for bed, hoping the familiarity of routine will calm my nerves, but it only serves to remind me that I'm doing this in the wrong place. That I can't be in my own home right now. That my front door is too busted to lock, that I'm not safe in there.

I grip the edge of the counter, taking deep breaths until I'm steady enough to finish up.

Heading back out, I find the living room empty, but there's noise coming from the bedroom.

"Austin?"

"Yeah, in here," he calls out. I guess it's okay to go in, then.

He's changing the sheets on his bed, tucking a faded blue fitted sheet under the corners of the queen-sized mattress. "Thought you'd want fresh sheets," he says off-handedly.

Tears pinprick my eyes at the simple gesture. That he'd offer me his bed to begin with. That he'd do something to make me feel more welcome when he's already done so much.

"Let me help you."

I unfold the top sheet and spread it wide over the mattress, letting him tuck in the ends.

He grabs one of the pillows and a folded blanket. "I'll take the couch."

I stare at the neatly made bed, the thought of trying to sleep here alone suddenly unbearable. "Will you stay with me?" I blurt out, turning to him.

He stills. "What?"

"I…" I cross my arms over my middle, firming my mouth so it won't tremble. "I don't want to be by myself."

He stares at me for a long moment, each passing second torturous.

"Whoever broke into my place could come back," I whisper. "I know it's asking a lot, but I'd feel safer with you here."

He nods slowly. "Yeah, okay."

My knees weaken as relief floods through me. "It probably sounds stupid, but I just have this feeling like… nothing bad can happen if I'm with you."

He looks down at the ground, but not before I catch his cheeks pinkening.

Crap. I embarrassed him.

"Um, is this what you normally put on the bed?" I ask, pointing to the blanket in his arms.

He seems to shake off whatever awkwardness I created. "I have a heavier comforter I was going to put on for you."

He grabs it from the closet and lays it out, then excuses himself to the bathroom.

I take a seat at the edge of the bed, burying my face in my hands. How did I end up here? A month ago, I'd never have believed I'd be spending a night at this guy's apartment.

Not that I'm *spending the night*. It's sleeping. I don't even know for sure if his offer extends another night in case they can't fix my door tomorrow.

God, what a mess.

"You okay?"

I look up, finding Austin in the doorway, the sweatpants he's changed into hanging low on his hips. How long have I been sitting here feeling sorry for myself?

"Yeah, fine. Just wondering which side of the bed you sleep on."

Does he ever have girls sleep over? I haven't noticed anyone since I moved in, but I wasn't paying attention.

How many women has he been with? It has to be a lot, right? It seemed like every other girl at Element was eyeing him. Mia's friend even outright asked him to dance with her.

But he'd chosen to stay with me all night.

Does that mean something?

"I don't have a preference. Whichever side you want is yours."

I nod, randomly choosing the right side, and slip under the covers.

"You ready to sleep?" he asks, hand hovering over the light switch.

A frisson of nervousness runs down my spine as I nod again and the room plunges into darkness.

Guess he doesn't have a nightlight.

He gets in on the other side, the sheets rustling.

"Goodnight," I whisper.

"Goodnight."

I shut my eyes, but it's no use. The only thing running through my brain is who wanted in and what they wanted to begin with.

I pull the comforter up tighter around my chin, consciously emptying my mind, but random flashes of memory still steal in.

The worry on Austin's face as I'd searched for him in the crowd after Joel's phone call.

My broken front door, the part near the lock torn up and splintered, as if someone had taken a crowbar to it.

The larger than life man opening my bedroom window.

"Tessa?"

My eyelids fly open, not that I can see anything in the pitch blackness. "Hmm?"

"You're breathing hard."

I am?

I check in with myself, realizing, yes, my pulse is racing, my breaths shallow. "Sorry."

"You okay?"

"Yeah."

Not even I believe the blatant lie, but what else am I supposed to say? I practically begged him to stay with me. I can't tell him now I'm having a mini-freakout.

I squeeze my eyes shut, but this time it's the police officer in my head, saying the intruder wasn't there to take anything. They were there to take *me*.

"I never did my relaxing routine tonight," Austin says, thankfully interrupting my train of thought. "For the study."

I focus on his words, pushing everything else out. "You do that before bed?"

"Mm-hmm. It helps me go to sleep."

"Really?" I don't know why, but hearing that makes my chest glow with pride a little.

"Yeah. If I did it out loud, would that bother you?"

I bite my lip, knowing what he's doing. "No, that'd be fine."

I slide a hand under my pillow, breathing in deeply. I like whatever laundry detergent he uses.

He starts with his scalp, describing aloud tensing and releasing each muscle group, and I follow along with him, letting the deep rumble of his voice wash over me, soothing me.

By the time he's down to his feet, exhaustion finally steals over me, my eyelids heavy as I sink into sleep, knowing I'm safe here with him.

CHAPTER EIGHTEEN

AUSTIN

TESSA GIVES me a shy smile as she loops her arms around my neck, matching the rhythm of her movements to mine. The other dancers surrounding us are hazy, this beautiful girl in my arms the only thing I can focus on. She steps closer, the sway of her hips in time with the beat of the song pounding through us, taunting me, the tips of her breasts brushing my torso every time she moves.

The shy smile turns seductive, a knowing glint in her eye telling me she understands exactly what she's doing.

When I bend down this time to kiss her, there's no shock on her face, no muscles going rigid. There's only need as she kisses me back, her hands cupping my jaw, moving down over my chest, up to my shoulders, in my hair. Her touch is everything I've ever wanted.

She presses her body flush against mine, and I moan, my dick rubbing against her, eager for more. She increases the pressure, my hands finding her waist and gripping for leverage, needing it harder, rougher.

She looks up at me, excitement in her eyes. She wants this, too.

My moan this time wakes me, the need in it embarrassingly loud in the quiet of the room. Tessa is pressed against me, her back to my front, her steady, even breaths indicating she's at least still asleep and didn't hear me.

The dream clears from my mind and I realize I'm hard, my dick nestled against her ass. I jerk back immediately, the dream suddenly making more sense. Not that I haven't dreamt about her before, but nothing as realistic as this.

She stirs but doesn't wake, and I quietly slip out of bed, letting memory guide me to the bathroom in the darkness of the room. Shutting the door behind me, I flip on the light, my erection bobbing in front of me, waiting for more of Tessa.

More of that delicious vanilla scent in my nose, more of her body heat warming me under the covers, more of her lithe figure pressed against me.

My dick doesn't seem to care that she's not actually mine, that it was a mistake for me to share a bed with her in the first place. But how could I deny her when she'd asked me to stay? When she'd said she was scared to be alone, even knowing what the result would be?

Because now I know what it's like to wake up next to her. To dream of her and find her there in reality. To have the chance to slide an arm around her waist and revel in the softness of her skin, cup the heavy weight of her breast, reach down and tangle my fingers through her nest of curls.

My dick perks up even more at that train of thought, and I curse myself, stepping over to the shower to flip the dial to hot, letting the water heat.

What I should have done was leave as soon as she fell asleep and gone to the couch. Then I wouldn't be dealing with any of this. Because now, I can't forget the feel of her, as quick as it was.

And I want more.

I strip and step under the heated spray, ignoring the raging urge to grip myself for as long as I can. I'm used to discipline. That's what training for boxing is all about.

But this is different. This is something I want. Something I… need.

The first stroke is excruciating in its pleasure, and I brace myself against the wall, holding back a guttural sound as I move from base to tip, over and over again, picturing Tessa.

Her looking up at me with those big, brown eyes as she reaches for me, her petite hand encircling me. Kissing me roughly as she strokes me, her sounds of satisfaction spurring me on. Undressing her slowly, learning her body, what makes her gasp, makes her moan, wanting to discover everything about her.

Need rises within me, my hand flying faster over my dick, breaths sawing in and out imagining what it'll be like to touch her the way I want, to sink into her softness, to watch how I affect her, the same as she affects me. Ignoring the fact that she doesn't feel that way about me at all. That she'd be horrified I'm envisioning her like this, but I'm too far gone to care.

Wishing she was here with me, body slick with soap as I crowd her into the back of the tub, nibbling on her neck. Listening to that beautiful laugh of hers, her leg rising to circle my hip so I can nestle into her. Having the freedom to touch her any way I want, for her to want to touch me, too.

Wanting her in the bedroom atop me, riding me for all she's worth. Wanting her under me, gripping my shoulders as I pound into her. Wanting her spread-eagle on the bed while I feast on her, drinking her down.

I bite my lip, restraining a groan as my hips jerk, cum shooting on the tile wall. Keeping silent so I won't wake her, won't cause her to suspect anything. How long can I keep being friends with her when the wanting only continues to grow?

I turn the shower nozzle to wash away any trace of my activity and dry off, realizing I didn't bring my clothes in with me to change into. I guess I can't walk naked to my closet like I usually do.

Wrapping the towel around my lower half, I open the bathroom door and pause, finding her sitting up in bed, already awake.

Her gaze travels over me, eyes wide, and I tighten my hold on the towel.

"I have to change." I point toward the walk-in closet, as if it's not obvious what I mean.

She nods, silent.

Could she hear what I was doing in there? Did I moan aloud? I can't remember now. I was too far gone.

I swallow hard, forcing myself to keep walking, and shut the door behind me, leaning against it.

What a start to the weekend.

The bed is empty as I return to the room, and this time I find her out in the living room on the phone. I'm guessing it's the apartment's management company from the sound of it.

I leave her be, giving Boots her breakfast, and surreptitiously wash up the few dirty dishes in the sink from the past couple of days.

Tessa joins me in a few minutes, resting her elbows on the counter next to me. "They can't get maintenance out to look at the door until Monday. I guess their normal guy requested this weekend off."

"Shit. That sucks." I rinse the last plate and set it in the drying rack. "You'll stay here, right?"

It's selfish of me to ask it of her when she probably has another friend to stay with, but I want her here.

"If you're offering, I'd love to. But I don't want to impose."

"You're not. Promise."

She lets out a sigh. "That's a relief, honestly. I'm not sure what I'd do otherwise."

I wipe my hands on the kitchen towel, avoiding her eye. "You wouldn't stay with Joel?"

She shakes her head. "He was being super weird last night. I don't know what's up with him lately. Maybe the study is stressing him out."

"Isn't he doing meditation for his part? Shouldn't he be more chill?"

She rolls her eyes. "You would think. I don't want to talk about him, though."

Fine by me. "You call out of work today?"

"No, but I told my boss I'd be in late. I need to get ready now, actually. But all my stuff…"

"You want me to go over again and get what you need?"

She straightens, crossing her arms over her middle. "No, I… I'm ready to go there myself. But could you, um…"

She scuffs her toe along the carpet in front of her.

"You want me to go with you?" I ask when it seems like she won't finish the question.

She looks up at me. "Would you?"

"Come on." I wrap an arm around her shoulder, pulling her into my side. "Let's get it over with while you're motivated."

She lets out a chuckle. "You're getting to know me a little too well."

I keep my smile at bay and lead her across the hall. Her door is slightly out of alignment, but it's easy enough to push open. Everything looks the same inside since the last time I was here, nothing obvious taken. She'd know better than me, though.

I glance behind me where she's standing in the doorway. She rubs her hands over her arms, appearing lost as she surveys her home.

I hold out a hand to her and she grabs onto it like it's a lifeline. Then again, maybe it is for her right now.

"You're safe, Tessa."

The lost look in her gaze fades as she focuses on me. "For how long, though?"

"What do you mean?"

"Why would someone break in and take nothing? That cop said they could have been looking for me."

"Why would anyone be looking for you?"

Her grip on me tightens. "That's what I don't understand. And how can I be sure they won't come back?"

I rub at my chest with my free hand, hating this powerlessness creeping through me. "I'm sorry I don't have answers." I struggle with what to say to make it better. Words have never been my strong suit. "But I'm always here for you. I'll protect you however I can."

Her eyes fill with tears.

Fuck. I said the wrong thing, didn't I?

She lets go of my hand and hugs my waist, squeezing me tightly as she sniffles.

I cautiously rest a palm on the back of her head, wrapping my other arm around her.

"I don't know what I did to deserve you," she mumbles against my chest.

What in the world is she talking about?

"You must think I'm crazy." She steps back, wiping at her eyes. "I'm crying. Again. I probably look hideous."

I sweep a thumb over her cheek, gathering a fallen drop. "You look beautiful. Like always."

She looks up at me from lowered lashes, her lips parting. This close, I can count each freckle along the bridge of her nose, wanting to smooth away the worry lines on her forehead and the brackets around the sides of her mouth.

This would be the moment. To bend down and kiss her. To show her how much I care about her. How much she means to me.

But after the way she reacted yesterday at Element, I can't trust my instincts. And with how vulnerable she is after everything that happened, it should be her that makes the first move.

Except, she doesn't.

Her gaze searches mine, but I have no idea what she's looking for, what she's thinking.

She steps back further, breaking eye contact. "You don't have to say stuff like that."

Does she not like compliments? Am I making her uncomfortable? Shit.

"Sorry."

She turns and goes to change into her work uniform, leaving me standing in the middle of the living room.

As much as I want her, I'll be her friend if that's what she needs.

Even if it kills me.

CHAPTER NINETEEN

TESSA

I WRESTLE WITH MY UNIFORM, cursing at it when the zipper snags halfway through zipping it. Can nothing go right today?

I take a deep breath, consciously relaxing the tightness in my shoulders, and finish getting dressed, not letting myself think about Austin. The way he'd called me beautiful. The way our faces had been so close. The way I could have sworn he was going to kiss me.

Wait. I'm not supposed to be thinking about that.

I'm obviously delusional. Trying to will into existence a chance to make up for the way I'd froze in the club yesterday. It was *me* looking up at him, making our faces so close. *Me* making a comment about how I looked awful. He was trying to make me feel better. Being a good friend. He outright said kissing me had been a mistake. That he'd simply been in the moment on the dance floor, forgetting that it was *me* he was dancing with.

What I need to do is get over it. I've got bigger things on my plate.

I finish getting ready and head off to work, losing track of time in the hustle and bustle of Saturday breakfast and brunch at the diner. For how slow my shifts are on Monday and Wednesday nights, the weekend makes up for it.

After a double shift that has my feet aching, I grab two burgers and fries to go with my employee discount, hoping the food somewhat evens out the inconvenience I'm putting Austin through.

As I park in front of our building, a tall, blonde girl catches my eye, struggling to get a large bag of cat food and an even larger container of cat litter out of the trunk of her car. I gather my things, watching her for a moment, then decide to intervene.

"Do you need help?"

She glances over at me, a grateful smile on her face. "That would be great. Thanks." There's something about her that seems familiar, though I can't quite place it.

I balance the cat food on top of the litter already in her arms, then shut her trunk. "Are you in one of the upstairs units?" If she lives up there, I should probably get to know her. Turns out it's a good thing to get close to your neighbors in case something goes wrong.

"No, I'm going here." She juts her chin forward in the direction of Austin's apartment.

My stomach sinks. "Oh. Me, too."

Who is she? A date? His girlfriend? Did I ever actually ask him if he's seeing someone?

She stops in the middle of the walkway, turning toward me. "You're going to Austin's?"

"Yeah, I'm staying with him."

She blinks at me uncomprehendingly. "Are we talking about the same guy? Austin Langford? Tall, blond, hardly talks to anyone?"

"Um…"

"What do you mean, *staying with*?" she interrupts. "Like staying the night? Living with him? Temporarily? Permanently? I can't believe he'd keep this from me."

Oh, God. Maybe she is a girlfriend. Why would she care so much otherwise?

"It was a sudden thing," I rush to say. I don't want him to get in trouble with whoever she is. "He's a friend. My neighbor—"

Austin's door opens, his head swiveling between us. "Are you harassing Tessa?"

The girl grins and finishes walking toward him, dumping the stuff she's carrying in his arms. "Now harassing is a strong word."

There's an easy rapport between them, my stomach sinking further.

He sets the items down and comes over to join me. "You okay?"

"Yeah." My gaze cuts to the girl, who's watching us with unabashed curiosity. "If you have plans, I can go—"

"No, no. She's leaving soon."

"Way to make a girl feel welcome," she says wryly.

He turns to her. "Don't act like you were going to stay."

"Yeah, but you didn't even invite me."

The way they're bickering, it's almost like they're… "Oh! You're his sister. Danielle." The resemblance is obvious now that I'm seeing them together.

"Who'd you think she was?" he asks, seeming genuinely perplexed.

"I don't know," I mumble. It seems silly to voice aloud my initial theory.

Danielle gives me a knowing smile but doesn't say anything.

"What, you thought…" He trails off, understanding dawning. "Oh, God, no." He rubs at the back of his neck. "I'm not dating anyone. I thought you knew that."

"I wasn't sure." Yes, we shared a bed last night. And he kissed me on the dance floor, even if it was a mistake. I guess that would have been pretty shitty of him to do if he was seeing someone.

"So, what's going on here?" Danielle asks, wagging a finger between me and Austin.

"Oh, my apartment." I gesture toward my busted door. "Someone broke in and maintenance can't come out to fix it until Monday. Austin's been so amazing helping me out."

She holds a hand to her chest. "Oh my God, you had a break-in? That's so scary. Were you home when it happened?"

"No, Austin and I were out."

A smile lurks around her mouth as she looks over at her brother. "Out, you say? Where at?"

"Um, Element."

She breathes out a laugh. "Hold up." She turns to Austin. "You went to a club? You?"

He merely looks at her, not responding. I guess there was truth in his statement that it wasn't his normal scene.

"Please tell me you danced." She looks at me next. "He danced, right?"

"Yeah…"

"Oh, I would've paid to see that."

Does she think he can't dance or something? "He's an amazing dancer. He was showing me what to do."

Austin groans and reaches for her, clapping a hand over her mouth. "Not a word out of you."

She grabs at his wrist, pulling it down to free her mouth. "I didn't do anything. I'm just talking with Tessa. It's Tessa, right?"

I nod.

"Don't you have that thing to do tonight?" he asks her.

Her gaze narrows. "What thing?"

"You know, that *thing*."

Is that some kind of sibling code?

Her lips thin. "Right. That. Guess I'll go, then." She takes a few steps toward her car, then turns back around. "But I'm free tomorrow. And I'd love to keep talking. How about you come over for dinner?" she asks me.

"I…" I look up at Austin, unsure how to answer, but his face is impassive. "If it's okay with Austin, I'd love to."

"Great. We'll eat around six at our dad's house. See you."

She strides off, leaving the two of us still out in the hallway. "I hope that was all right to say yes. If it's not, I totally understand."

"Why wouldn't it be?" He holds the door open for me, waiting till I'm inside to lock up.

I set my stuff down on his kitchen counter. "You seemed sort of annoyed."

"With her. Not you. She was trying to start trouble."

"What do you mean?"

His lips twist. "She's a busybody. Always sticking her nose in other people's business."

"She does that to you a lot?"

"She tries. But I normally don't have anything going on."

"And now I'm here."

He gives me a soft smile. "And now you're here."

I bite my lip, a small spark glowing in my chest. "I like being here."

"I like you here, too."

The spark burns hotter. He means as a friend, right?

I'm half-tempted to ask him, but my stomach chooses that moment to let out a loud rumble. Right. Dinner.

"I brought home some food for us. I figured burgers and fries were a safe bet since you ordered that last time you were in."

"You remember what I ordered?"

Oh, crap. Busted. "I… I'm a server. It's my job to remember stuff like that." Even though he wasn't sitting in my section. And I pretty much avoided him that whole time, other than when I literally ran into him.

"Well, thanks. That sounds way better than the frozen pizza I had planned."

I work on plating our food, smiling to myself for what tomorrow night holds. Dinner with his family. His sister certainly seems fun. And it'll be a chance to get to know him better. To get closer to him.

As long as I don't end up embarrassing myself in the process.

I snuggle in further to the wall of warmth along my back, pleasantly in that in-between state of dreaming and waking. Austin must keep the heat cranked on during the night. Why else would I be so deliciously toasty?

It's not only my back, but my side and stomach too, a comforting weight surrounding me that has me relaxing further into the bed. Have I ever slept so well at home? What kind of mattress does he have that makes it so much better?

Austin shifts behind me, and that's when I realize all that warmth is him. It's his front along my back. His arm slung over my side. His palm resting on my stomach. And with the way he just moved, it's *him*, pressed against my ass, hot and hard.

Oh, God. I squeeze my eyes shut, not that he'd be able to tell I'm awake. It's pitch black in this room. But I don't want this to end.

A ball of excitement rolls around in my lower belly as I cautiously move back, feeling him stiff against me. His hand shifts with my movement, a little further down, and I bite my lip to contain the moan that wants to escape. With how big his hands are, he's awfully close to…

An ache pulses deep within me, wanting to rock against him, for his hand to move south, for some of this growing pressure to release.

God, what am I thinking? Now is not the time. He's doing me a favor letting me stay here. Especially in the same bed after I begged him Friday night. And yeah, he's got morning wood, but that's a biological reaction, not because of me.

Even so, I can't help my response, unable to keep still with him hard against me like this. It's too much.

I press back, the pressure simultaneously relieving even as it gets worse. He makes a low, sleepy sound of contentment, my breath catching with how sensual it sounds. I move again and his palm on my lower stomach flexes, so close to where I actually want it.

He mumbles my name, followed by a soft *mmm* noise, and I grin into the darkness, excitement and guilt warring within me. I shouldn't be doing this.

Shouldn't be taking advantage of him when he's unaware. But it's not like I maneuvered myself into this position. He's the one who's touching me. The one who has me tucked securely against him. The one whose hard cock is nestled snugly against the cleft of my ass.

I rock against him twice more, wishing I could do it harder, but when his slow, steady breaths stop and his torso stiffens, I freeze.

"Tessa?" His voice isn't sleepy anymore.

I do my best to feign sleep, and he must believe it because he rolls away from me, cursing softly.

I lay motionless as he gets up and goes to the bathroom, my heart pounding as a thin light from under the door turns on a moment later.

What the hell did I just do? What was I thinking?

I was thinking it felt good. Right. Necessary. The way our bodies fit together, the feelings he inspires in me…

I roll over on my back, pressing the heels of my palms over my eyes. I need to get myself under control. Yeah, I'm attracted to him. But that doesn't mean it goes the other way. He said he didn't want to ruin things between us and here I am almost doing the same thing.

As long as I'm here, I need to behave.

Even when that ache within me keeps growing.

CHAPTER TWENTY

AUSTIN

I WIPE the sweat from my forehead, glad Lawrence gave me a good workout today. Now, Uncle Marty needs to recruit some better opponents for me to spar with here.

"I'm taking a few guys out of town for a tournament next weekend," Lawrence says as he puts the punching mitts away. "You're welcome to come."

What if Tessa's door still isn't fixed by then? "Nah, I've got plans."

"All right, let me know if you change your mind. I'm trying to convince Lexie to let Ethan go, too."

I grin. "She got him on a tight leash?"

"Oh, yeah. But he likes it."

To be honest, I wouldn't mind being on Tessa's leash.

Okay, that sounded weird. But half of me already feels like I'm under her pull. I'd woken again this morning hard against her. I must have been moving in my sleep because I was so turned on, it had been all I could do to retreat to the bathroom and jerk off in the shower to relieve myself.

I need to stop thinking about her like that. Need to stop wanting her so badly. But what the hell am I supposed to do when she's snuggled up to me every night?

Things will get better at least when she's back in her apartment. Until then, I have to keep my hands to myself.

Grabbing my phone out of my gym bag, I find a text from Danielle asking me to pick up shredded cheese for the tacos she's making for dinner. Fuck, I'd half-forgotten about that.

I walk over to Uncle Marty's empty office and close the door behind me as I call her, needing to set some ground rules for tonight.

"Hey," she answers, "you get my text about the cheese? Can you believe Dad doesn't have any? I mean, not even slices. What is he, a barbarian?"

I ignore her, getting to the point. "Why'd you invite Tessa over for dinner? I know you got my hint that I wanted you to leave."

She scoffs. "I was doing you a favor. You're welcome, by the way."

A favor? Is she delusional?

"You can't tell me you're not into her," she continues.

And she figured that out from the five-minute conversation we had in the hallway? "She's a friend."

"The two aren't mutually exclusive. You like her."

I'm silent, knowing she doesn't need a response.

"You don't have to confirm. I can tell."

Is she a psychic or something? "How?"

She lets out a light laugh. "You barely talk to anyone. There's no way you'd let some girl stay with you if you didn't want to bone her."

"Jesus, Danielle. I'm not an animal. She's going through a rough time and I'm helping her out."

"By going out to clubs with her?"

I groan. Why is she so fucking infuriating? "Why do you care, anyway?"

"Because I'm your wingwoman tonight."

"You absolutely are not." God only knows what she'll say.

"You want her to like you, right? She's halfway there already, I can tell."

"Seems like you can tell a lot of things," I mutter.

"Yeah, actually. I can. It's called a woman's intuition."

When has she ever acted like a woman in her life? "Just don't embarrass me."

"You think that little of me?"

"I don't know what the hell you're doing." What I'm doing either, for that matter.

"I'm setting you two up. Duh."

No. She'll only make things worse. "I don't need your help."

She lets out an exaggerated sigh. "Listen, I love you, but I saw you with girls in high school. You stand there like a statue."

I rub my forehead. "Things are different with her. She's easy to talk to."

"Yeah? Tell me about her."

Yeah, right. "You're only going to make fun of me." That's what she does.

"No, I won't."

I roll my eyes, knowing she won't let it go if I don't say something. "She's smart. Got a full ride scholarship and all that. Plans on going to grad school after graduating next year."

"What else?"

What else does she want to hear? How I can't stop thinking about her? How I've loved every minute she's been at my house? We stayed up late last night watching movies, Boots curled up on her lap, talking about nothing in particular, but I still enjoyed listening to her words, her laugh. Just wanted to be next to her.

"She's the kind of person you want to be around," I find myself telling Danielle. "She's interested in what you say. She builds you up. She's giving." I chuckle to myself, thinking about all the times she's said the wrong thing. "She's funny, even when she doesn't mean to be. And beautiful. I mean, you saw her. But she also has this inner beauty. She's got this… I don't know what to call it. A pure soul or something. She sees the good in people." Even when they don't deserve it. "She's innocent, but not. I can't explain it. She's dealt with some real stuff, things I can't imagine, but she still stays so positive."

I pause when I realize I've been rambling. Danielle's going to give me so much shit, despite her promise not to.

"Austin…" She clears her throat, uncharacteristically serious. "I think you might be in love with her."

No, that's crazy. I've never been in love. Never come anywhere close to it. For Christ's sake, Tessa doesn't even like me romantically. I still can't get out of my head the utter shock on her face when I'd kissed her. The way she'd stiffened. The way she hasn't brought it up since. She must want to pretend like it never happened.

"I'm not in love with her."

"Are you sure?"

"Of course. She doesn't…" I take a deep breath. "She doesn't feel that way about me. I kissed her and she… didn't respond."

"Shit, Austin. I'm sorry."

"No, it's fine. It was a long shot, anyway. She's way too good for me."

"That's not true. Listen, I can talk to her—"

"No. I don't want to make her uncomfortable, especially since she's staying with me. Just leave it alone."

She sighs. "If that's what you want."

Yeah, that's what I want. And she better not make things worse.

Tessa makes the last turn toward our apartment complex, my stomach comfortably full of tacos. If nothing else, Danielle's a good cook.

"I liked your family. It was so nice of them to include me."

I nod, crossing my arms over my chest. "Danielle really liked you." Too much, actually. The two of them had instantly clicked.

"She was so funny. You guys are polar opposites, but you were finishing each other's sentences, too. I always wished I had someone like that."

"It gets old sometimes, trust me. But she's got my back when I need her."

"And you have hers?"

"Of course. She's my little sister."

She glances over at me, grinning. "Have you ever had to go into super protective brother mode with her?"

I stroke my beard, thinking about it. "With a few guys in high school. But she's pretty good at taking care of herself. She doesn't take shit from anyone."

"I wish I could be like that."

"You need me to lay the smackdown on someone?"

She laughs. "My own personal hitman?"

"Whatever you need."

"Are Boy Scouts allowed to do that?"

I groan. "I was in second grade. And Danielle shouldn't have told you about that."

"Why not? It's cute."

Cute? Is she serious?

"Well, I'll call on your services if I ever need you, okay?"

She parks in front of our building, the cold nipping at us as we make our way inside.

I strip off my jacket as soon as we get in and turn the heat up. "You want to watch another movie tonight?"

"Oh, I'd love to, but I have to study. I've got a test in Behavioral Genetics tomorrow morning."

Right. That doesn't sound hard at all. "Need help?"

She smiles. "You'll quiz me?"

"Sure." Not that I have the first clue about whatever her class is.

"Great." She grabs her backpack and pulls out a binder that's about two inches thick. "Everything for this section is behind the blue tab."

Jesus, this weighs a ton. Opening it up, the whole thing is color coordinated, with a legend at the front that explains what each color means. "Are you always this organized?"

"When it's important, yeah. I don't mess around with my classes. If I do, I could lose my scholarship."

"You can lose those?" I thought they gave you a bunch of money off the bat.

"I have to maintain a certain GPA for them to keep paying my tuition."

"I wouldn't stand a chance, then."

"You're too hard on yourself," she says softly, taking a seat on the couch. "Okay, I'm ready. Let's see how well I'll do tomorrow."

I sit on the opposite cushion, facing her, and open the binder to the blue tab, my head swimming as I skim through her notes. Alleles, carriers, zygotes… What the hell am I looking at?

I randomly flip through the section and pick a paragraph on a page. "How do genes regulate protein synthesis?" What did I just read?

"They specify which amino acids will join together and in what order."

"Uh…"

"It's right, trust me."

I'll have to take her word for it. "Okay, what are polymorphisms?"

"Mutations in more than one percent of the population."

Mutations?

I flip through again. "What's one thing that doesn't change even as you develop new physical and behavioral characteristics?"

"Your genotype. Well, unless you have a mutation."

"What do you mean by mutation? Like comic book stuff?"

She laughs. "No. If you fall in a radioactive vat, you're more likely to die from complications than suddenly have super strength or whatever. But mutations happen all the time. They're happening within us right now."

"I'm… mutating?"

"Yeah. They're technically called gene variants. Every time your body creates new cells, there's a chance they'll change slightly when they divide and multiply. Usually, the change is detected and repaired, and if not, the cell will die. But if it doesn't and those variants create new cells of their own, that's when trouble can happen."

"What kind of trouble?" Back in high school, I tuned out most things my teachers said, but I don't remember anyone talking about stuff like this.

"Cancer is the most common gene variant."

"So… your body's making cancer cells all the time and there's nothing you can do about it?"

She winces. "I mean, you can limit your exposure to the things that cause mutations. UV rays, cigarettes, radiation. Stuff like that."

The last two aren't a problem, but should I start wearing sunscreen?

Nah, I probably won't.

"How do you remember all this?"

She shrugs. "It's interesting to me."

"Aren't you a psychology major, though? This is biology you're talking about, right?"

"Well, there's a lot of overlap between the processes of the body and how it affects the mind. I mean, look at the study you're in and the relaxation techniques. The way your muscles are contracting and releasing has a direct correlation with your perceived stress levels."

"Is that the kind of stuff you want to study when you go to grad school?"

"Yeah, I'd love to get into a program where I could do that sort of research."

God, she's so fucking smart. How could I ever keep up with her?

"What is it?" she asks, her brows knit together.

Shit. Did I make a face or something?

I shake my head. "Nothing."

She nudges my arm. "No, really. Tell me."

"I just…" I wipe a suddenly sweaty palm down my leg. "I have no idea what this stuff means. These questions I'm asking you." I hold up the binder, as if it holds the secrets to the universe. "You're the smartest girl I've ever met."

Her head tilts to the side. "Okay, first of all, I find it refreshing that you're not pretending to understand it."

"What?"

She rolls her eyes. "Do you know how many times I've worked on group projects and a guy takes charge and acts like he knows everything? And then halfway through when it becomes embarrassingly obvious that he's full of shit, someone else has to redo it all. Usually me. So, I'm just saying I appreciate that you're not so egotistical you can't admit when you're out of your league with something, you know?"

Does she mean out of my league with this stuff for her test? Or out of my league with her?

Or both?

"Everyone has to start somewhere," she continues. "That's how you learn. How you grow. And if you decide to do the college thing, that mindset will help you so much."

"That it's okay to start at the bottom?"

She nods. "And don't be afraid to ask for help. The worst anyone can say is no and then you move on."

I swallow heavily. Is that her way of saying that she's moved past me kissing her? She said no and now it's over and done with?

"And second of all, I am not that smart. As we've talked about *previously*," she says with emphasis, a teasing note in her voice, "book smarts aren't everything. There's plenty of stuff I don't know about. You can't talk to me about boxing, right? I'd be lost. Or motorcycles? Forget it."

"That's true. But those things aren't important."

She lifts one shoulder in a shrug. "Importance is in the eye of the beholder."

I study her, considering her words. Does she have any idea how important she is to me?

I swallow as another thought occurs to me. How important am I to her?

CHAPTER TWENTY-ONE

AUSTIN

I NEED to stop thinking about stuff like this. I'm supposed to be helping her.

I turn back to the binder in my hands. "Sorry, I got off track."

"That's okay. I like talking to you."

I thumb through the pages, unsure what to ask her next. "You know, Danielle was surprised by how much I talk to you. I never know the right thing to say to people, so I usually keep my mouth shut."

Her lips quirk. "I should take that advice. Keeping my mouth shut so I don't say the wrong thing. But you don't have a problem with not knowing what to say. You always seem to know exactly what I need to hear."

"I do?"

"Yeah. I've been a mess when it comes to my apartment, but you're so level-headed about it all. You've been the only thing keeping me sane."

"I just want to make sure you're okay," I murmur.

She gives me a soft smile. "I am now. Thanks to you." She looks down at her lap, looping a loose string on her shirt around her finger. "Your dad talked a lot about boxing at dinner tonight."

Well, that's a change in topic. What's she getting at? "Yeah."

"You said he doesn't listen, but have you actually talked to him about how you feel? About how you don't want to do it long term?"

I let out a sigh, rubbing my forehead. "I don't want to get into it with him."

"How will he know if you don't tell him?"

My jaw tightens.

"I don't want to make you mad," she whispers. "But you were giving him these one-word responses like you were annoyed. And then Danielle would change the subject when she could." Her finger twists and twists around the string, the tip red after she unravels it. "You said you wanted to make sure I'm okay, and I want the same for you."

Ah, shit. "I'm not mad. Not at you."

"At your dad?"

I shake my head. "At myself. I should've said something a long time ago."

"Have you mentioned anything about college to him?"

I chuckle, though there's no humor in it. "Langford men don't go to college. We're a salt of the earth family."

"Does he really say that?"

I nod.

"What's his job?"

"He's a mechanic."

"Did he used to be a boxer? Is that why he's pushing you to do that?"

"No, but my uncle was."

"Oh, right. Marty."

My brows raise. "You know him?" That's what her tone implied.

"Yeah, that day I came to the gym. He gave me a tour of the place."

Why would he do that?

"So why can't you talk to your dad? Are you afraid he won't love or respect you if you don't follow what he wants from you?"

God, she asks hard questions.

"I haven't consciously thought that." I take a deep breath, letting it out slowly. "But maybe. I don't want to make things uncomfortable. For me or Danielle. It's better to keep the status quo."

She looks at me solemnly. "You're not a big risk taker, are you?"

Look what my last risk got me. Rejected on the dance floor. At least it hasn't affected the two of us acting like normal. If anything, we're closer than ever.

I shrug. "In the ring I do. But calculated risks. You have to. In real life…" She probably thinks I'm a coward.

"I understand. It's scary to put yourself out there, especially when it'll make waves. But if you ever want to plan out what to say to him, I'm happy to listen. To spitball ideas or whatever."

I nod, ignoring the ache in my chest at her kindness. "I looked more at the material you gave me about the community college."

Her eyes sparkle. "Yeah? You seriously considering it?"

"The business program looks good. I figure it's broad enough that I can use it for anything."

"That's smart. Will you apply for the summer semester?"

I wipe my palms on my pants, still thrown off by how fast this decision came together. "Yeah, I think so. Only one class, though. To make sure it's something I actually want to do. And online so it doesn't interfere with work."

She reaches out to squeeze my arm, her fingers warm. "That's a big step. It sounds like you've put some thought into this."

"You've inspired me."

She points to herself. "Me?"

"Yeah. You make me… want more out of my life."

Her lips part slightly. "I don't know what to say. There's nothing special about me."

"I think there is."

She swallows, looking unnerved.

Shit. Did I make her uncomfortable again?

I stand, placing her binder on the coffee table. "I'll let you study for real now on your own. You want the bedroom or the living room?"

"I…" She shakes her head. "I'll take the bedroom so you can watch TV out here." She stands and picks up her binder. "Thanks for talking with me."

She moves forward and gives me a brief hug, just long enough for her vanilla scent to envelop me, then disappears into my room.

I blow out a breath, lacing my hands behind my neck. How the hell did that conversation turn so personal? It seems like more and more lately things have been turning in that direction. This… vulnerability with her has been unexpected but not unwelcome.

The only thing is, where is it leading?

Something warm and soft shifts against me, consciousness gradually returning. And yep, for the third day in a row… I'm hard. Am I going to wake like this every time?

My arm is around Tessa, my front to her back, holding her securely to me.

But this time, there's no mistaking that she's the one moving, her ass rubbing against my dick, the pressure incredible. No wonder I'm turned on.

Is she asleep? She must be, right? She obviously wouldn't do this if she was awake. Would it be awful if I let her keep doing it? This might be the only chance I get to feel her like this, sliding up and down my shaft, pressing back firmly.

Is she dreaming about me? Is that too much to hope for?

My fingers flex on her stomach, unable to help myself, wanting to move against her, too.

But it seems as if I've broken the spell, her movements slowing. It's so quiet, her breaths are audible, not a steady, rhythmic sound like she's asleep.

The past two mornings I've rolled away from her as soon as I realized what was happening, but this time I stay where I am, neither of us acknowledging the compromising position we're in as the seconds tick by.

It takes everything in me to keep still, to not grind against her the way she was doing to me, waiting for her to make the first move, to decide what will happen. She's sure to get out of the bed at any moment, to wake up enough to realize what's going on.

But against all odds, her hand shifts, coming to rest over mine, her fingers soft and delicate. She gives the slightest pressure, pushing my hand down, and I move it without resistance, in awe as she guides it to the juncture of her thighs. Is this really happening?

She presses back against me again, then forward into my hand, telling me with her body what she wants, and I softly rub her over her pajama pants, enjoying the way her breathing grows rougher, the way she rocks against me.

I keep quiet, too afraid she'll come to her senses if I ask her what she's thinking, taking this moment for what it is... even though I'm not sure what it is. Not that I'm complaining. I can't deny this possibility crossed my mind that first night she asked to sleep together.

As she presses her ass against my front, I finally allow myself to move too, a low groan issuing from me as I grind on her. Christ, that's good.

She lets go of me, but it's too dark in here to see where she moves her hand. God, I wish I could see her body shifting in time with mine right now. I slip my hand under her pants, rubbing her over her underwear, and she inhales sharply, her hips thrusting forward.

She makes these little sounds of pleasure, spurring me on, and I breach the last barrier, lifting aside the edge of her panties to tease her seam, finding her slippery with arousal.

She jerks back against me, moaning, and as I enter a finger inside her, she's already coming, her inner walls pulsing around my middle finger.

She stops moving, silent as she gets her breathing under control, and I let go of her, waiting for her cue on what to do next.

Where do we go from here? Was this a one-off occurrence? Did she wake up horny and needed a quick release, not considering the consequences?

How will this change things?

My alarm goes off on my phone, signaling it's time to wake, and I roll over, sitting up to grab it from my bedside table and shut it off. My erection bobs between my legs, wanting more, but I ignore it. "I have to get ready for work." They're the first words we've spoken, despite everything we did.

"Okay," she whispers.

I pause for a moment, seeing if she'll say anything else, but she doesn't.

She said I always know exactly what to say to her, but my mind is blank. Guilt flashes through me, knowing I shouldn't have done this. I don't want her to feel awkward now. Not that I coerced her. She was the one who made the first move, after all. And really, how could I have denied the chance to feel her so intimately?

I look over my shoulder, but it's too dark to see her. My mouth opens and closes, but I don't know what to say.

I get up instead and head into the bathroom, shutting the door behind me before I turn on the light. Maybe it's better to say nothing for now. To think about it in the shower, to wait for the right words to come. This is too important to mess up.

I glance at my reflection in the mirror, my cheeks flushed, dick straining at my sweatpants. Looks like I'll be taking care of things in here for the third morning in a row.

CHAPTER TWENTY-TWO

TESSA

I PUSH open the lecture hall door and step outside, taking in a lungful of wintry air to clear my head. It was all I could do the last hour to focus on my test and not relive the incident this morning.

Rocking against his hard body. His hand sneaking under my waistband to skillfully rub me. The way I'd come *embarrassingly* quick.

I hold my hands to my burning cheeks, hoping anyone passing by on the sidewalk attributes it to the cold weather and not my remembered mortification. From the time I'd realized he was awake to when I'd come couldn't have been more than two minutes, tops.

What must he think? I'd practically forced him to touch me, pushing his hand down like that. Yeah, he continued on his own afterward, but then I'd climaxed almost as soon as he slipped under my panties. Who comes that fast?

And then, when he'd left to shower, all I could think of was how awkward it would be when he came out of the bathroom. Of how I'd have to explain myself. So… I'd left. Retreated to my apartment across the hall, despite the creepy crawlies that had overtaken me as soon as I'd stepped inside. Rushed to get ready and left way earlier than I needed for class, probably before he'd even finished showering.

I pull out my phone, finding no messages. What did I expect, though? I'd *fled* his apartment after leaving him high and dry. Why would he contact me first? It should be me saying something.

But what do I even say? Thanks for the orgasm? Let's do it again, soon?

I drop onto a free bench, burying my head in my hands. I have an hour until my Statistics class. An hour to craft the perfect thing to say to him. To explain why I left. Why I pressured him into doing it in the first place. Why I want to do it again.

No. Not that. If I couldn't handle what we did this morning, how can I ask for anything more? How can I even be sure he *wants* to do anything more? Maybe he only did it because he felt bad for me. Because I was so obviously desperate. He hadn't even mentioned doing something for him. Shouldn't a guy have wanted to get off, too?

Wow, am I seriously complaining about that? That this sexy, considerate, amazingly sweet guy got me off and didn't ask for anything in return? What a hardship.

My phone rings and I fumble to grab it, for some reason believing it's Austin. I drop it on the ground, praying I didn't break the screen, and finally answer it, not recognizing the number.

"Is this Ms. Hooper?" a man asks.

"Yes." Oh, God. It's not a telemarketer, is it?

"This is Roy with maintenance. We received your request to fix your door and wanted to let you know we can have it done by Friday."

It takes me a moment to process his words. "Can't you fix the lock today?"

"It's not only the lock," he says, sounding unconcerned. "The whole door needs to be replaced. Looks like someone took a crowbar to it."

"So, my apartment's unusable for almost a week?" Is that legal?

"There's nothing wrong with the inside. It's still livable."

"No, it's not." It comes out with more force than I intend, but with everything on my mind lately, I'm on edge. "Someone broke in. I feel unsafe in my own home. I can't sleep there at night."

"Ma'am, I understand—"

"No, you don't." A girl passing by gives me a troubled look, so I lower my voice. "My mother died in a home invasion when I was younger. This is my worst nightmare come to life. Someone broke into your shitty apartment doors, so it's your job to fix it as soon as you can. And with better locks than last time."

There's more deference in his tone as he says, "I apologize. I'll try to fast track this as much as possible."

"And I want a discount on my rent this month," I blurt out, caught up in the moment.

"I'll see what I can do."

I'm breathing hard by the time I hang up, my heart pounding, but I'm proud of standing up for myself like that. For asking for what I want.

Now only if I could do that in all aspects of my life.

"Tessa?"

I glance up to find Mia half a dozen feet away, bundled up in a wool peacoat. "Hey."

"Everything okay?"

She glances at my phone and back at me. What must I look like to have someone stop and ask me that?

"Yeah, I'm fine. I was on the phone with maintenance at my apartment. I—" I pause, realizing I never told her I was leaving Element Friday night. "Oh my God, I didn't tell you what happened."

She takes a seat next to me. "I heard about it. Austin texted Tyler and Ethan to let them know what was going on."

Thank God he'd had his head on straight. He'd been so wonderful, so in control. Meanwhile, I'd been a hot mess.

"Yeah, so they still have to replace my door. It's been a crazy weekend."

"I'm so sorry that happened to you. Do you have a temporary lock on your door or something?"

"No, I've been staying with Austin."

Her brows raise. "Oh."

Is that a bad *oh*? Or a good one?

Recognition seems to hit her. "So that's why he bought you that drink at the club. I thought that was strange. Oh, and I told Kelsey you guys weren't together. Sorry."

"Oh, no. It's fine. I mean, we aren't together. Just friends."

I think. Are we still friends after what happened this morning? For some reason, I don't want to say anything to Mia about it. It's embarrassing as hell, for one. And it also seems... private.

She waves her hands in front of her face. "Sorry, I'm making assumptions all over the place. I guess we haven't talked much lately, have we? You've got a lot to catch me up on if you're friends enough to stay over at his house."

I breathe out a shaky laugh. Yeah, a lot has changed, hasn't it? Like how I can't even imagine my life without him now. How integral he's become.

I don't tell her those things, though. I talk instead about the self-defense moves he's been teaching me. About helping him with college stuff. About

Boots and his family and hanging out with him. About how badly I'd misjudged him that day I was on the phone with her. How he's nothing like I thought he was.

"I have a confession," Mia says, her fingers twisting in front of her. "I kind of told him a while ago that… Well, because I didn't want him to think…"

"What?"

"That something had happened to you when you were younger. But I didn't say what. I just didn't want him to think you were scared of *him*."

Her hands won't stop fidgeting in her lap. Has she been worried about that?

"Hey, don't stress about it. I told him weeks ago. It's fine."

She gives me a relieved smile. "Okay, good. I wasn't sure if I should say anything, but I didn't want him to take it personally. He really is a nice guy."

I can't explain why, but her high regard of him doesn't help my mood any. It's a good thing that he's nice to other girls, too. That he's a nice guy all around.

But a tiny part of me wishes that all his helpfulness, all his attention, was special to *me*. That it was because he likes *me*.

My God, I'm mental.

I glance around, wanting to change the topic, and my gaze lands on the couple walking hand in hand about twenty feet away. Wait, I know that guy. "Is that Dr. Hanover?"

Mia looks in the direction I'm pointing. "Yeah. Tyler and I took his Research Methods class together. I had such a huge crush on him then."

"On Dr. Hanover?" I mean, I guess he's good looking. But he's such a hardass, it cancels out any of his looks. I still have nightmares about being called on in his class.

She nudges my arm. "No, Tyler. Besides, Dr. Hanover has a girlfriend." She points to their retreating backs. "I heard she was his student when they started dating."

"Really?" He seems like such a rule follower. Maybe it was only his own rules that others had to follow, though. "Is that allowed?"

She shrugs. "They must not be too worried about it. She might have already graduated by now. I'm not sure."

"I guess the heart wants what the heart wants." Sometimes there's no rhyme or reason to it. Like when you know the other person is way out of your league, but you still… hope for something more.

But at what point do you have to face reality?

I stand in front of Austin's door, debating if I should knock or sleep at my own place tonight, lock be damned. No, I can't do that. I wouldn't sleep at all. Wouldn't have his warm body to snuggle up to. His arm over my torso holding me securely to him. So safe in his embrace…

I blink, realizing the door is open and Austin's standing there, looking at me. How long was I out of it?

"Did I knock?" I ask, genuinely unsure.

He rubs at the back of his neck, his bicep popping in his short-sleeved tee. No, don't look at that.

"I heard you in the hallway. Thought you'd want to come in."

"Yeah, thanks."

I step past him, awkwardness descending over me. I never texted him today. Never explained any of the craziness from this morning. Would I be awful if I waited to see what he says about it first?

"I'm going to get a shower," I murmur, unzipping my jacket. "I smell like greasy diner food."

He nods and I retreat to the bedroom, delaying the conversation we have to have at some point. Grabbing my pajamas, I head into the bathroom and do everything possible I don't normally do like deep condition my hair, shave my legs, and exfoliate.

After blow drying my hair, I finally go out to face my fate. He's scrolling on his phone, but puts it down as soon as he spots me. "You need dinner? I made a frozen pizza earlier."

I wander over to the couch, curling up on the other end opposite him. "No, I ate at the diner."

He picks up a half-empty beer bottle on the table and takes a swig. "I forgot you were working tonight at first."

"Yeah, I always work Monday and Wednesday nights."

He messes with the label of his bottle, peeling it back, a ghost of a smile over his lips. "Thought you might be avoiding me."

"No…" Okay, that's obviously a lie. "Well, maybe a little." I take a deep breath. "About this morning…" I trail off, no idea where I'm going with the sentence.

He nods, still looking at his beer. "Do you regret it?"

"No." Wait, does he? Is that why he hasn't reached out either? "I just don't want things to be weird between us."

He shakes his head. "No, it won't."

"So… we're good?"

He sets the bottle back down on the coffee table. "Yeah."

An unsettled feeling floats around in my stomach, still not sure if that resolved the issue. What did I think would happen tonight? That I'd come home and he'd declare his love for me or something? Get real.

"Okay," I whisper, crossing my arms over my chest.

"Did you hear anything about your door?" he asks after a moment.

"Yeah. It'll be ready Friday at the latest, but hopefully sooner."

He nods. "Well, my place is open to you for however long you need it."

A pang settles deep in my chest. "Thanks."

There's an extended pause of awkward silence and then he stands. "Think I'll go to bed now."

This early? "I-I'll probably study for a bit."

"Take as long as you need."

After he adjourns to the bedroom, I sag against the arm of the couch, disappointment and frustration warring within me. I was able to ask for what I wanted with the maintenance guy today. Why can't I do the same with Austin?

And what would I even ask him? If we can do stuff in bed together again? That'll go over real well. I couldn't even say anything this morning as it was happening.

Maybe tomorrow will be better. Maybe I'll come up with a new way to broach the subject. Yeah, we said things are good between us, but they're obviously not. Not if my stomach is a ball of confusion right now.

I just have to think of a different angle to address it.

No pressure.

CHAPTER TWENTY-THREE

AUSTIN

"I COULD HAVE SWORN I made enough copies," Tessa mutters, searching through the papers and folders on her desk.

I stand and put on my jacket, watching her shuffle through a folder she's already looked through twice. "It's no big deal. I can memorize the instructions."

"I know it's somewhere, but I guess I'll have to give it to you tonight. It has all the things we talked about today with differential relaxation. Mostly about relaxing during your daily activities and isolating the muscles needed for specific tasks while keeping the rest of you relaxed. And then what you can expect next week with rapid relaxation and your final questionnaire."

"Yeah, I'll get it later. No problem."

"Okay, thanks." She gives me a nervous smile. "I made plans with Mia tonight, so I won't be home for a few hours."

I stick my hands in my pockets, looking down at my scuffed work boots. "Cool. I'll probably head over to the gym for a while, then." Anything to get this restlessness out of my system.

Last night had been fucking awful during the few minutes we'd interacted. She'd been so nervous, like she was trying to let me down easy. It was all I could do to stick around for as long as I did. Before she told me she wasn't thinking clearly. Before she told me it was a mistake. I couldn't bear to hear that.

I glance up to find her staring at me, her expression solemn.

"What is it?"

"You're so hard to read," she murmurs.

Me? "What do you mean?"

"I don't know, I…" She shakes her head. "I've been thinking a lot about our conversation last night. Or, rather, that there was more I should have said."

"You can always talk to me." Even when it's something difficult to hear. Something I'm dreading to hear. I don't want her to feel nervous around me again.

"I know. And that's part of it. You've been so wonderful through all of this. Like, an incredible friend. I'm so grateful you're letting me stay with you. And then I—" She takes a deep breath, her lower lip trembling. "I'm probably over-thinking it, but I'm pretty sure I fucked everything up yesterday morning. I pressured you and I never asked if you were okay with it—"

"Hey, hey." I wrap her in my arms, my heart thudding as she rests her head against my chest. "I wouldn't have done it if I didn't want to."

She sniffles against my jacket. "I was just so caught up in the moment, and I've been replaying it in my mind and my stomach has been in knots trying to think of a way to explain it. And I hate not talking to you because we've gotten so close, and I don't want to jeopardize anything."

The more she talks, the more my belly sinks with disappointment. She said last night she didn't regret it, but clearly, she does.

"Tessa, you're fine. Everything's fine. You don't have to worry about me."

She leans back, her nose pink as she sniffs again. "I always worry about—" She pauses, blinking up at me. "Wait. Did you say you wanted to do it?"

"Uh…" What the fuck do I say now that she basically said it was a mistake?

"I mean, you didn't even get anything out of it."

"Of course I did," I reply without thinking.

Her eyes widen. "What?"

Ah, shit. It's not like I can tell her I'd do whatever she wants in bed. That I'd gotten more satisfaction out of that brief encounter with her than anything in memory. That all I want is another chance to touch her.

There's a knock at the door and Joel peeks his head in. "Hey, just seeing if you're finished."

Tessa wipes at her eyes and steps away, returning to her desk. "Yeah, all done. I only have to clean up my stuff here. I made a mess earlier looking for some papers."

Joel glances between us expectantly, but I don't want to get involved in his drama again. "See you at home," I murmur to Tessa before heading out.

Joel holds the door open for me, something about it setting me on edge. Like I'm being kicked out.

I shake off the feeling and speed through the lobby, but as I start down the stairs, there's a noise behind me. I glance back, finding Joel shutting the stairwell door.

"Hey, you got a sec?" he asks.

I nod, wondering what the hell he's up to. There's something about him that's… smarmy.

"Tessa still at your place?"

"Yeah." Despite his best attempts to keep that from happening.

"How's she doing?"

Oh, so he actually cares? "As well as expected, I guess."

He crosses his arms, looking over his shoulder for a moment to check behind him. "She's a good girl. I wouldn't want her to get mixed up with someone who isn't right for her, you know?"

My jaw hardens. "You mean me?"

His head tilts to the side in mock concern. "All I'm saying is she's been through a traumatic experience. She's vulnerable. She might have some vision of a knight in shining armor kind of thing. But it's not real."

My hands flex at my sides into fists, but I consciously let them go and take in a deep breath. "Look, it's obvious to everyone but Tessa that you're into her. But she doesn't feel the same way about you. Let it go, already. She's insistent you're just friends."

The fake concern drops from his face. "Like the way she tells me she's just friends with you?"

"I'm not talking about me."

"And I bet you're not in any rush to have her leave your place, are you?"

He wants to be a prick? Fine. I can be one, too. "No, I'm not. I love waking up with her every morning. You know we're sharing a bed, right?"

He sneers, but I don't get the satisfaction I thought I would from throwing that in his face. Instead, there's a dull ache in the pit of my stomach.

I shouldn't have said that. Anything between me and Tessa is between us only.

"I have to go," I mutter, turning around and rushing down the stairs.

What if he tries to make things difficult for her now, even more than he already has? What if it affects their study?

I make my way to the parking lot and my phone vibrates in my pocket. Oh, God. What if Joel went and tattled to her?

It's not Tessa calling me, though. It's Dad.

"Hello?" I answer, unsure why he's reaching out. We're not exactly a chat on the phone father and son duo.

"Hey, I found out about a tournament a couple of hours away."

I sigh, rolling my shoulders back to release the tension that's already formed there. "Yeah, Lawrence mentioned it to me."

"So, you're going, then?"

I pinch the bridge of my nose, finally reaching my bike. I swear to God if I ever have kids, I'll never hound them like this.

Opening my mouth to make some noncommittal answer like I always do, I pause, Tessa's words from two nights ago coming back to me. *How will he know if you don't tell him?*

"No," I say slowly, the word feeling foreign. "I'm not."

"Why?"

I could tell him I'm not interested in tournaments anymore. That I won't be fighting professionally. That it was never my plan for the future.

But instead, I say, "I have other things going on." A tangle of guilt and shame mix in the pit of my stomach, but I push it aside, not wanting to get into it with him.

When will I, though? I can't put it off forever.

"What's more important than preparing for going pro?" he asks, his tone genuinely confused as to what could take precedence over boxing.

"I…" I glance around the parking lot, but there's no one here to help me out. Why didn't I take Tessa up on her offer to come up with something to say to him?

Maybe it's because I'm already on edge from getting into it with Joel, but I blurt out, "I'm not going pro."

There's silence from the other end, then a weird sounding chuckle. "What are you talking about?"

Again, it's Tessa's voice that comes to me, asking me if I think Dad won't love or respect me if I don't follow what he wants. But more importantly, how can I respect myself if I'm not doing what I want? If I'm living for him and not myself?

"I never wanted to go pro," I tell him, filled with more resolve than I expected.

"Of course you did," he counters. "You've spent years training for this."

"Because you pushed me into it." Now that I've started, it's like a dam breaks. "It's the only thing you've ever cared about with me. You treat Danielle like an actual person, but I've only been a boxer to you. Beginning, middle, and end. There's nothing else that defines me, nothing else you talk to me about. I've only ever been one thing to you and I'm sick of it."

I'm breathing heavy, glad now there's no one in the parking lot to witness my outburst. I've never spoken to him like this. Dreamed of it, yes, but never followed through.

Things are changing, though. Like I told Tessa, she's inspired me. I want something different for my life.

"I have to go," I tell him, hanging up. The dread that always accompanies conversations with him is absent this time, lightness floating through me in its place, like after completing Tessa's relaxation routine.

If I'd known it would feel this good to finally speak my mind to him, I would have done it years ago.

I straddle my bike and head to the gym, more than ready to work out. Despite not wanting to box professionally, I still like it as a hobby.

One of the trainers, Steve, gives me a funny look as he passes me on the stairs down to the basement level, but I don't think much of it as I go in and make my way to the office to grab my spare gym bag.

Uncle Marty looks up from his desk at me, his mouth a grim slash across his face.

"Everything okay?" He's usually pretty stoic, but not like this.

He sighs deeply. "Just got some bad news."

I take a seat, sensing he wants to talk. "What's going on?"

"Steve's quitting."

My brows raise. He's the second-best trainer here, after Lawrence.

"Told me he can't work this weekend because he has to pack up his house. His wife got a new job across the country and the start date's pretty sudden."

"Sorry to hear that."

"Now I'm out a cornerman for the tournament." He drums his fingers against his desk. "I have to find someone to replace him in the next few days. Someone who's familiar with the guys here, who knows their fighting styles, their strengths and weaknesses, their…"

He trails off, eyeing me speculatively. What's he thinking?

"You're not competing this weekend, right? Could you help me out?"

"You want me to be a cornerman?" That's a legit job. He ever only has Steve or Lawrence do it.

"The other trainers are already scheduled here, and I can't have Lawrence do it all since some of the matches are at the same time. You'd be doing me a big favor."

"I…" I can't believe he's asking me. "You trust me to do it right?"

He picks up a pen and taps it on the desk. "As much as anyone that works for me. Hell, probably more. You're good at recognizing patterns and seeing what opponents are setting up. Coming up with a game plan on the fly, pivoting fast. I've seen you coaching some of the guys here, especially Ethan. You're good at it. You give them actionable steps to improve without any bullshit."

The tips of my ears go hot. "Uh, thanks." I had no idea he was paying that close attention.

My mind races through the options. Even if Tessa's apartment isn't ready by then, she can stay at my place without me. She'll understand. And Uncle Marty needs me. It's the least I can do for him. "Yeah, I'll be a cornerman this weekend."

He nods, relief on his face. "Thanks. Now that I think about it, how'd you like to replace Steve full time?"

I blink at him, unprepared for this turn of events. Wasn't I just thinking I wanted a change, though? "I…"

He holds up a hand. "Take a few days to mull it over. The tournament will give you a taste for what the job will be like."

Working at the gym full time? That sounds amazing. And it's not as if I plan on going anywhere in my current job. "Yeah, okay. I'll wait until Monday to tell you for sure, but I'm leaning toward yes."

He smacks a palm down on the desk. "Excellent. Now if I can only find someone to replace me."

"What? You're quitting?"

"No, no." He waves off my concern. "But I can't keep doing this forever. And I'm getting tired of all the day-to-day headaches. I've got Lexie doing accounting, but I need a general manager to take the rest off my plate."

My pulse picks up. This feels important, somehow. "What would they do?"

"Off the top of my head? Hiring, managing, ordering, payroll, memberships, marketing, facilities issues. I'm sure I'm forgetting a few other things, too. But it'll be tough to find someone who knows boxing well enough that's got business sense, too. I don't want to bring in some guy that has a fancy management degree but can't tell the difference between a hook and a cross."

"You putting out any feelers?" Uncle Marty knows everyone in a fifty-mile radius that has anything to do with boxing.

"Nah. Just been on the back of my mind lately."

"What time frame are you looking at?"

His brows narrow. "If I didn't know better, I'd say you have someone in mind."

I wipe my palms on my pants to get the sweat off. "I… You met my friend Tessa, right?"

He frowns at me. "Petite girl? Long hair? You think she's interested in the job?"

"What? No." I rub at my forehead, debating how to word this. "She's been helping me look into college stuff. She's like the smartest person I know and she says I can do it. I'd already decided to take a class in business this summer at the community college and… I don't know. If you're willing to wait, maybe I could take some more courses and in the meantime shadow you and learn the ropes about what you do."

He studies me, rubbing a hand over his jaw. At least he isn't laughing in my face. "Your dad know about the college class?" he finally asks.

I shake my head. "I wasn't going to say anything yet. Not until it's a done deal." Our conversation earlier was enough of a revelation for him.

His lips tip up at the corners. "Smart plan. It all sounds like a smart plan, actually." He rubs at the back of his neck. "You know I never had kids. And even though you're my nephew, I always thought of you as a little more than that, especially after your mom…" He clears his throat brusquely. "It would mean the world to me to pass this place on to you one day if you wanted. But you couldn't be here and go pro. I wouldn't want you to give up your dream."

I swallow heavily. Damn, I wasn't expecting all this coming here tonight. I was only planning on blowing off some steam. "It was Dad's dream. Not mine." Might as well let the cat out of the bag now.

His brows raise. "Really?"

I shrug. "You know how he is."

He nods. "Fair enough. Well, we'll see how the weekend goes and if you like it, then I'll get you settled in Steve's role in a week or so. And then we can talk about learning the backside of the business and eventually taking on more responsibility."

We discuss a few more logistics, like job duties, salary, and benefits, and I shake his hand before I leave, impatience already bubbling within me.

I step outside and pull out my phone, halfway ready to text Tessa and tell her the good news before remembering the state of things between us. Even with our conversation at the Stress Lab earlier, it doesn't seem fully resolved.

You know what? Fuck it. If she doesn't want it to be weird, it won't be. I've gotten good at pretending around her.

Me: *Just got myself a job as a trainer at my uncle's boxing gym. I'm going to take those business classes at the community college and work my way up to general manager one day.*

I put my phone away, sure I won't hear from her for a while since she's hanging out with Mia, but it vibrates in my pocket before I can even step back inside.

Tessa: *OMG congratulations! We have to celebrate tonight.*

There are a bunch of emojis following her sentence. Happy face, confetti… a pink heart. My gaze sticks on it before I shake my head and turn off the screen. I've turned into a sap when it comes to her.

See, things are normal between us now. I share good news with her and she's happy for me. That's the way it should be. We can move past any awkwardness. It doesn't have to ruin our friendship.

Even if I wish she wanted more.

CHAPTER TWENTY-FOUR

TESSA

KNOCKING ON AUSTIN'S DOOR, I'm careful to balance the container of cupcakes in my hand. It'd be just my luck to drop it before I get inside.

As he opens the door, his gaze immediately zeroes in on the dessert.

"Congratulations!" I thrust the sweets at him, glad I have a ready-made excuse to talk about anything other than the elephant in the room. We never finished our conversation earlier.

He gives a defeated sigh and takes them from me, a smile lurking over his lips. "Seriously?"

"Yeah, this is a big deal. A whole career change with a chance to move up. It's exciting."

His mouth quirks up on one side. "Thanks." He moves to hug me, surprising me a bit after everything that's recently happened. I don't think he's ever initiated a hug that wasn't a direct result of me freaking out or crying.

Wow, what does that say about me?

I happily step into his arms, getting caught up for a moment in how good he smells. There's something about his embrace that just feels… right.

His arm had been around me yesterday morning too, keeping me safe and secure against him as we'd slept. And then again as we'd…

But there'd been nothing of that when I'd gone to bed last night. He'd already been asleep, turned away from me.

"You want to break into these now?" he asks, releasing me.

I mourn the loss of him briefly, careful not to let him see. "Yeah. I never turn down cupcakes."

"I can't believe you got this." He sets them down on the kitchen counter and opens the package. "How are we going to eat a dozen of these?"

"Well, not with that attitude you won't." I grab one and peel back the wrapper, indulging in a delicious bite of buttercream frosting and chocolate cake. "Damn, that's good," I mumble, spraying crumbs everywhere. Oops.

His brows knit with concern, but there's amusement in his gaze, too. "You've got some frosting… here."

He reaches forward and thumbs away a dollop from the corner of my mouth, licking it off his finger.

My belly dips low, eyes widening. Did he do that to be sexy? Because if he did, it worked.

We stare at each other for a moment, until he finally says, "Sorry. I don't know why I did that."

I want to tell him that I liked it. That I want him to do it again. That he could use his tongue next time.

Oh, God. I'm awful.

"No, it's fine." I set the rest of my cupcake down and take off my jacket, suddenly warm. "So, do you have a start date for the new job?"

He tells me about his plans to put in notice at his current job and go to the tournament this weekend as a cornerman.

"And what's that?"

"It's like a coach during a fight. I psych them up, preparing them mentally and physically. Create a strategy for them once we discover who their opponent is. Motivate them between rounds, give tactical advice. That kind of stuff."

"Well, I'm sure you'll be great. You've been an amazing coach to me during our self-defense training."

"Yeah, but that's just messing around. This is professional, you know?"

I gaze up at him, taking in the sudden worry on his face. "Why do you doubt yourself?"

"I'm not, I…" He scrapes a hand through his hair, the artfully messy waves falling back into place. How does it naturally do that?

He doesn't finish his thought, so I add to mine instead. "You hardly ever talk about yourself unless I prompt it. You never accept compliments. You should give yourself more credit."

He nods, looking down as he fiddles with my discarded cupcake wrapper on the counter. "The stuff I do, what I'm good at… it's not anywhere on your level."

I squint at him. "Didn't I tell you the other day that importance is in the eye of the beholder?"

He lets out a brief chuckle of acknowledgment. "You know, I did one more thing today, too."

"Yeah?"

"I told my dad I don't want to go pro."

My brows pop up. "Really?"

He nods. "The stuff you said the other night… I had to act on it. I couldn't let it go on any longer."

I reach out and give his arm a squeeze. Purely for congratulatory purposes, of course. "I'm proud of you. I'm sure it was difficult."

"Once I started actually telling him, it was the easiest thing in the world."

"What'd he say?"

He winces sheepishly. "I kind of hung up on him before he could say anything."

"He didn't call you back?"

He shakes his head.

Hmm, that's not good. "Well, the hard part's over, right?"

"Yeah," he murmurs softly. "It is."

His gaze lingers over me, and a flush steals across my face in response. When will I be able to control myself fully around him?

I turn my chin down so he can't see and say, "You know, I don't have to study tonight. We could watch a movie again."

"Yeah, we could do that."

I let him pick something, but I can barely pay attention as we sit on the couch, thinking instead about the way he was looking at me, about the hug he gave me, about those glorious few minutes in bed yesterday morning as he touched me.

I'd confessed to him at the Stress Lab that I couldn't stop replaying that scene in my mind, and it continues now. The sensation of his hard shaft against my backside as he'd rubbed me with slow, torturous circles. The rising need for him.

"Tessa?"

I blink, turning to him.

"You okay?"

What was I doing to make him think I'm not? "Yeah, I'm fine."

"You seem kind of out of it. We can pick a different movie if you want."

"No, this one is great." Crap. I don't even remember what we're watching.

He pauses the movie. "Okay, tell me what's going on." He motions toward the screen.

"Um…" Crap. Crap. Triple crap. "Maybe I should head to bed. I didn't get much sleep last night." That's the truth, at least. I'd been too worried thinking about what I should say to him today.

His brows raise the slightest bit. "All right. Let's go to bed."

I bite my lip, that wavering feeling in my stomach going haywire. He makes it sound like we're going there *together*. Which we are, I guess. Just not the way it sounds.

Restlessness courses through me as I go through the motions of getting ready for bed, practically bursting with it as I lay down. He's within arm's reach on the other side of the mattress, so close yet so far. I wish I could ask him to touch me again, to touch him, too. To tell him I desperately want to make up for that awful kiss at Element where I froze up.

After what happened yesterday and what he said earlier… would he want that, too?

"Austin?" I whisper into the darkness. I can't take this balancing on the edge anymore.

"Yeah?"

"At the Stress Lab today, we never really finished our conversation."

"We didn't?"

I grip the blanket, pulling it tighter around me. "No. I was worried I'd pressured you yesterday morning and you said you wouldn't have done it if you didn't want to. And I just want to know what you meant by that. You said you got something out of it, too."

My heart is pounding, practically beating out of my chest, but at least he can't tell how nervous I am in the darkness of the room.

"I… liked doing that for you."

He did?

"Would you want to do anything like that again?" I ask. I press my lips tightly together, hardly able to believe I said that.

"You want me to touch you? To… get you off?"

His voice is lower than normal, the words sending a shiver through me. And though there's a note of disbelief, I swear there's also something like longing, too.

"Yes," I whisper, my cheeks singeing the pillowcase. "And maybe I could touch you, too."

The silence in the room is deafening, the seconds ticking by slower than usual. Did I misread him? Was I projecting my own wants too hard?

The sheets rustle, and I can sense him closer, his body heat warming me.

"You can always touch me."

My heart is in my throat as the backs of his fingers lightly caress my jaw, goosebumps racing down my arms, and then he's half-leaning over me, cupping the back of my head. His lips brush over mine, featherlight, the same way they did at Element, testing, making sure I'm okay with it.

But this time, there's no freezing on my end. I deepen the kiss, angling myself toward him, and he makes a low sound of satisfaction, my belly dipping with desire. This is what I wanted.

I revel in the sensation of his lips on mine, his mouth warm and minty. His fingers sift through my hair, scraping softly against my scalp, and I let out a guttural noise of pleasure, unable to help myself.

He pauses, then does it again, and I press closer to him, running a hand over his broad chest. His body seems even bigger in the dark as I pass over his pecs and down his stomach, toying with the edge of his shirt. Would it be too much if I...

He seems to read my mind as he drags it over his head, leaving his torso beautifully bare. I trace the ridges of his abdomen and around his sides to the hard muscles of his back, enjoying the sounds of contentment he makes as I explore.

He kisses me greedily, his hand moving from my hair, down my neck and the length of my arms. He settles a palm on my stomach, his thumb brushing the underside of my breast, and I inhale sharply, startled by the bolt of lust that steals through me.

He leans back slightly. "Is that okay?"

"Yes," I murmur, tugging him forward. "More than okay."

His hand creeps up, anticipation running rampant through me as he settles his big palm over me, squeezing gently.

I make an unintelligible noise, straining toward him, wanting more. He slips under my shirt and does it again, his bare hand on my skin heavenly.

I arch into his touch, sliding my hands into the soft strands of his hair, my breaths growing harsher the longer he continues. He thumbs a nipple into a hardened peak, then the other, the wanting rising within me.

I sneak a hand south, needing relief, and he stops me, nudging my hand away. "That's my job."

I bite my lip, holding back a moan. God, he sounds sexy.

His fingers trail down my stomach to my waistband, and I grip the pillow as he snakes under and rubs me softly. My thighs fall open, hips lifting as his middle finger slides under my panties to tease me. My body's on sensory overload, a groan escaping me as he steadily sinks in and out. I'm so freaking wet, it would be embarrassing if I wasn't so turned on.

He builds me up, adding a second finger, trailing kisses over my neck, and I squirm against the sheets, wishing this would never end. Wanting to stay connected with him forever.

"Let me touch you, too," I whisper, shifting so I can reach him.

He continues to stroke me as my hands roam over his torso and down to the vee on his lower abdomen. I'd caught sight of it that morning he'd stepped into the room in only his towel, desperately wanting to touch it, and now I have the chance, my thumbs tracing the dip that disappears into his sweatpants.

I cup him, enjoying the falter in his strokes for a moment, and outline the shape of his cock, anticipating the first touch of him.

I play with the string at the waistband, drawing out untying it, and he makes this low, growly sound that sends a fresh wave of arousal through me.

Pulling the front of his pants down, I lightly trace a finger down his long length, his breath hitching. I smile, finding his mouth in the darkness to kiss him, and wrap my fingers around his cock, sliding from base to tip.

"Fuck, Tessa," he mutters against my lips, reverence in his voice.

He thrusts into my hand, eager for my touch, and I give him what he wants, stroking him in time with the way his fingers move inside me.

Without the benefit of sight, every other sense seems to amplify, from the scent of musk in the air to the roughness of our breaths in the quiet of the room. I can't believe we're doing this, that it's really happening. That this incredibly sexy man agreed to do this, that he's actually enjoying it, too.

A tingling sensation races through me as his thumb rubs my clit, a maelstrom of emotion swirling within me, words rising to my lips I dare not speak.

I've wanted you for so long.

I need you more than I thought was possible.

I think I'm falling...

That crest looms close on the horizon and I try to hold it at bay, wanting him to come with me, but it's too strong. It pulls me under and I let go of him, my hips arching to wring every ounce of pleasure I can out of the moment, his fingers continuing to pump in and out until the end.

My chest is heaving when he releases me, and I slump against the mattress. "That was amazing."

"Glad you liked it."

I roll to the side and reach for him again, loving the velvet over steel feel of him.

He twists his upper body so he can kiss me, his tongue sliding into my mouth, and I smile against his lips, reveling in how close we are. How right this feels. Like we were made to be doing this.

Made for each other.

I continue to stroke him, picking up my pace until his hips go jerky. His hand covers mine, angling himself up, and he groans long and low as he comes, the sound incredibly erotic. I want him to make that sound for me every night. To hear it softly in my ear. To feel the vibrations of his voice against my skin. To make the same sound for him as I climax.

Will there be another chance to do this again? Now that I've had a taste, I only want more.

"Give me a sec to clean up," he says, kissing me one last time before he leaves the bed.

I take stock of my body once I'm alone, enjoying the lingering bliss that floats through me, still riding the high from my orgasm. My breasts are sensitive from his attention earlier, and I gently cup them, realizing I'm fully clothed. Oh my God, we never even undressed to do all that. All he did was take his shirt off.

A thrill runs through me at the reminder of how fast everything moved tonight. At how on board he was with it all. At that need-to-have-you-now feeling we both had. At how natural it was between us.

The light clicks off in the bathroom and then he's slipping under the covers, holding out an arm to me. I snuggle against his chest and yawn, fatigue stealing over me.

"I won't be able to sleep alone after this," I mumble, a sense of safety pervading me being in his arms like this.

"You always have a place here with me if you need it."

I smile sleepily, letting his steady breaths lull me under, until there's nothing but gentle darkness to carry me through till morning.

CHAPTER TWENTY-FIVE

TESSA

LETTING OUT A QUIET *MMM* SOUND, I slide my arm across the soft sheets and stretch, luxuriating in the drowsy contentment of waking. When I encounter something furry, though, I snatch my hand back, fully alert.

Boots is peering at me through narrowed eyes, as if I committed a grievous sin against her.

"Sorry."

I scratch her behind her ears until she's appeased, and she curls up again in a ball on Austin's empty side of the bed.

Wait. Where is he?

The bedroom door is open, light filtering in from the living room, and I cautiously slip out of bed, poking my head around the corner. The wild excitement from last night has faded, apprehension replacing it. Will Austin be as cool with everything we did now that the moment has passed?

The apartment is eerily silent, and as I explore a little more, it's apparent I'm alone. Disappointment sinks hot in my stomach before I tell myself I'm being silly. He probably had to go to work. It's not like he could hang out here all day with me.

Oh, shit. What time is it? I have to get to class.

I rush back to his room and pick up my phone to check the time, discovering a text from him.

Austin: *There are waffles in the freezer for breakfast if you're hungry. See you tonight.*

Okay, so he's cool with me staying over again, which means he's cool with what we did, which means… What does it mean?

I can't deny that I like him. Like, *seriously* like him. Like… maybe more than like him?

Oh, God. Now's not the time to think about this. I've got ten minutes to get out the door.

I pop a couple of waffles in the toaster and get ready for the day, making sure to grab my work uniform out of the closet for later.

As I lock the front door, a man across the hall gets my attention. It's the apartment complex's maintenance guy. "Miss Hooper?"

"Yes?"

He glances between my door and Austin's, clearly confused.

"I've been staying with my neighbor," I explain awkwardly. "While I wait for you to fix my door."

He nods. "Well, good news. I have your replacement door in my truck, so everything will be fixed up and ready to go in a couple of hours. Got one with a deadbolt, so no one should be able to get in again."

"Oh." That means I won't have a reason to sleep over at Austin's anymore. And right as we…

"Do you need it done sooner?" he asks anxiously. "I promise I'll work on it as fast as I can."

Oh, crap. "No, you're fine. Thank you for making it a priority. I'm still a little rattled by the whole thing."

"Sorry again about everything that happened, Miss. We've never had someone break into a door like this before."

"Not exactly what I wanted to be first at," I say, the joke falling flat when he doesn't smile. Okay, time to go, then. "I have to run."

"Right. I'll leave your new key at the front office when I'm finished."

"Thanks."

I rush to my car, hoping I get to class on time, and slide into my seat for Behavioral Genetics right as the teacher starts. I try my best to focus on today's lecture, but all I can do is relive last night's once in a lifetime experience. The way he'd touched me… it was like he was in my head, knowing exactly what I wanted when I wanted it. Using the right pressure, the right speed… Have I ever been so turned on before?

Austin is everything I've wanted in a guy. Sexy, sweet, caring, protective. How could I have ever looked at him and been scared? Thought there was something dangerous about him? He's one of the kindest people I've met, so at odds with the tough guy image I first attributed to him.

And if he was willing to do all that with me last night, he must be attracted to me, right? At least a little? I still don't understand it, but I can't deny the facts.

Logically, I know I need to talk to him about what's going on between us. I should have done it last night, but I had other things on my mind. And, really, what's the worst that could happen?

He might say he's not interested in me like that, a voice in my head says. *That he was turned on in the moment and it was only a quick hookup for him.*

That's true. I mean, how much easier could I have made it for him? I was already in his bed and *asked* him outright to do it. With how sexy he is, he must get girls all the time. Case in point, Mia's friend hit on him right in front of me at Element.

But the thing is, I don't want this to be a quick hookup. If I'm being honest with myself, I'm halfway in love with him already. I want something more with him. He ticks all my boxes. He somehow makes me feel more alive than I've ever been, while at the same time the safest. And after so much upheaval in my life, someone I can be myself with is all I've ever wanted.

I take a deep breath, glancing around at my classmates. Is anyone else in here having an existential crisis at the moment?

When do I tell him? *How* do I tell him? I've never confessed serious feelings for a guy before. Never put myself out there like that. And nothing's ever felt so important either. What if I screw it up? What if he doesn't feel the same way? How can I go back to being just friends with him if it turns out he doesn't want a relationship?

Because that's what I want with him. To solidify this closeness that's grown between us over the last month. And where before I was sure he wasn't interested in me romantically, there seems to be a chance now. That maybe mousy, awkward, foot-in-her-mouth me could get such an amazing guy.

I just have to ask him.

Yeah, that's not terrifying at all.

I pull out my phone, debating what to say. I can't spring something like this on him over text, right? I should start out small.

Me: *Thanks for the waffles this morning. They hit the spot.*

I press send, then immediately regret it. That was the dumbest thing to say.

Then again, if I haven't run him off by now with all the embarrassing things I've done, I don't think this text will be the one to do it.

I stare at the screen, waiting for a response, but there's nothing. I should probably be paying attention to the lecture, but it's too late for that. My focus is shot.

I rub my fingers over my temples, then dive for my phone as it lights up.

Austin: *You're welcome to everything in my apartment.*

Including him?

I nearly groan aloud. God, I'm awful.

Me: *I'll have to bring you something from the diner again to make up for it.*

Austin: *You don't owe me anything, but I won't say no to another burger and fries.*

I smile to myself, something about the idea of getting food for him seeming intimate. Like I'm coming home and… Wait. His place isn't my home anymore, is it? My door will be fixed today.

Me: *I ran into the maintenance guy earlier. He's replacing my door.*

He doesn't text back right away, but there are still the three little dots like he's typing.

What is he thinking? Is he sorry to see me go? Happy to have his apartment to himself again?

Austin: *Are you moving back to your place tonight?*

That's the question, isn't it? If I'm being honest, I don't want to, but it's not like I can play house with him forever. I'm paying for an apartment across the hall.

Me: *I'm not sure yet. I won't be home from work until about nine-thirty.*

I won't mention that I could easily pack up everything of mine I've brought over to his place in less than ten minutes.

Austin: *Will you be able to sleep alone?*

My chest fills with warmth at his question. And while he probably means it in a caring, concerned way, I can't help but want to answer no for purely selfish reasons. To have one more night with him. To feel his body against mine. To touch him again and have him touch me in return.

My fingers hesitate over the keyboard screen, then decide to just ask him.

Me: *Could you stay at my place tonight with me?*

I mean, it's a legitimate question. That first night of the break-in, I really did need him close while I slept. And those feelings could very well return tonight, despite the new deadbolt on the door. He doesn't have to know I don't mean the question completely innocently.

Austin: *Can't think of anywhere else I'd rather be.*

My cheeks heat. Is he flirting? Or am I misinterpreting that?

I glance around the room and tilt my phone screen down, not that anyone's paying attention to me, and take a chance.

Me: *I don't know how much sleeping I'll be doing tonight.*

I hit send, prepared to tell him it's only because I'll be anxious about being in my home after everything that's happened if he asks what I mean.

Even though that's not what I mean.

Austin: *You need a distraction?*

Me: *You have anything in mind?*

Austin: *I can think of a few things.*

There's a winking emoji at the end of his sentence and I bite my lip, shifting in my seat at his flirty words.

Me: *Like things we did last night?*

Austin: *That's definitely on the list.*

Me: *Oh, you've got a list?*

Austin: *Of all the things I want to do to you? Yeah.*

My jaw drops. Where has this sexually suggestive Austin come from? And how can I get him to stay?

Me: *Do you have a copy of this list I can read?*

Austin: *Sorry, the only copy's in my head. Guess you'll have to find out by me showing you.*

Me: *Can I get a hint? You've got me excited.*

Austin: *It involves my tongue on you.*

A flush runs over me. Oh my God, are we sexting? I can't do this in class, right? And yet...

Me: *Where?*

Austin: *Where do you want?*

I stare at the screen, this whole thing becoming suddenly real. Didn't I want this, though? For something to happen between us?

And why am I being prudish? I gave the man a hand job last night, for Christ's sake. He fingered me until I was floating on a cloud of bliss. I fell asleep in his arms, more content than I've been in a long time. What's a little text message in comparison?

Me: *My pussy.*

I flip my phone over on my desk, my cheeks scorching. I just asked Austin to go down on me tonight. Wasn't I supposed to be telling him I like him? That I want a relationship with him?

In light of this new development, though... I'm dying to see how this plays out.

I turn my phone over, discovering another text from him.

Austin: *You've got me so fucking hard in the break room at work. How am I going to go back out on the floor?*

I let loose a goofy grin. Do I really affect him that much?

Me: *If it makes you feel better, I'm surrounded by fifty other students in class right now and my face is tomato-red.*

Austin: *You never have to be embarrassed talking to me about this. I love hearing it.*

See, he always knows exactly what to say to get me off the ledge.

Austin: *Listen, my break is over, but maybe we could continue this conversation tonight?*

A thrill runs through me. Tonight. When we'll actually be doing this stuff.

Me: *Absolutely. Can't wait.*

Austin: *Me, too.*

I set my phone down and press my hands to my cheeks, surreptitiously glancing around, but no one's paying attention to me. Thank God.

I glance at the clock on the other side of the room, my heart sinking at the time. I've still got three classes and a shift at work to get through before I see Austin. How the hell am I going to focus?

And, more importantly, what exactly will tonight entail?

CHAPTER TWENTY-SIX

AUSTIN

"ALL RIGHT, that's the last paper to sign," Uncle Marty says, gathering my paperwork. "Want to see how I file everything?"

I rub at my eyes, the beginnings of a headache forming after looking at legal fine print for so long. "Maybe some other time." Instead of signing things without reading them like I always do, I actually read through all the forms and asked questions, figuring I should understand what it all means if this will one day be my job. Paperwork that would usually take five to ten minutes somehow stretched out into an hour and a half as we went through it all line by line.

"How about we take a break?" he asks as he steps over to his filing cabinet. "That was a lot for me, too. I don't normally think much about all this legalese stuff. But you seemed to pick it up quick."

Did I? It didn't feel like it to me.

He files the papers, then looks back at me. "How late can you stay tonight?"

Not too late. I still want to go home and shower before Tessa gets off work. "I've got plans at nine-thirty. So I need to be out of here before nine."

God, I can't fucking wait for later.

"Let me guess. With that girl that came in here a few weeks ago? The one you mentioned yesterday?"

How the hell is all my family reading my mind lately when it comes to Tessa? "Yeah," I admit. "How'd you know?"

"You've got a lovesick smile on your face."

The smile I didn't realize was there drops. "No, I don't."

He laughs, eyes crinkling at the corners. "I heard from Lawrence how Johnson finally landed one on you that day she came in."

Why's he bringing that up now?

"First time he said he's ever seen you distracted in the ring."

Jesus. You get hit one time…

"So, what do you two have planned for tonight? Netflix and chill?"

I groan. "No one says that anymore."

"Yeah, but you didn't say no."

"Uncle Marty…"

He raises his hands in defeat. "Sorry, sorry. But I've never had the chance to tease you before. I haven't seen you show real interest in a girl."

I nod, looking down at my shoes. "She's pretty amazing. But we're not a couple or anything. She… Well, I actually thought she wasn't interested in me until recently." As in last night. "I'm going to ask her out tonight. Like on an official date. Not just hanging out at home."

He rubs his mouth, unsuccessfully hiding a smile. "Good luck. How about you get going now so you have time to get ready? If you've got that on your mind, I won't get much more out of you."

He doesn't think I'm slacking on the job already, does he? "No, I can—"

"It's a good thing," he says. "You deserve it. She seems like a nice girl."

"Thanks," I murmur, getting up from my seat. "And just letting you know, I'm working on a plan for my guys this weekend at the tournament."

"Glad to see the initiative. Now go prepare for your other *plans*."

I finally let loose a grin, nerves floating in my stomach. It's a good kind of nervousness, though. One that's tinged with excitement and possibility. Anything could happen tonight.

I head out on the main floor, getting stopped by Ethan before I make it out the door.

"Can I talk to you?" He glances around, eyeing everyone suspiciously. "In private?"

"Uh, okay."

What's this about?

He grabs his jacket off the coat rack and I follow suit, walking up the basement steps behind him toward the parking lot.

He stops at his SUV, turning to me. "Sorry about the secrecy, but I didn't want anyone to overhear. I heard you're replacing Steve this weekend. Is that true?"

I nod, watching him stroke his beard. The fading bruise I gave him last week in the ring is barely visible on his cheek.

"I want you as my cornerman for the tournament," he says, surprising the hell out of me.

"But you have Lawrence." Everyone fights for him. I'm taking all the guys that aren't lucky enough to get him.

"I know. He's great at guiding me when I'm practicing here at the gym. But…" He looks around again, but we're the only ones in the lot. "You know how I bombed pretty bad at the last tournament, right?"

"Yeah." It was his first time, though. Lots of guys need more practice before they win.

"Not that Lawrence could have made much of a difference because of who my opponent was and all, but I wish I'd had more guidance in the ring during the fight. So that's why I'd rather have you. I need your eyes looking at the big picture. Telling me what the guy has planned and what I should watch out for. And once I get punched a few times and my brain starts scrambling, what I should do to get back on track. Is that cool with you?"

"Yeah, of course." I'm flattered, especially since he lobbied so hard to get Lawrence in the first place as his primary trainer.

He sighs in relief. "Good."

"What are you going to tell Lawrence, though?"

He grimaces. "That's the thing. It's a delicate situation. He's my girlfriend's dad, so I can't burn any bridges. I was thinking of telling him I want to support you during your first tournament as a cornerman. So don't blab anything to him about why I'm really switching."

I mime locking my lips with a key.

"So you're quitting your regular job and everything? You'll be a trainer full-time?"

"Yeah, at first. Uncle Marty and I talked about me possibly becoming general manager one day, then taking over for him."

He nods, looking impressed. "Congrats. You'll be good at it. And maybe you can get some things updated around here. Lexie keeps complaining about all the stuff she suggests to Marty to improve the place that he doesn't want to deal with."

"One thing at a time, man."

He grins. "Right. My match is Sunday afternoon, so start coming up with some strategy for me, okay?"

I nod. Shouldn't be hard. I'm pretty familiar with Ethan's strengths and weaknesses. Just have to see who he's paired with.

"And hopefully I'm not fighting some Russian monster robot," he says, shaking his head.

Who the hell did he fight last time?

"I've got you covered, don't worry."

We say goodbye and I head home, those nerves from earlier returning and multiplying the closer it gets to nine-thirty. I shouldn't be nervous. Tessa made it pretty clear she's on board with the plan for tonight. I mean, she asked me to lick her pussy. I still can't believe my sweet, innocent Tessa said that. Talk about an instant hard-on. What else will she say once we're in bed? Is she a dirty talker?

Fuck, am I? I've never felt compelled to before, but as soon as she'd mentioned what we did last night, it was like a switch had flipped and all I'd wanted to do was have us acknowledge this attraction between us. The one I could have sworn was only in my mind. But after everything that's happened so far…

I pull up in front of our building and head inside to shower, finding a text from her when I get out.

Tessa: *On my way home now. See you soon!*

Damn, she sounds eager. Almost as much as me. That's just how I want her, too.

I pace the apartment a few times before I force myself to sit on the couch and be still. I go through the relaxation sequence Tessa taught me weeks ago, my belly jumping when there's finally a knock on the door.

I open it, finding Tessa's face bright with excitement on the other side. I lean down and kiss her, not worrying about whether or not it's the right thing to do, the enthusiasm in her response spurring me on.

She leans back slightly, her lips in a wide grin. "I like that kind of greeting."

I kiss her again, needing one more taste to tide me over. "I like giving it. I missed you today."

She lets her purse drop on the floor next to her and reaches up to wrap her hands over my shoulders. "I missed you, too." She pulls my head down to meet her halfway, murmuring, "I've been thinking about you all day."

All right, I can't hold back anymore. I run my palms down her backside until they reach the backs of her thighs, and bend to pick her up, wrapping her legs around my waist.

She makes a sound of pleasure as I shut the door and press her against it, letting my lips trail down the column of her neck, that vanilla scent of hers driving me wild.

"Austin," she pants, arching to give me better access. "I'm still in my coat and work uniform. Let me at least change."

"Why? I'm just going to take it off you soon."

She whimpers, her grip on me tightening, but I slide her down my body, loving how fast her breaths are coming. That I affect her so much.

"You need help packing your stuff?"

She looks up at me, a rosy flush across her cheeks. "I'll just grab the essentials."

Heading into the bathroom, she returns after half a minute with a tote bag full of items. "Okay, ready."

"That's it?" I know she had to have brought over more than that.

"I'll get the rest later. When I have more time."

The unspoken implication that she's impatient because she's ready for what I have planned for tonight hangs heavy in the air, the two of us staring at each other for a moment before I open the front door and usher her across the hall.

She slips a hand in her coat pocket and pulls out a shiny silver key, holding it up. "Hot off the press," she jokes before sliding it in the lock.

"Have you gone in yet?"

She shakes her head. "Not since you were last here with me." She pauses before turning the key, then wipes her palm on her coat. "I'm glad you're here."

"Of course."

I keep forgetting there's an actual purpose to me staying over here. It's her first night back since everything happened.

"You want me to go in first?" I ask when she continues to stand there, her hand hovering over the knob.

"No, I'm fine." She pushes past her reserve and opens the door, walking in and flicking on the light. "Honestly, I'm okay. I know I'll be safe with you here."

Pride swells within my chest. How far we've come that I've earned that kind of trust from her.

She sets down her bag and removes her coat, draping it on the arm of the couch, then turns to me, a shy smile lurking over her lips. "I liked your texts earlier."

I close the door behind me and make my way over to her. "Yeah?"

She steps closer, running her hands up my forearms. "I was a little surprised, though. We've never texted like that before." There's a note of excitement in her voice I love hearing.

"I figured after last night you'd be okay with it."

"More than okay," she murmurs, hands now on my shoulders, the tips of her breasts brushing my chest with how close she is. "Are you still offering that distraction?"

She reaches on tiptoes to kiss me, her seductive tone making my belly drop low with arousal. She wants this as much as I do. How did I get so goddamn lucky?

I slip a hand into her hair to cup her head as I deepen the kiss, the other sliding down her back to press our lower halves together. We stay that way until we're both breathing heavy, the kiss turning rougher, wilder. God, she gets me going so quickly.

I pick her up again, her legs automatically wrapping around my waist as I walk to her bedroom and lay her down on the soft duvet. Her uniform rides up as I nestle between her thighs, grinding against her as we make out, the desire within me pooling higher the longer we continue.

"You ready for more?" I ask her, wanting so badly to undress her and fully explore her body.

"Yes," she pants, arching under me as my lips skim her soft skin.

I tug lightly at her uniform. "How does this come off?"

"There's a zipper in the back."

She twists underneath me so she's on her stomach, and I move her hair aside, pressing a kiss to the nape of her neck as I draw the zipper down. I unhook her bra while I'm at it, my lips traveling down her spine.

I flip her over and strip her until she's bare for me. Just enough light spills through the open bedroom doorway to see her, my gaze devouring her nude body. I mentally trace the curve of her hip, the dip of her navel, up to her perfect breasts, impressing this moment upon my memory. "You're so beautiful."

She watches me, her gaze flicking over my face, then whispers, "You really mean that, don't you?"

"Of course."

She shifts atop the duvet. "I thought you were only saying that before to make me feel better."

"Tessa…" I lean down and lay a soft kiss on her lips. "You're the most beautiful woman I've ever met. Inside and out."

Her brows notch together, gaze still studying me. "No one's ever thought that about me. I… I've always been the plain girl. The one who fades into the background."

I caress her cheek, sweeping a thumb over her bottom lip. God, I've wanted to do that for so long. "You're the only girl I see. The only one I want."

CHAPTER TWENTY-SEVEN

AUSTIN

SHE REACHES FOR ME, the passion in her kiss making my heart sing. My hands roam over her body, exploring with no reservations, finally letting myself believe she truly wants me, too.

Shaping the soft weight of her breasts, I trail kisses down her chest, sucking a nipple into my mouth, loving the gasp of pleasure she makes.

She runs her fingers through my hair as I lave attention on the other one, circling the hard bud with my tongue, then gently lapping. She moans my name, holding my head in place, and I take my time worshipping her until her hips shift restlessly, seeking relief.

I make my way down her body, kissing every available surface until I reach the juncture of her thighs, anticipation racing through me.

I skim a hand up her calf and part her legs, my lips following, pressing a trail of kisses to where I want to be.

Her hands grip the pillow, watching me with unabashed interest as I spread her wider.

"You ready?" I ask, watching her closely. We've gone from purely friends to this in a matter of days, it seems like.

She nods, her eyes wide as I nestle between her legs, bringing her thighs over my shoulders. Parting her folds, I give her a long lick, enjoying the gasp of pleasure she makes.

I work my tongue on her slowly, adjusting my movements to her sounds of contentment, the way she angles her hips. Learning what makes her whole body tense and what has her relaxing into the mattress. I build her up over long minutes, reading her in the way I do best, using that kinesthetic knowledge she says I have to discover everything she likes until she's gasping my name, her hips bucking as her fingers grasp at the duvet.

I back off, giving her time to recover, and nip at the sensitive skin of her inner thighs, glancing up at her. She's panting, her legs spread eagle on the bed with one arm over her eyes. I go in again, watching her moan for me as I flick my tongue over her clit, hips lifting, seeking more.

"You like that?" I ask, knowing full well she does.

She nods, murmuring, "I love everything you do. I didn't know it could be this good." She clutches at her pillow. "It's like I'm having an out of body experience or something."

I chuckle to myself. "Tessa, this is only round one."

She whimpers, her neck arching as I nuzzle her and suck gently on her clit. I build her up again, this time taking her over the edge, her hand in my hair, gripping the strands tightly as she comes, bucking under me.

She moans my name, satisfaction coursing through me. There's nothing I want more than to make this woman happy.

She tugs me up next to her when she recovers, kissing me greedily. "That was incredible. More than incredible. I don't have a word for it."

I sweep her hair back from her face, taking in the brightness of her eyes, the dusting of freckles over her nose, the way her lips are swollen from my kisses. "I know exactly what you mean."

She runs a hand over my torso, down to the waistband of my jeans. "Can you… I mean, would you mind…" She toys with the button and I catch her meaning.

"You want me to undress?"

She nods, biting her lip as I strip. I'm conscious of my body in a way I'm not normally, hoping my size doesn't scare her again.

That doesn't seem to be on her mind at all, though, as she gives me a once-over, lust in her gaze. "I want to do the same for you," she murmurs seductively.

My brain takes a moment to connect what she's saying. "The same…"

She scoots closer, laying a hand on my thigh. "To give you a blow job."

My dick is at full attention, ready for whatever she has in mind, but I still want to make sure we're on the same page first. "Trust me, I'd absolutely love that, but I'm not expecting anything in return, okay? You don't have to do it because I went down on you."

She nods, giving me a quick kiss. "I want to. Making you feel good makes me feel good. I just…" Her fingers trace up and down my thigh, so close to where my dick wants her. "I've never done this before, so if you could tell me what to do…"

My mind short-circuits, still fixated on her offer. "I don't know," I answer honestly. "I've never gotten one before."

She stares at me, her eyes widening. "But you're a sex god."

Even in the dim lighting, the darkening of her cheeks is apparent. Is that how she sees me?

"What?" It's the only thing I can say in response, unsure where she got that kind of idea.

"W-what you just did to me," she stutters. "Yesterday, too. It was beyond anything I've ever imagined. You must've been with a lot of girls to get that good."

Now it's my cheeks that turn hot. "No, I… I don't pick up women." I take a deep breath. "You're the first girl I've been this close with."

She moves closer, curling herself around me. "Then how are you so good?"

I stroke a hand down her arm, savoring the freedom with which I can touch her right now. "You tell me with your body everything I need to know. You're incredibly responsive."

She runs a palm over my pecs and down the trail of hair on my lower stomach. "I am?"

I nod. "I can tell what you like from your breaths, your moans, the way your hips move." As my fingers brush over her back, she snuggles more tightly into my side. "You show me with your body language what turns you on, what you want more of. And I know how to read you."

"I can't believe you can tell all of that." Her hand on my lower stomach moves further south, dangerously close to my dick. "So, how can I learn what you like?"

I swallow hard as her delicate fingers wrap around me, lightly pumping up and down. "I don't know," I mumble, every ounce of my focus on the movement of her hand. "What you're doing is amazing."

"This?" She shifts so she's kneeling next to me. "I'm barely touching you."

"You could breathe on me and I'd come," I answer without thinking about it.

She grins, biting at her lip. "What about this?"

She positions herself over me, enveloping the head of my cock in her mouth.

"Fucking Christ." My hips lift, body on sensory overload, especially as I glance down and find her watching me with a knowing look. She's the Tessa from my dream the other night, a sensual seductress I can't get enough of. "Keep doing that. Exactly like that."

She makes a soft *mmm* of acknowledgment, growing more daring over the next several minutes as she explores me, pushing me to the limits of my control with the way she moves her tongue and lips on me. I grip the headboard behind me, the sight of her bobbing up and down on my cock the hottest thing I've ever seen.

She's intent on her task, sucking me harder, gripping me tighter as we continue on. I swear I'd never know this was her first time doing this, but then again, it's mine, too. I have a sneaking suspicion it wouldn't be this way with anyone else, either. The chemistry between us is more than I could have hoped for.

I groan as her mouth moves all the way down on me, the suction like nothing I've experienced. A tingle races down my spine, my grip on the headboard tightening. If I let go, I'm not sure what I'll do.

"Tessa," I choke out, trying desperately not to grind my hips into her face. "I can't hold back much longer."

She releases me, giving a long, slow lick to the length of my shaft. "Give me everything you've got. I'm ready for you."

Oh, fuck.

As she takes me in again, her tongue swirling around the head, the longing within me grows higher. I shut my eyes, wanting this moment to last forever, but too soon I'm past the edge and coming in her mouth, wave after wave washing over me. Opening my eyes, I find her greedily drinking me down, an expression of bliss on her face.

I tremble with the strength of my orgasm, weakness overtaking me as I sink into the mattress afterward, fully spent. "Holy shit," I mutter, running a hand through my hair.

She wipes at the corner of her mouth, the action sending a bolt of possession through me.

"Come here," I whisper, pulling her up to straddle my lap as I sit against the headboard.

I take my time skimming my hands over her body, exploring every dip, every hollow, every inch of perfect, creamy skin. I kiss her deliciously slow, building her up gradually for the second round I have planned for her. "You're incredible. That was better than I ever dreamed it would be."

It feels natural to say this stuff to her now when I would have never dared to be this open before. It seems we breached the last barrier between us tonight.

Her cheeks pinken but she smiles, sliding her palms over my shoulders. "I discovered what you meant by taking my cues from you to find out what you like."

My hands move up to cup her breasts, and her lips part, breath hitching for a moment. "Yeah? So you found out my tells?" I can't recall doing anything specific, but I was so goddamn turned on, it wouldn't surprise me if I did.

"It was the sounds you made. These low moans or these cute grunts. You'd whisper my name or groan. All I had to do was listen to tell what you like, but you did it so much, it seemed like you liked everything."

I stare at her, embarrassment washing over me for a moment. "I did all that? I don't remember saying anything."

She bites at her bottom lip, unsuccessfully hiding a grin. "You were very vocal. But I loved it. I can't wait to hear you again."

That sense of possession rolls over me once more at the mention of a next time. That this is the start of something lasting between us.

"Do you have plans tomorrow night?" I ask, remembering my ultimate goal.

"No. Why?"

I smooth my hands down her back, reveling in the softness of her skin. "Will you go out to dinner with me?"

"Like a date?"

I swallow hard, nerves coursing through me. I can't mess this up. "Yeah. Like a date."

The smile she gives me in response has relief splashing hot in the pit of my stomach. "I'd love that."

I maneuver her off of me, rolling over so she's underneath, her body pliant and eager for me to do what I will.

I make my way down, stopping directly above her pussy, and look up at her, excitement on her face.

"You ready for round two?"

She nods before I'm finished with my question, her hips straining toward me, and I mentally chuckle, loving how free she's been with me tonight.

I settle into position, my heart buoyant at the thought of our date tomorrow.

I'm the luckiest bastard in the world, with the girl of my dreams finally within reach.

And things are only going up from here.

I glance at the clock for the tenth time in the last hour, the minutes ticking by painfully slow, and avoid my manager's eye. Yeah, I've been phoning it in today, but what's he going to do—fire me? I already handed in my notice.

Mentally, I'm on Tessa's doorstep, picking her up for our date. I'd told her this morning to change into something nice when she gets home from her psych study, planning to take her somewhere fancy. The good thing about being a homebody is I have plenty saved in the bank. I want to spoil Tessa tonight. She deserves everything.

Should I stop at the store after work and grab some condoms? I don't want to be presumptuous, but based on her response in bed last night, it couldn't hurt to be prepared. Will she be ready to go for that tonight? Despite it only being our first official date, we've been through so much already. She knows me inside and out by now. There's no one else I've wanted like her.

Danielle's words from last week come back to me about how she thought I was in love with Tessa, and though I dismissed it at the time thinking there was no way Tessa felt the same, the sentiment doesn't seem so unbelievable now. Was Danielle on to something? Could she see what I couldn't?

Because the more I think about it, the more right it feels. This growing closeness, this overwhelming need for her… It's been leading to this point.

God, I can't fucking wait for tonight.

My phone buzzes in my pocket, a grin crossing my face as I see it's a text from Tessa.

"I'm taking my break," I tell my manager, already halfway across the warehouse floor. Maybe she sent something that needs to be viewed in private again.

I step outside the loading dock door, my smile falling as I read her text.

Tessa: *Listen, this is uncomfortable to say, but I've been thinking about it a lot and I don't see anything long-term happening with us. We're too different. It'd be better if we're just friends.*

I blink at my phone, too shell-shocked to fully process her words. What the hell is she talking about? I thought we were in sync finally. Her enthusiasm last night was off the charts. She called me a fucking sex god. And, most importantly, she agreed to that date tonight. Is she backing out now?

I press the call option, but it only rings once before it goes straight to voicemail. So she's declining my calls?

Me: *I'm not sure what's going on, but I'd like to talk about this.*

Tessa: *I'm too embarrassed to discuss this in person. I was caught up in the moment of something new, but I realize now it won't work out. Please respect my decision.*

My mind races, lightheadedness settling over me as my thumbs trip over themselves to text back. This doesn't make any sense.

Me: *I feel a connection with you I've never felt with another girl. Yeah, we're different, but you said yourself that doesn't matter.*

Tessa: *I was saying that to be nice. I don't want to draw this out. It's better if it's a clean break. I'm done discussing it.*

I swallow hard past the thickness in my throat, her punch to my gut harder than anything I've received in the ring. Normally, I'm good at rolling with whatever's thrown at me, but this… Jesus, how could she have changed her mind so quickly? Especially after what we've shared the last few days.

Me: *You're the most important person in the world to me. Can we at least talk about it tonight?*

My mouth trembles as I press send and I firm my jaw, bracing myself, my clenched fists leaving half-moon indentations in my palms before I realize what I'm doing. Despite her insistence on being done talking about it, I need to say my piece. This can't be over before it had a chance.

Me: *I'm in love with you, Tessa. I'll do anything to make this work.*

There's silence from her end for a solid minute, my stomach rising and falling in nauseous, anticipatory waves, the tightness in my chest growing and growing until I'm sure I'll burst with it.

Tessa: *I don't feel the same way. Like I said, I'm done discussing it. Don't bring it up again.*

I slump against the wall, the fight leaving me as tears sting hot in the corners of my eyes. I let them build, a numbness stealing over me as I sink to the concrete path outside the loading dock door, blindsided.

What the fuck just happened? What changed between when I kissed her goodbye this morning and now? How could she seem like a completely different person? That's not the Tessa I know.

I eventually remember myself and brush at my face, not acknowledging my body's response. Glancing at the time, I realize I should head back inside. My break is long over. Why would she even text me this now? Shouldn't she be in her study at the Stress Lab?

My limbs are heavy as I force myself to get up and return to work, avoiding speaking with anyone until my shift is over. I'm already mentally making a plan to go to the gym later and knock the fucking crap out of a punching bag, desperately needing a distraction from the Tessa-shaped hole in my heart.

I thought I knew her, that this was the start of something real, but maybe I was only seeing what I wanted to see. Maybe I wanted her so badly, my vision was clouded. But she couldn't have made it any clearer.

There's no future for us.

CHAPTER TWENTY-EIGHT

TESSA

I RUMMAGE through my bag for the third time, not that I expect my phone to magically appear when it clearly wasn't here the first two times. Where the hell is it?

There's a knock on my office door, and Joel peeks his head in. "Here are the questionnaires to hand out next week." He holds up a thick manilla folder filled with papers. I still don't understand why our participants can't answer their final questions electronically.

"You sent me on a wild goose chase earlier looking for them."

He gives me a sheepish grin, shrugging his shoulders up. "Sorry. I thought Kelly had them. Turns out she had given them to Dr. Price."

I roll my lips between my teeth, not saying anything. I'd almost been late for my first participant after he'd asked me to go searching for them.

Things are still strained between us, but he'd at least apologized for his behavior last weekend. After we're finished working on this study, though… It's time to end this friendship. Something about him has changed.

"Everything okay?" he asks as I turn back to my bag.

"I can't find my phone," I mutter. "It should be in here."

"Did you take it out? Maybe it dropped somewhere."

Before I can tell him I don't want his help, he's searching around on the desk, messing up the piles of papers I'd neatly sorted. I sigh, letting him do whatever, and go through the folders in my backpack, wondering if it somehow slipped into one of the pockets.

Joel moves behind me and crawls under the desk, then says, "Aha!"

He hands me my phone, gratitude and confusion warring within me. How did it get under there? I swear I don't remember taking it out of my bag.

"Thanks," I tell him as sincerely as I can. "I wouldn't have thought to look there."

He nods, wiping the dust off his jeans. "No problem. And I want to say sorry again for everything that happened this weekend. You back in your place now?"

"Yeah, they fixed the door. I moved my stuff last night." Not everything, but he doesn't need to know that. Or that Austin will sleep over again after our date.

"Do you need help putting things back?" he asks, a hopeful note in his voice.

"I've got it covered. And I have plans tonight," I add, before he can ask to hang out. I need to be more direct with him.

He doesn't seem as put off as I thought he'd be, though, and surprisingly keeps mum about Austin. Instead, he simply shrugs, some kind of weird smile playing about his lips.

"Well, I'm available if your plans fall through."

Right. Don't think so, but okay.

"I'll see you Tuesday," I say, shouldering my bag as I exit.

Joel is quickly pushed out of my mind on the drive home as thoughts of my date with Austin take over. He told me to dress up for dinner tonight, so he must be taking me somewhere nice. I've never had a reason to go to a fancy restaurant before. And I can't think of anyone I'd rather go with than him.

Butterflies float through my belly, and I let loose a stupid smile by myself in the car. As silly as it is, especially considering everything we've already done, it means a lot to me that he asked me out on something official like this. I swear he'd sounded nervous asking me, though that had endeared him to me even more. It's a definite shift in our relationship, and one that's very welcome.

I pull up to our complex, catching sight of him locking up his apartment. Is he ready to go already?

"Hey," I shout, waving to catch his attention.

He pauses, but doesn't respond as he glances over from his spot by the door.

I approach him, my steps slowing as I spy the workout clothes he's got on under his jacket. That's not exactly fancy attire.

"Are we still on for dinner?" I ask, pretty sure what the answer is based on his clothing, but needing to ask it anyway.

"No." He leaves it at that, his jaw clenched. What's going on?

"Did I get the days mixed up?" I'm pretty sure he said tonight, but maybe I misheard him in my postcoital haze.

His gaze narrows, almost like he's… mad. But why?

"You still want to go out to eat?" he asks tightly.

"Um… yeah." Did I miss something?

He makes a scoffing noise, sticking his hands in his pockets. "I'm not exactly in the mood."

Well, that's obvious. What's going on with him? "Is everything okay? You seem off."

His teeth grind together, annoyance flashing over his face. "I need some space."

"Oh."

I stare at him, though he's determined not to meet my eye, and my stomach sinks until it's a puddle somewhere around my feet. What changed since this morning? Did things get too real last night? Does he regret what we did? He must if he's acting like this.

"I…" I pause to take a breath, unsure what to say. "I'm sorry to hear that."

An awkwardness descends over us, the ease I've felt with him lately vanishing. It's like he's radiating irritation. With me? Or something else?

"I have to get to the gym," he mutters, moving past me and toward his motorcycle.

I stare after him, mutely watching as he straddles his bike and takes off. He didn't even wait for a response from me. Barely acknowledged our date. Barely acknowledged *me*.

Something has to be wrong. That wasn't the Austin I know. That wasn't my sweet, caring guy who's always there for me. It's like he was a stranger, the frostiness in his gaze nearly unbearable.

I blindly stumble into my apartment, grabbing a throw pillow to hug to my chest as I sink into the couch cushions. I'm guessing that means he won't be sleeping over tonight, either.

I glance at my bedroom door, then away, not wanting to think about that yet. Why does he need space?

My first urge is to follow him to the gym and figure out what's going on with him, but he asked for space. I can't outright ignore that, right? If our conversation just now is any indication, showing up at his new workplace demanding to talk probably won't go over well.

Maybe he needs a day to cool off from whatever happened and he'll be ready to speak tomorrow.

It's the only plan I've got going for me.

"Welcome to Kate's Kitchen. How many in your party?"

The guy standing at the front entryway looks behind him, but there's no one there. "Just me."

"Great. Please follow me."

I'm on autopilot as I seat him in my section and place a menu and roll of silverware on the table, then take his drink order.

Dragging my feet over to the soda machine, I scoop ice into a cup and depress the Coke nozzle, staring at the little brown bubbles.

"I've never seen Zombie Tessa before," Lexie remarks, dropping her tray on the counter behind us.

I glance toward her and away, not in the mood to talk.

"You're even too out of it to ask me to take that guy for you."

"What?" I would shake my head to clear it, but it wouldn't do any good. Between unsuccessfully trying to sleep alone in my apartment the past two nights and worrying about Austin, I'm running on empty.

She points toward the man I sat. "You always ask someone else to take your tables with big guys."

I look again at the man, realizing yes, he's humongous. Bodybuilder size. For once, I didn't recoil or flinch or evade like I usually do. Is that because Austin helped me overcome my fear? Or because I'm going on over fifty hours of little to no sleep?

I shrug, not giving her an explanation, and bring the guy's Coke to him, then take his order of a burger and fries.

My pencil falters over my notepad. That's what Austin ordered here.

I mentally slap myself. Jesus Christ, get a grip. I've got a job to do.

I return behind the counter and enter the order in the system, my mind unwittingly returning to my encounter with Austin last night. I'd knocked on his door under the pretense of needing to get the rest of my belongings, but he hadn't even given me a chance to ask to talk before he'd left, saying he was going for a run and would be back later. Like, just up and left his apartment with me standing there in the hallway.

Why in the world is he so desperate to avoid me?

"What's up with you?" Lexie asks, in a talkative mood for a change.

"Tired."

"Austin keep you up?"

My finger hovers over the computer terminal for a moment before I force myself to continue inputting the order. "No."

"Hmm." She crosses her arms over her chest, eyeing me carefully. "I saw you two on the dance floor at Element last weekend. It looked like you were getting cozy before you had to leave."

God, was that only a week ago? It seems like a lifetime.

"We're not together," I whisper, finishing ringing my customer up.

She straightens. "Shit, I'm sorry. I was just teasing. I didn't realize it was serious."

"What makes you think that?"

She glances around us and lowers her voice. "Because you look like you're about to cry. You need to take a break or something?"

I twist my lips, suppressing any emotion that rises to the surface. I can't be sad in front of customers. "I'm fine."

It's clear from her expression that she doesn't believe me, not that I was convincing to begin with. "Do you... want to talk about it?"

"No." God, I sound like him now with my clipped answers. "Really, I'll be okay. We weren't on the same page about things, I guess." What other answer do I have for her?

Maybe I was too clingy, taking over his life, acting like a girlfriend when he never said he wanted that. My brain keeps trying to come up with a reason why everything went south so suddenly.

She reaches out and pats my shoulder awkwardly. "I'm sorry."

"Thanks. I, um, I'm going to clean something." Anything to make the next two hours of my shift fly by. Then again, what do I have waiting for me at home?

I keep myself busy until it's time to go, dread curling in my stomach as I pull up to my apartment. Will it be another sleepless night?

Austin's bike is missing from his usual spot, a different car parked in it instead. Wait, isn't that...

"Hey, Tessa," Danielle says brightly, walking toward the parking lot from Austin's doorway.

"Hey," I reply weakly, smoothing my hands over my stained apron. I'd spilled ketchup all over it right before leaving work. "What brings you by?"

"I'm taking care of Boots while Austin's at his tournament. You would think she'd be fine for one night, but he's becoming a crazy cat dad."

A pang of sadness bolts through me. Does Austin's invitation to come over anytime to see Boots still hold?

"I was surprised he asked me," she continues. "I figured you'd do it."

I shake my head, leaving it at that.

Her brows notch together as she steps closer, concern on her face. "Are you okay?"

How many people are going to ask me that? How awful do I look? "Just having trouble sleeping at home since the break-in."

"Right. Totally understandable." She watches me for another moment and cocks her head. "This might sound weird, but you're welcome to come over to my apartment. My roommate's at her boyfriend's tonight, so you could crash in her bed. Or the couch, whatever."

I open my mouth to tell her it's a kind offer but I can't accept, and instead blurt out, "Yeah, I'd like that."

Her face brightens. "It'll be like a sleepover!"

She gives me her address and I go inside to pack a bag, wondering what the hell I'm doing. I barely know her. I'm sleeping in some random girl's bed. But the thought of being here another night by myself... I can't do it. Especially when every time I close my eyes, all I remember is the last time Austin was there with me. How happy I was. How safe and secure. How right it felt.

But apparently, he didn't feel the same way.

Thirty minutes later, I'm propped on Danielle's couch with a ton of pillows behind me, a sweet lab and beagle mix lounged across my lap, snuffling in his sleep. I stroke his silky ears as Danielle navigates through her Netflix queue to find something for us to watch.

"So what's going on with you and my brother?" she asks casually, as if it's not an incredibly loaded question.

I shrug. "Nothing." It's mostly the truth... sort of.

"You're not into him?"

I'm silent, debating what to say, and end up admitting, "I am." It's not like it's a secret.

She sets the remote down. "Then what's the problem? He's *super* into you."

That's what it seemed like Wednesday, but after that... "I thought things were going well, but then he changed his mind or something. Asked me out on a date one night and said he needed space the next."

She frowns. "What happened?"

"I have no idea."

"You haven't talked to him about it?"

I give the dog on my lap a scratch behind his ears, and he stretches out contentedly. "I want to, but he keeps leaving when I try."

"That's so weird. Austin's not a wishy-washy kind of guy. And he definitely likes you, trust me. Maybe you didn't make it clear enough that you like him?"

I gave the man a blow job, for Christ's sake. How much clearer could I get? "He knows how I feel."

Her lips twist. "You have to beat him over the head with it sometimes. How about I call him?"

She already has her phone out and is tapping at the screen before I can respond, my eyes widening as the line rings and she puts it on speakerphone. I didn't even agree to this.

Relief and disappointment mingle together in the pit of my stomach as it eventually goes to voicemail. "He's probably busy with the tournament."

"This late? Nah, all the matches are finished by now."

She hits redial and this time he answers on the fourth ring. "Yeah?"

Danielle holds a finger to her lips, indicating for me to be quiet. Not a problem.

"Hey, do you and Tessa want to come over to Dad's for dinner tomorrow night?"

"I'm working a tournament this weekend. I can't make it."

"How about Monday? I'd like to hang out with Tessa again. I liked her a lot." She winks theatrically at me, smiling, but I'm too nervous to smile back.

"You should probably call her yourself, then."

My heart sinks at the irritation in his voice.

"Did something happen?"

"No." There's that word again in that curt tone.

She frowns, annoyance on her face. "Did you ever ask her out?"

There's silence, the moment prolonging. I swallow compulsively, leaning in to hear what he'll say.

"It didn't work out. Listen, I have to go. Uncle Marty has me on the clock. I'll talk to you when I get back."

He hangs up and Danielle mutters, "Rude," as she sets her phone down beside her. "He's normally vague, but that was ridiculous even for him. Sorry I couldn't get a clearer answer for you."

"Thank you for trying. That was really nice of you. And for inviting me over."

"Yeah, of course."

I stroke the dog's soft fur, realizing I'm so out of it, I don't remember his name. "Has Austin said anything about me to you?" I blurt out, wanting some questions answered, propriety be damned.

"Yeah. We talked on the phone about you last week. He was gushing about you. He's never spoken about anyone like that."

"So why did he say it didn't work out? We had this amazing time Wednesday, and by the next night it was like a switch had flipped." I hate to be dumping my problems on her like this, but I don't know what else to do.

She sighs. "Austin's never been one to talk about himself, especially unprompted. He's an observer, not a participator. You'll have to drag the truth out of him."

"You heard him. He won't talk to me. Or even about me."

She purses her lips, then snaps her fingers. "Go to the tournament tomorrow. Confront him when he can't run."

Wow, she's hardcore.

"He's working. I'm not going to show up and be a stalker."

"You want answers, right? Catch him between matches. He's not working then."

"I…" How much longer can I continue in this state of uncertainty?

I dig my phone out of my back pocket, upsetting the sleeping dog for a moment, and call Austin, but it immediately goes to voicemail.

Danielle raises her brows, making a tsking noise. "Declining your calls?"

I groan, my grip tightening on the phone. This is so ridiculous. Why am I so hung up on him, anyway?

Because you've never met anyone like him.

Because he ticks all your boxes and then some.

Because you're falling in love with him.

I bring a hand to my chest, rubbing at my breastbone, and pull up my messages with Lexie.

Me: *Are you driving to the tournament tomorrow to see Ethan?*

Lexie: *Yeah.*

Me: *Can I ride with you? I'll pay for gas.*

Lexie: *Can you be ready to go by two? It's a two-hour drive over there and Ethan's match is at five, so I want to have some buffer time.*

Perfect. My shift ends at two, anyway.

Me: *Pick me up at the diner at two?*

Lexie: *See you then.*

I glance over at Danielle. "I'm going to the tournament."

She grins widely. "Awesome. But don't let him wriggle away. Get a straight answer out of him."

I nod, determination stealing over me. Whether he likes it or not, we're talking tomorrow.

CHAPTER TWENTY-NINE

AUSTIN

"WHAT ARE the chances I get two Russian fighting machines in a row?" Ethan complains, waving his already wrapped hand in the air. "Daniel Vasiliev? That's Russian, right?"

"Could be," I hedge, trying not to feed too much into his conspiracy theory. Ever since he learned his upcoming opponent's name, he's been a ball of nerves.

"The universe is out to get me. I'll have two losses in a row."

"You'll be fine," I tell him in an even voice. He needs to calm down.

"You think he's related to Sokolov? It can't be a coincidence, right?"

"Stop thinking about it. It's time to focus and warm up."

I lead him through light drills until he's limber, not giving him a chance to worry.

"Now, I talked to a buddy of mine who knows this guy—"

"How long has he been fighting?" he interrupts.

"Don't worry about that."

His face falls. "That means longer than me."

Yeah, he's right. Somehow, he keeps getting matched with guys more experienced than him. "Okay, but you have something he doesn't have."

"What?"

"Me. And I've got a strategy for you. I did some digging, and this guy's a southpaw."

"Shit, are you serious?"

Left-handed guys usually have the advantage in a fight because they have more experience against someone of an opposite style.

"Better you know now, right? I've got two things I want you to focus on to beat him, okay?"

He nods seriously.

"Get your front foot on the outside. If you control that position, you control the fight. Throw some punches and while he's busy blocking, step outside. The other thing is to counter his left hand. Don't just avoid it—counter it."

"Should I use my right or left?"

He seems flustered, when I know for a fact if we were training back at Uncle Marty's he wouldn't have a problem. Tournaments can mess with your head when the pressure's on.

"Your best punch is with your right hand, but be ready for his left cross. Every time he throws it at you, pull your head to the outside and come back with a counter right. Got it?"

"Foot on the outside, counter his left," he mutters to himself. "How much time do I have?"

I glance at the clock in the corner of the locker room. "About fifteen minutes."

"I'm going to find Lexie. She should be out in the crowd by now."

He moves past me and I sit on a bench, resting my elbows on my knees. The frenetic pace of the last two days is nearly at an end since Ethan is my last match of the day. At least I had this distraction to keep me from thinking of...

Fuck.

The memory of me sitting outside the loading dock at work Thursday afternoon returns, staring at my texts from Tessa as if they'll magically change.

I push it aside, only to be met with meeting up with her in our apartment hallway, asking me about dinner, of all things. How could she think I'd want to do that after she'd stomped all over my heart?

She said she wanted to go back to being friends, but how can I do that when I still crave her so badly? It's better to avoid her, at least until the worst of this has passed. The only problem is, it's not getting better, especially when there are so many reminders of her. Christ, Danielle had even called last night asking about her. I can't get away from her.

And once I go back home tonight, with her right across the hall... How will this work? How can I get over her when she's always around?

I step out of the locker room, searching for Ethan in the crowd to see if he wants any more advice, but my gaze gets stuck on a petite brunette, out of place among the rough and tumble attendees with her delicate features. Her long hair sweeps over one shoulder, head turned to the side as she looks around the sports complex, like she's searching for something.

What's she doing here?

I take a step toward her before I remember myself, forgetting for a moment how things stand between us. She's not mine to go over and kiss her in greeting the way I want. She made it clear she doesn't want that. Doesn't even want me to mention it.

She turns her head, gaze meeting mine like a magnet, recognition flaring in her eyes. Getting up from her spot in the bleachers, she moves past the people in her row, rushing down the stairs in her haste to reach me until she's suddenly in front of me, the freckles on her face pronounced with how pale she is.

"Hi," she says, breaths coming fast.

"Why are you here?" It's all I can think to say. I'd gotten a random call from her last night that I'd ignored, but she'd probably made it by accident, anyway.

Her hands twist together distractingly. "I wanted to talk to you."

Oh, so she wants to talk now? When I'm working? "I thought I said I needed space."

"I… I don't understand why you said that."

Is she for real?

"Is there somewhere we could go that's more private?" she asks.

"I'm working. Ethan's match is in less than ten minutes."

"Please. I came all this way to see you."

"I didn't ask you to."

Her mouth turns down at the corners, lips trembling.

I sigh and mutter, "Come on." I lead her over past the locker room door to an empty spot. "What is it?" Maybe it's better to get this out of the way now so I can focus on the match.

"Why are you so upset with me?"

My jaw clenches and I have to take a moment to compose myself so I don't lash out. "I'm trying to respect your wishes, but you're making it hard. I can't be around you right now."

"Why?"

The anger that's been building for the past few days rises to the surface, a dark cloud forming over me, but she surprisingly doesn't back away. "Because you blew me off."

Her gaze narrows. "What? If anyone, you're the one who blew *me* off. I was ready to go out and then you say you need space and you're going to the gym. What was that about?"

"Why would I go on a date with a friend?" That's all she sees me as, right? She said we were too different, that things wouldn't work out long-term. That she wants to go back to being friends. But I don't want that.

She swallows hard, hurt overtaking her face. "You don't at least want to give a date a try?"

Go out on a date with her as a friend? What's the point? "You go on dates with someone you like. Romantically. Emotionally. Someone you want a future with. Not with someone who doesn't feel the same way." She made it clear we're not on the same page.

Her nostrils flare, eyes filling with tears, and she looks down, hiding her face. "So that's it?"

I shrug and cross my arms over my chest, willing myself not to comfort her. What does she want me to say? This was her decision. "I guess."

"I'm sorry I misread things between us," she whispers, wiping at her eyes. "Was it only sexual for you?"

What? "No, of course not." I wanted everything with her.

"So, sex and friendship, but no romantic feelings? Why'd you ask me on that date, then?"

What the hell is she talking about?

The announcer for Ethan's fight comes over the loudspeaker, letting the crowd know that the Hudson versus Vasiliev match is in five minutes in ring two. It jolts me out of this nonsensical argument we're having, and I step back, ready to leave. "I have to go. Ethan needs me."

She reaches out, her fingertips chilly against my forearm. "Can we please talk about this more later? I feel like I'm losing you."

A scoffing sound escapes me unintentionally. "What did you think was going to happen when I told you I loved you and you basically said you didn't care?"

Her mouth opens and closes, eyes wide, but I don't have time for these weird games she's been playing. I move past her toward the ring, Ethan already by the side giving one last kiss to Lexie.

"Enough of that," I tell him, holding the ropes open for him to slip through.

"Sorry Mister Boss Man," Lexie drawls, stepping back. "Good luck, Snookums," she murmurs to her boyfriend.

Ethan grins, apparently liking that nickname. Whatever floats their boat, I guess.

"You work it out with Tessa?" Lexie asks me. "She's really torn up about you."

Why is every girl I know asking me about her? Including Tessa herself? "What, she's mad that she only wants to be friends and I don't?"

She gives me a quizzical look. "You mean *you* only want to be friends and *she* doesn't."

My heart stops for a moment before it resumes beating. "What are you talking about?"

"She told me all about it on the car ride over. Two hours is a *long* time to be driving with someone who has a lot to get off their chest."

"She told you what?"

"That she was all ready for your date and then you changed your mind."

What? Something in my brain's not connecting. "No, *she* did."

"Maybe we could continue this after the fight?" Ethan asks. "As riveting as the *he said, she said* shtick is, we need to get going."

Shit. He's right.

I search through the stands, but I don't see Tessa. Is this why our conversation earlier was so confusing?

My head's not in the game as I slip through the ropes behind Ethan, still parsing through Lexie's words. Tessa thinks I'm the one who only wants to be friends? I'm the one who changed my mind about the date? How could she think that? She literally said she only wants to be friends.

I reach in my pocket for my phone, then remember it's in my bag in the locker room. It's probably for the best that I can't check her texts, anyway. I'm supposed to be working.

I size Ethan's opponent up, his shadowboxing in the corner clearly designed to intimidate more than actually warm him up. Glancing over at Ethan, it seems to be effective, but he hasn't been in as many fights as me to tell the difference.

"He's all show," I whisper, putting his mouthguard in for him. "Take a deep breath and get all your nerves out. You know what to do and how to beat him. You've got this."

He nods, punching his gloves together, and steps into the middle of the ring to join the ref and Vasiliev.

I tune out everything but Ethan's opponent, studying him. His facial expression and the way he carries himself screams cocky and aggressive. The arrogance we can deal with, but the aggressiveness worries me. Lawrence said Ethan didn't do well against that kind of competitor last time.

My gaze flicks to Vasiliev's cornerman, a middle-aged man I recognize from tournaments before, though I don't know his name. His ears are all torn up, indicating he was a former pro boxer, meaning he must have a fair amount of experience. That doesn't bode well for Ethan, either.

The ref starts the first round and Vasiliev immediately comes in aggressive like I suspected he would, jabbing Ethan in the face. His act of intimidation works, throwing Ethan off-kilter.

Ethan goes into defensive mode, backing up as his opponent approaches again, rattling him.

"Counter him," I shout, praying Ethan hears me. "Get away from the corner."

He snaps out of it, maneuvering to the middle of the ring, and throws his first punch of the fight, which is easily blocked by Vasiliev. He jabs again, and Vasiliev finally stops advancing on him as he keeps the jabs coming, pressuring him.

"Good," I yell. "Foot on the outside." He needs all the leverage he can get.

Vasiliev throws a left hook and this time Ethan counters like he's supposed to, making him retreat even more. Ethan's never been this aggressive in the ring, but it serves him well here.

His opponent realizes what he's doing, though, and plants himself, refusing to move back any further. The two trade blows but nothing connects, both skillfully dodging each others punches. They're at a standstill, something needing to change in order for the fight to advance.

"Slip under and circle around," I yell out.

Ethan thankfully hears me and does what I say at the next opportunity as Vasiliev throws a right. He retaliates with a left, the two switching dominant sides for a moment, and Vasiliev ducks to avoid the punch.

Ethan anticipates the dodge and easily recovers, slipping to the left until he's almost behind his opponent. Vasiliev comes out of his duck, not realizing Ethan's there, and Ethan uses the opportunity to throw a right uppercut, connecting with his jaw.

Vasiliev backs off, his dander up now, and steadies himself before coming forward and going on the attack. He takes a reckless chance leaving himself exposed, but it pays off as Ethan is caught off guard, and he lands a one-two blow that has Ethan retreating.

The fight continues for the rest of the round this way, each gaining the advantage, only to lose it as the other person retaliates. I shout out a reminder to Ethan to keep his guard up when his hands slip too low from a defensive position, and continue to study Vasiliev for weaknesses. Ethan needs every ounce of strategy I can give him during the break between rounds.

Things are still at a stalemate as the clock ticks down close to ten seconds. He has to do something soon.

"Go big," I yell, knowing it doesn't matter how exposed he leaves himself with so little time left.

Ethan rains down blows and jumps back as the bell rings before Vasiliev can retaliate.

Fuck, yeah. That's how you end a round.

I slip through the ropes and set down a stool for Ethan, taking his mouthguard out so he can talk. "Focus on relaxing for the next minute. You're doing a hell of a job out there."

He nods and I towel off his face, then hold an ice pack to the back of his neck to cool him off.

"Fuck, that feels good." He lets out a long sigh. "This guy's an animal."

"You are, too. And I've got some tips for you."

"Good."

"First thing—when he throws his right, he doesn't keep his left close enough to his face to block. He hasn't thrown rights that often, but be aware of that so you can land some hits."

"What else?"

"When you throw your right hooks, he leans back too far to avoid it, leaving his torso exposed. Aim low to take advantage of that."

We go over a few other things I noticed until it's time for him to head in again. I grab my stuff and get out of there, watching him, but there's this tingle on the nape of my neck.

I look out into the crowd and there Tessa is, sitting next to Lexie. She waves at me as I catch her eye and my heart gives a squeeze, caught up in the mixture of hope and concern on her face, apparent even from this distance.

I turn away, not wanting to get distracted, but the urge to glance back at her is incredibly strong.

What the hell was Lexie talking about earlier? That I was the one who wanted to be friends with Tessa and she didn't? Why would Tessa lie about that?

What if she's not lying, though? Tessa's always been truthful with me. But that completely negates her texts, then.

I look over my shoulder and raise my hand back. She smiles, her face beaming.

There's a fluttering in my chest in response and I quickly tamp it down, reminding myself that she crushed my heart just days ago. I shouldn't get my hopes up.

And for now, I've got a match to win for Ethan.

CHAPTER THIRTY

TESSA

I BOUNCE IN MY SEAT, watching the second round of Ethan's fight with bated breath—not that I have a clue who's doing better. The two guys seem well matched, trading blows with a precision I'd never be capable of.

But as exciting as the action is, my gaze continually draws back to Austin on the sidelines. He stares eagle-eyed at the ring, yelling something to Ethan, but I can't make it out over the din of the crowd.

He raises his arms to link his hands behind his head, biceps popping in his sleeveless tank, and I bite my lip, wondering if he looks especially sexy because I've been missing him or because he said he loved me.

I mean, he said that, right? I didn't hallucinate it or anything, did I? It had come out of nowhere and doesn't match up at all with how he's been acting, but it has to mean something.

Why would he say I didn't care, though? Why in the world would he think I'd dismiss him if he ever said that? He made it seem like he's said it previously, but I definitely would have remembered that. Did I miss something?

There's a collective gasp from the crowd and I tune back into the ring. Ethan's opponent clutches at his side and backs away, avoiding Ethan's advance.

"What happened?"

"Ethan landed a liver shot," Lexie says, pride in her voice. "That's what did him in last time."

"Will the other guy be okay?"

"Hopefully not."

I frown, then realize where I'm at. Duh.

The guy comes back at Ethan, landing a punch to his jaw, and Lexie groans. "Must not have been too hard of a shot," she mutters.

I glance at Austin, but his face is impassive. If his fighter doesn't win, does he get penalized? He just started this job and isn't even there full-time yet.

Lexie's hands clench together in front of her, knuckles white as she watches her boyfriend get pummeled, then rain down a series of blows of his own.

"Who's winning?" I whisper, unsure if it's insensitive to ask in case Ethan's losing.

"No clear winner so far," she says, gaze never leaving the ring. "It'll probably come down to points."

"It doesn't go until one of them gets knocked out?"

"That's pro boxing. But yeah, if that happens before the end of the third round, they'll call it."

"Could Ethan get knocked out?"

She huffs a laugh. "If he does, it'll be a shitty ride home. He's riding with us on the way back."

"How long are you staying after his fight?"

"You mean how long do you have to talk to Austin?"

I give her a sheepish grin. "Yes."

"Ethan will probably have to take a few pictures afterward, especially if he wins. And he's definitely taking a shower before he gets in the car with us for two hours. So, I don't know, twenty minutes?"

"Okay, call me when you're about to leave and I'll meet you in the parking lot."

She nods. "You know, Austin said you only want to be friends with him when I talked to him before the fight."

I turn to her, not even pretending to pay attention to the match now. "And you couldn't have led with that when I first sat down?"

"The match had already started," she says, gesturing in front of her.

"What do you mean I only want to be friends with him? Why would he think that?"

"I don't know. I'm just the messenger."

I wince, realizing too late I'm practically yelling at her. "Sorry. This is all stressing me out."

"Talk to him."

"I'm trying. Trust me."

Whether he likes it or not, I'm getting to the bottom of this sudden change in personality today.

I'm quiet as the second round ends, watching Austin tend to Ethan in the corner of the ring. He speaks intently to him, Ethan's head bobbing at whatever he's saying, and as the final round starts, Ethan goes in with a renewed spirit.

The advantage seems to continually swap back and forth between the two men, and Lexie mutters something under her breath about hooks and crosses I can't quite make out.

When the bell rings after three rounds, I'm still not sure who won.

"They have to tally up the points," Lexie explains when I ask her. "Based on the number of clean punches they landed."

"How do you think he did?"

She chews on her bottom lip. "I think he had more hits, but I'm biased. And after his last match, he needs this win."

We wait with bated breath as they total up the points and bring both guys back in the ring.

"And your winner is…" The announcer pauses for dramatic effect. "Ethan Hudson."

Lexie jumps up from her seat, loudly clapping and cheering. I've never seen her so animated.

I cheer too, but it's just as much for Austin as it is for Ethan. Hopefully, he's in a good enough mood now to talk. Our conversation earlier had only raised more questions than it answered, especially when adding in what Lexie said.

My stomach roils unpleasantly as I walk down the bleacher stairs, nerves coursing through me, and I stumble on the last step. A helpful arm reaches out to catch me, and I look up into familiar gray eyes, though they're not the ones I was hoping for.

"Mr. Langford," I stutter. "What are you doing here?"

He raises his brows and I wince.

"I'm sorry, that sounded rude. You're obviously here for Austin."

Did the two of them ever talk again about him not going pro? If they did in the last couple of days… I guess Austin wouldn't have said anything to me about it.

"When Marty mentioned Austin would be here," he says, "I thought he'd changed his mind about fighting. I didn't realize he'd be working."

"Yeah, he's the new trainer…" I trail off when it's apparent this is news to him. "Maybe you should talk to—"

"Dad."

I glance up at Austin, his gaze flicking between me and his father, finally settling on the latter. "How'd you know I'd be here?"

His dad sticks his hands in his pockets. "Marty."

Austin doesn't say anything in response and I bite at my lip, not sure how to make this less awkward. "I can give you two privacy if you want to talk."

Mr. Langford shakes his head. "No, I just wanted to say you did good out there coaching. You'll be a great trainer."

Austin blinks a couple of times, bewilderment on his face. "Thanks."

He shrugs his shoulders. "Maybe you can come over for dinner sometime this week?"

"Yeah, okay."

"The both of you, if you want," his dad says, nodding to me.

I smile noncommittally, pretty sure I shouldn't accept without Austin's approval.

"I'll see you, then."

He turns around and leaves, disappearing into the crowd, and Austin and I look at each other with twin expressions of confusion.

"He drove two hours out here just to say that and leave?" I ask. "Did you guys talk again after Tuesday?"

"No, he never reached out. I didn't either, though. I—" He stops, a change coming over him, his shoulders stiffening.

I laugh, despite myself. If I don't, I'll probably cry. "You forgot you're not talking to me, didn't you?"

His brows narrow. "You're the one that doesn't want to talk."

What? "I've been asking you to talk for days."

"You literally told me not to bring it up."

I shake my head, so confused by all of this. "I don't know what you're talking about. It's like we keep having two different conversations."

"Your texts," he says, like it's obvious.

"What texts?"

He looks down at the ground, his voice lowering. "The ones from Thursday."

"You mean Wednesday? The—" I glance around, but no one's paying attention to us. "The naughty ones?"

He glances up, heat flaring in his gaze for a moment, gone as quick as it came. So he's not unaffected by me, then.

"No, Thursday. The night after…. everything."

I pull my phone out of my back pocket, searching through our texts. "I didn't text you that day."

I show him the screen for proof, not sure what else to do. I'm at a loss here. "Can you show me what you're talking about?"

He stares at me, the anger that's been lingering around him the last few days clearing. "You didn't send those texts?"

"What'd they say?"

His gaze searches mine for a moment. "Come on." He grabs my hand, the first physical contact I've had with him in days, and leads me through the crowd. I intertwine my fingers with his and he falters for a second, then squeezes my hand in return. The tight ball of tension in my chest loosens the slightest bit at his gesture.

He stops in the same hallway we talked in earlier, a sign taped to the door in front of us indicating it's the men's locker room, then turns to me. "Let me grab my phone."

He doesn't leave right away, though.

"What is it?" I ask, looking up at him. I can't interpret the expression on his face.

"I… Nothing." He lets go of my hand and disappears inside, leaving me alone. I cross my arms, ignoring the strange looks from guys entering and exiting the locker room, my heartbeat picking up the longer he's gone. What are these mysterious messages? How could there be something he thinks is from me that I didn't send?

"Here," he says when he returns, handing me his phone. He won't look me in the eye, instead staring at his feet.

At the top of the screen is my contact information with the right phone number, so there's that, at least. And there are our previous messages from Wednesday… My face heats slightly, but I continue down, any redness on my cheeks fading as I read what it says.

My hand comes up to cover my gasp and I race through the rest of the texts, disoriented. "I don't understand. I didn't say any of this." I force myself to swallow against the pain in the back of my throat. "I would *never* say this."

I move in front of him, forcing him to meet my eye. Now that the anger's gone, there's only hurt left on his face, my stomach dropping in response.

"Austin, you have to believe me. That's the opposite of how I feel. I want something serious with you more than anything." I swallow again, the good parts of those texts giving me hope. He said I'm the most important person in the world to him. That he'd do anything to make this work.

That he loves me.

A range of emotions crosses his face before longing overtakes the others. "I want to believe you," he whispers.

"You can. I promise. We'll get to the bottom of this together."

His gaze searches mine for what seems like forever, my stomach on the edge of tipping over, and he finally nods, my knees weakening as relief floods through me.

I reach for him, standing on tiptoes to hug him tight, and his arms encircle my waist, supporting me.

Tears sting at the corner of my eyes, but for the first time in days, they're ones of happiness now. "I've missed you. I had no idea why you wouldn't speak to me."

"I thought it's what you wanted. And I was hurting. You... you broke my heart. Or, I thought you did."

I run a comforting hand over his back, wishing I could erase all the heartache from the last few days. "Those things you wrote..."

He stiffens for a moment before I soothe away the tightness. "Yeah?"

"I feel the same way. That there's this connection between us. You're the most important person in the world to me, too."

He squeezes me tighter, releasing a breath. "Tessa..." There's enough emotion in that one word to fill a book. "I—"

A group of guys enter the hallway, loud in the echoey space, and make their way into the locker room. None of them are paying attention to us, but it makes me aware that we're locked in an embrace with a crowd of people just beyond us.

"Maybe this should wait till later," he murmurs.

"Right. Sorry." I let go of him, but he doesn't move away.

"There's one thing I need to do now, though." His hand slides in my hair, cradling my head as he kisses me briefly, but deeply.

I smile up at him, and he returns it, a weight lifted off him compared to how he's been the past few days. "I love when you kiss me."

He leans down, whispering in that lovely, deep voice, "Can I kiss you more tonight?"

A tingle races down my spine, thoughts competing for space in my head about where exactly he can kiss me. There's no need to censor my words with him anymore, though. "I want you to kiss me everywhere."

CHAPTER THIRTY-ONE

TESSA

AUSTIN GROANS, burying his face in the crook of my neck, and I take a moment to delight in this closeness. What would have happened if we hadn't cleared this up?

"How did those texts come from my number?"

He moves back, sobering. "I have no idea. I guess a hacker could do it? I don't know how any of that works."

I chew on my lip, suddenly wishing I understood more about cyber security. "Me neither."

"Well, simplest question first. Did anyone else have your phone on Thursday?"

"No, it was with me the whole day. When were the texts sent?"

"Right after four during your psych study. I thought it was weird that you were texting me then."

I rub my temples, trying to remember back to that day. "No, I never even took it out of my bag. I—" I freeze, recalling what happened. "Wait."

He steps in closer, concerned. "What is it?"

"At the end of the study, I was looking for my phone. I couldn't find it anywhere, even though I knew it was in my bag. And Joel found it under the desk."

Austin's brows raise. "*Joel* found it? The guy who hates me?"

My jaw drops as my mind races to connect the dots. "He'd come in before the study started and asked me to get something from the Stress Lab's reception-ist. I didn't think anything of leaving my bag in the room. He must have taken my phone while I was gone."

"Then texted me, told me to never mention it again to you in person, and deleted the evidence from your phone."

"And brought it back after and pretended to find it. Oh my God, I can't believe this."

His lips twist wryly. "Well, that makes a lot of fucking sense now. He cornered me after the study on Tuesday. Tried to tell me he didn't want you getting mixed up with me. I—" He pauses, scrubbing a hand down his face. "Shit. This is my fault."

"It's not your fault he thinks that way."

"No, I…" He presses his lips together tightly for a moment. "I goaded him. He was trying to piss me off and I told him you and I were sharing a bed."

Yeah, with the way he's been acting lately, that might have put him over the edge. Even so, our relationship isn't any of his business. "I don't see why he cares so much."

Austin sighs, his head cocking to the side. "Tessa, he likes you. It's really obvious."

"No, we're friends. I've never thought about Joel like that."

"Well, he's thought about you like that. I guarantee it. And it seems like he was trying to get me out of the picture. Maybe he thinks I stole you or something."

I throw my hands up, tired of all this needless drama. "It was never a competition." Even if he does like me… which I guess sort of makes sense now that I think about it. "I told him there was nothing going on between you and me because he kept being so ridiculous about it. And, you know…" I glance down, suddenly shy. "At the time, I was sure you didn't feel the same way about me."

"Tessa…" His finger slips under my chin, tilting my head up to look at him. "I never thought you'd go for a guy like me. When I kissed you at Element and you didn't respond—"

"I'm sorry. I was in shock. I couldn't believe you were actually kissing me. But then you said it was a mistake."

His lips tip up at the corners. "I guess we could have been together sooner if we'd just confessed what we were feeling."

A weak chuckle escapes me. "A novel idea, right?"

His hand moves to the side of my neck and down my arm until he's holding my hand. "I know you saw it in those texts, but I want to tell you that I—"

My phone rings, startling us in the echoey hallway, and my heart beats fast at his murmured tone. Was he going to mention the part where he said he loves me?

"Sorry, that's probably Lexie," I rush to say, grabbing my phone out of my back pocket. "Hello?"

"We're at the car," Lexie says. "Where are you?"

Crap. Has it been that long already? "I'll be there in a minute. Thanks."

I hang up, looking up at Austin. "Lexie's ready to go."

He nods somberly. "Wish I'd brought my extra helmet now so you could ride back with me."

"I'll see you tonight. Come over to my place whenever you're ready."

The air between us thickens, both of us aware of exactly what we'll be doing later.

"Maybe, um…" I glance around, not that there's anyone nearby, and reach on my tiptoes to whisper in his ear, "Maybe you could pick up some… you know… protection? If you're ready for that, I mean."

His arm wraps around my waist to pull me close against his hard body, palm squeezing my ass for a moment. "Yeah. I can definitely do that." His voice is deliciously rough, full of promise for the night to come.

He hugs me tight, the worry from the last few days melting away under the strength of his embrace. "I love you, Tessa."

My eyes squeeze shut as I burrow into his chest, my heart filling exponentially. "I love you, too." God, it feels so right to say it aloud. "And I really have to go now. Lexie's going to leave without me."

He lets me go, giving me a kiss to satisfy me for the next few hours. "See you tonight."

I walk away, glancing back once at him to blow him a kiss, buoyant inside. It definitely paid to come out here today and get this straightened out.

And now, I finally have something to look forward to.

***

Okay, fresh sheets on the bed? Check.

Candles lit? Yep.

Legs shaved? It was the first thing I did.

Now I just need the man.

I unload the dishwasher for something to do, trying to keep myself occupied so my mind doesn't leap to illogical conclusions. Like what if he changed his mind and doesn't believe me about the texts? What if he realizes this is all more trouble than it's worth? What if…

The knock on the front door has me abandoning the dishes without a second thought. I kiss Austin immediately, not giving him a chance to change his mind. Based on his response, though, he didn't have any thoughts of changing it as he picks me up and carries me into my bedroom without a word, kissing me with a passion I didn't know I could inspire in a man.

I give back as good as I'm getting, not wanting to waste a moment of tonight. It feels like I've been waiting for this forever.

He sets me on the edge of the bed and steps back to strip off his shirt, revealing that hard body. I delight in each inch of skin he reveals, from the ridges of his abdomen to his defined pecs, up to the heavy breadth of his shoulders. I can't believe this sexy man is mine.

"I want you," he murmurs, leaning down to kiss me. "I spent the whole ride home thinking about you." His hands move to my waist, sliding under my shirt. "All the things I want to do to you. How good our first time will be." He pulls my top off, my skin overheated from the way he's looking at me. "How much I can't wait to taste your pussy again. How it'll feel to sink inside you. To fill you up."

My breaths are harsh in the quiet of the room as he slides my bra straps down and unhooks the back. I fling my bra to the floor, exhaling roughly as his big palms cover me, squeezing gently.

He kneels in front of me. "You said you wanted me to kiss you everywhere, right?" His mouth is poised over my left breast, so close all I'd have to do is lean forward the slightest bit.

"Uh huh," I answer, unable to come up with an equally seductive reply when he has my wits so addled.

He doesn't call me out on my less than stellar response, instead pressing his heavenly lips to me. I grip the duvet, the fabric twisting under my fingers as he worships my breasts, using his mouth to drive me wild.

At some point, the rest of my clothes are off, though I swear I don't remember that happening, too caught up in the desire growing within me.

His hands gently nudge my thighs apart as he sucks my nipple, then laves it with small kisses. He breaks away, holding eye contact with me as his fingers travel up my inner thigh and tease my pussy with barely there passes. My lower half tenses with anticipation and I mumble his name, not sure what I'm asking for, just knowing I want more of this wild recklessness that keeps building.

He increases the pressure of his fingers, rubbing my clit now, and leans forward to brush his lips against mine. "You ready for me to kiss you here?" he murmurs, sinking a finger deep inside me.

I nod, spreading my legs wider, and he travels down my body, making good on my request for him to kiss me everywhere.

At the first touch of his tongue, I buck, the sensation just as amazing as the last time he did this. Holy crap, how can it be this good?

His hands move to hold my thighs open as he licks me again with the flat of his tongue, delightfully slow over the sensitive area. Goosebumps wash over me, and I do my best to relax, leaning back on my elbows to watch him. I can't imagine I'll ever see anything sexier than this mountain of a man pleasuring me.

Resting my feet on his shoulders, my thighs quiver as he builds me up over long, torturous minutes until I'm panting, ready for release. I mumble his name, unsure what I'm even trying to convey, and squirm against the duvet.

"You're almost there, baby," he murmurs, somehow knowing what I needed to hear. "You ready to come?"

I nod frantically, my back arching as he adds his middle finger, pumping in and out while sucking on my clit.

"Oh, fuck," I cry out as my orgasm overtakes me. I collapse on the bed, my eyes squeezed shut as I tremble, tingles racing up my limbs.

He continues until I'm spent, then leans back, stroking his hands down my legs. I squint at him, finding him watching me, his gaze roaming over my body, desire on his face. I still can't get over that he looks at *me* that way. That as sexy as he is, he somehow finds me equally desirable.

And tonight, he's all mine.

CHAPTER THIRTY-TWO

AUSTIN

LUST AND LOVE course through me, the way she's looking at me turning me on even more.

She sits up, kneeling on the edge of the bed, and reaches toward me, smoothing her hands over my chest. "I love when you go down on me."

I brush her hair back behind her shoulders, pressing a kiss to the delicate column of her neck. "I'll do it every night from now on." And I'll die a happy man doing it.

She makes a sound of contentment. "And I loved how you talked dirty to me when we first got started."

"I know."

"You do?"

Why does she seem surprised? She's so easy to read now that I know what to look for. "You said you liked those texts we sent Wednesday. I figured you'd like it even more in person."

"I do." Her fingers trail down my abs, over my sides, and up my back. "You're so sexy."

I press in closer, wanting more of her touch. "Tessa, that's you." I grip her ass and squeeze, loving the *mmm* noise she makes in response.

"I can't believe you're my boyfriend," she murmurs, almost to herself.

My belly dips low. That's the first time she's called me that.

She leans back, hands still resting on my shoulders as her gaze searches mine. "I mean, are you? We haven't discussed it yet."

"Yes. Absolutely. I want that." I practically trip over the words in my haste to get them out.

She bites at her bottom lip, trying to hide a smile. "And I can be your girlfriend?"

"There's nothing I want more." I kiss her deeply, needing that connection.

She smiles against my lips. "You say the sweetest things."

My thumbs circle her hip bones, shifting her back to create more space between us. "But you wanted dirty tonight, didn't you?"

Her breath hitches. "Yes."

I move my right hand down her lower belly, her hips angling toward me. "Tell me what you want."

"You. All of you."

"You want my cock here?" I tease her seam, the area slippery with arousal. "In your pussy?"

She nods, her breathing picking up.

"Lay back on the bed."

She does as I say, watching me raptly as I pull a condom out of my pocket and undress, then roll it on. Her legs widen for me as I join her on the mattress, creating room for me.

I settle between her thighs, propping myself on my elbows as I glide my dick over her pussy, not entering her just yet.

"Tell me you're as excited for this as I am."

She moans, gripping my shoulders tightly. "I want you so bad. More than I thought was possible."

Desire pulses through me as I position myself at her entrance, my need for her stretching my limits. "If I'm too rough with you, let me know." She's so petite, a part of me is afraid I'll hurt her somehow.

She shakes her head solemnly. "I want you out of control. Give me everything you have."

A groan escapes me, her words painting a vivid picture in my mind of the two of us moving as one, sweat-soaked, chasing a high only the other one can supply.

I enter her slowly, sliding in easily with how wet she is, but I still hold myself back, giving her time to adjust to me.

She pants, her eyes widening, and her nails dig into my shoulders the slightest bit, the sweet sting both revving me up and making me pause.

"You okay?"

"Uh huh." She squirms underneath me torturously. "You're just bigger than I expected."

"Do you want to stop?"

"No. Give me a second."

I lean on one elbow, bringing my free hand to her breasts, shaping the soft weight. She arches into my touch, the action pushing me deeper, and she moans, moving at her own pace. It's everything I can do not to grind into her, letting her relax until the tenseness in her body is gone.

"Okay, I'm ready."

I pull out and back in, building up a steady rhythm, taking my cues from her to what she wants. When she widens her legs, I deepen my strokes. When she pulls me closer, I skim my lips over the shell of her ear, enjoying the way she trembles in response.

She runs her hands over my chest and upward, sifting through my hair, my scalp tingling. "I love how you fuck me," she whispers, the seductive tone of her voice sending a wave of arousal through me.

A strangled sound makes its way up my throat, but I keep myself in check.

"How deep you go inside me. How full I am."

Christ. If she talks any more about how I feel inside her…

"Next time, I want to ride you, okay?"

I groan, imagining what it'll be like to watch her on top of me, breasts bouncing, working herself on my cock…

My hips pick up the pace, no longer as careful with my movements. I grip her waist, using my hold on her for leverage as I pump into her, and the low, answering sound of contentment she makes only spurs me on more.

"Harder," she whispers, tilting her hips so there's more friction against her pubic bone. "I want all of you."

Her plea unlocks something within me, and I become close to feral, rutting against her, wanting to consume her. I've never in my life felt this frenzied. Nothing in the ring has ever matched this level of primal need I have for her.

She's right there with me, though, her movements frantic, sounds of satisfaction rising in volume, each of us feeding off one another until we're out of control like she wanted. The more eager she gets, the more I give her what she wants, whispering in her ear everything that comes to mind. How I can't wait to fuck her in my apartment next. In the shower. On the couch. In the kitchen. How I want her on top of me, below me, on her knees, bent over. How I want to eat her out again, her tugging on my hair as I drink her down. How I want her mouth on my cock, driving me wild as she sucks me dry.

"Austin," she cries, clutching at my shoulders as her hips buck. "I'm coming."

Her pussy tightens around me, milking me, and it sends me over the edge too, lost in the feel of her. I kiss her, unable to get enough, telling her over and over between kisses that I love her. I need her to understand how much she means to me. How essential she is.

My stream of consciousness turns in a different direction, brokenly whispering how the past few days were the hardest I've ever gone through. How much I missed her. How desperate I am for her. How she's the best thing that's ever happened to me.

She trembles, looking up at me with luminous eyes. "You're the best thing that's ever happened to me, too."

I automatically start to deny her statement, but she stops me, laying a finger on my lips. "I do my best not to let it affect me, but ever since my mom died, I've had no one. No family, no true ties to anyone else. And then you came along." Her fingers brush over my cheek and tuck a lock of my hair back behind my ear where it's fallen loose. "Trust me when I say you mean *everything* to me."

My chest swells, my throat thick as I swallow hard. There's so much love in her gaze, it's a wonder I didn't see it before.

"I love you," she whispers, the words filling in all the cracks still left in my heart. Though she told me it earlier after Ethan's match, it doesn't truly hit home until now.

"I love you, too," I reply, wrapping her in my embrace, wishing we could stay like this forever.

I bask in her presence, running light fingers over her back, enjoying her sleepy sighs. And as she drifts off in my arms, a sense of peace steals over me I've never quite felt. This is where I'm meant to be. With this woman.

As long as I have her, everything else will work out.

I pull into the driveway beside Dad's truck and shut my bike off, keeping it steady as Tessa dismounts behind me. There's a big grin on her face as she takes her helmet off and fluffs out her hair.

"Do I have you hooked?" I ask her as I take off my own helmet and lock them both up.

She laughs, coming in close to wrap her arms around my waist. "I like riding with you."

I lean down and kiss her, unable to help myself. At what point will I stop wanting to do that every five minutes? "Should I get you your own helmet and jacket?" She can't keep using her winter coat. It would tear too easily if something were to happen.

She skims her hands over my back, sliding along the cool leather. "I'd like that."

Danielle's car pulls in next to us, and as she gets out, there's a cat who ate the canary smile on her face. "Hello, lovebirds."

I sigh, letting go of Tessa. "Hi, Danielle."

"Are you ready to sing my praises? I totally got the two of you together."

Tessa laughs. "Oh, wise and noble Danielle. Your advice was amazing. I didn't take no for an answer and pulled the truth out of him."

"And? What was going through your thick skull?" she asks me.

I'd only texted her that we were doing dinner tonight at Dad's house, but not any details about what had gone down.

I explain to her about the texts, her eyes widening. "Oh my God," she exclaims, turning to Tessa. "Your lab partner did that?"

"We're pretty sure. He's the only person who had access to my phone that day and has a motive."

"That's crazy. Have you confronted him about it?"

"Not yet. I…" Tessa crosses her arms, hunching her shoulders forward. I wrap an arm around her, tugging her into my side. "I'm going to talk to him about it after the study tomorrow."

"And then what?"

She shrugs. "Our friendship is definitely over. I can't trust him anymore. But I don't want this to affect our study. I really want to get it published."

"Sounds like you're stuck between a rock and a hard place."

Tessa chuckles in response, a note of desperation in it. "Yeah, I am."

I give her shoulder a squeeze. "Let's head inside. We can worry about Joel tomorrow."

For now, I have a bigger problem on my mind. I have to talk to Dad.

As we make our way up the driveway, I catch Danielle's arm, pulling her aside for a moment. "Thanks for taking care of Tessa on Saturday. It means a lot to me."

She waves me off. "Don't get mushy. It was nothing."

She speeds ahead to unlock the door and I sigh. We're not exactly a family that talks about our feelings, but still.

Dad's out on the back porch grilling when we enter, and Danielle automatically heads to the kitchen to set the table.

"Are you going to talk to your dad?" Tessa whispers.

I nod, even though I'm unsure what to say.

"Do you want me to go with you?" she asks when I make no move to head out there.

"No, I've got it." I wipe my palms on my jeans, bracing myself.

"Do you have a plan?" It's clear from her tone she knows I don't, but her voice is kind, anyway. "Should we go over talking points?"

Talking points? Dad would laugh his ass off if he knew I was inside going over talking points to use with him.

"No, I just need to get it over with." I give her a quick kiss. "I'll be back in a minute."

"I'll go help Danielle," she says, looking at me worriedly. How unprepared do I look?

I take the plunge and head over to the slider, welcoming the cool air outside.

Dad glances up from flipping the burgers, then shuts the grill lid. "Hey."

"Hey."

I stick my hands in my pockets, my mind drawing a blank on what to say next. The last time he'd called, I'd yelled at him. And then he'd shown up to the tournament to watch me coach and praised me. I still can't make sense of it. Shouldn't he be mad?

"Did Tessa come with you?" he asks, throwing me off. He wants to talk about her?

"Yeah. She's helping Danielle in the kitchen."

He nods. "Is her apartment not ready?"

"It is. But we're, um, dating now. So she'll probably be around here with me more often. She doesn't have any family, so I wanted to include her—"

"That's fine. She seems like a nice girl." He crosses his arms over his chest as a breeze blows past. "You've never brought a girlfriend home before."

"I've never felt serious about anyone else. She's the one, you know?"

His brows lift as his lips quirk to one side. "Guess I shouldn't be surprised. I fell hard for your mom right away. Maybe it's something the Langford men do."

That's right. The Langford men always do things a certain way. "About our phone call last week…"

He holds up a hand. "I'm sorry. I'm man enough to admit I was wrong."

I stare at him, stunned. He's wrong?

"Looking back, I put a lot of pressure on you, didn't I? But you were thriving. You lived and breathed boxing. I was only trying to encourage what I thought you wanted."

"I…" I clear my throat when the words won't come out. "I should have been more open about how I felt. It was fine when I was younger, but after a certain point I wanted to do other things and you wouldn't let me. You told me not to bother to study for tests because my grades wouldn't matter once I was a pro boxer. That I didn't need to hang out with friends because I should be training instead. I couldn't join any sports teams in school because they would interfere with tournaments."

He looks down at his feet, nodding. "I fucked up. I realize that now. I thought you needed that push to make you great. I didn't know I was pushing you away the whole time."

"So you're okay with me not going pro?"

"Of course, if that's what you want."

I rub the back of my neck, hardly able to believe years of living under this mental weight are gone like that.

"Can you forgive me?" he asks quietly. The way he sounds… It's like my answer matters to him.

"Yeah. We both played a part in it. And I'm sorry if I let you down—"

"No, you never have. I don't want you to ever think you've disappointed me."

I swallow hard when the thickness in my throat won't go away. That keeps happening too often lately. "Okay."

He lifts the grill lid and pokes at the burgers. "I talked to Marty on my way home last night. He said you're coaching for him now."

"Yeah. I'll start full time in about a week."

"He mentioned something too about you taking over for him one day?"

"It's a possibility. I'm going to take some business classes at the community college and see how I do."

He pauses with his tongs in mid-air. "You're going to college?"

"It's only one class for now, to see if I'm any good at it. Tessa's helping me sign up for the summer semester."

He covers the grill again to keep out the cold air, silent. Is he mad?

"Uncle Marty said he'd work my schedule around my classes," I continue, needing to fill the silence. "And he'll tell me the best ones I should take, like general business management."

"Sounds like you've got it all planned out."

Where before I would have left it at that, not wanting to make waves, I instead ask, "Do you have a problem with it?"

He looks up, his forehead wrinkling. "No. It's just… You made all these plans for your future and I had no clue about any of it. I need to do better about asking how *you're* doing, not how boxing is going."

I turn my head, catching sight of Danielle and Tessa peeking through the blinds of the living room window. What the hell are they doing? Tessa doesn't need to pick up Danielle's bad habits. I put my back to them so I'm not distracted.

"I mean, I've usually got nothing going on. It's only lately things have been happening. Ever since I got roped into Tessa's study, really."

He gives me a confused look. "What study?"

That's right. I never told him about that. I figured he'd only ask why I was wasting my time with that instead of training.

As the burgers finish cooking, I tell him about the relaxation techniques I've been learning. It's probably the first solo conversation we've had in years that doesn't directly relate to boxing, and as we head back inside with the food, a sense of peace fills me I wasn't expecting.

"You look happy," Tessa murmurs, pulling me aside before we go into the kitchen. "Everything went okay, then?"

"You mean you couldn't tell from spying on me through the blinds?"

She bites at her bottom lip, having the grace to look at least a little ashamed. "Danielle said—"

"It's fine." See, I knew it was my sister who instigated it. "It went okay. As good as something like that can go, right?"

She nods, looping her arm through mine. "I'm proud of you for talking to him about it."

She said the same thing the night I'd told him I didn't want to go pro over the phone, too. "You give me too much credit."

"And you don't give yourself enough."

I lean down, giving her a long kiss. "I love you."

She beams up at me, her dark eyes sparkling. "Love you, too."

"Is this what I have to look forward to?" Danielle asks with a smile, interrupting us as she pokes her head out of the kitchen. "PDA every time you're over here? Maybe I shouldn't have been so quick to get you two back on track."

I move over to sling my arm around Danielle's shoulders. "You brought this on yourself, wingwoman."

She chuckles. "I guess I did."

She can tease me all she wants about Tessa. I don't mind. It only means Tessa's here with me, safe and sound.

A bubble of uneasiness crops up in the pit of my stomach at the thought of her safety and what'll happen with Joel tomorrow. The guy's not going to run away, tail tucked between his legs. Not if he went so far as to steal her phone and send me those texts. My instincts never lead me wrong in the ring, and they're screaming at me now that something's on the horizon.

The only thing is, I don't know what.

CHAPTER THIRTY-THREE

TESSA

"ALL RIGHT, THAT'S IT," I announce to Austin. "You're officially finished with the study."

He gets up from his seat, pushing the sleeves of his henley up his forearms. "It was the best study I've ever been a part of."

"You mean the only one."

He flashes me a smile, my heart warming. "That, too."

I move out from behind my desk and hug him, gathering strength. "I have to talk to Joel now."

"Are you positive you don't want me to go with you? I want to make sure you're safe."

I hug him tighter. It's still a little strange to have someone else this concerned for me when I'm used to handling everything on my own. "I already told you. I think he'll respond better if it's only me there. I don't want him on edge from the get-go assuming we're ganging up on him."

"Okay. I'll be waiting in the lobby when you're finished, then. Good luck."

He kisses me, my heart fluttering at the way he pours all his love into the kiss.

"Love you," I whisper, pressing my forehead to his.

"Love you, too."

I take a second to pull myself together after he leaves, then head to the room next door. Joel is packing his bag, smiling as he looks up and notices me.

"Hey, you never texted me back."

I blink, thrown off for a moment before I remember that he had texted asking if I wanted to hang out Thursday night. I'd been so upset over Austin canceling our date, though, I'd forgotten all about it. No wonder he'd asked that after sabotaging my plans.

"You know, my phone's been acting weird lately."

"Oh, no problem. We can get together tonight."

A snort escapes me, despite everything. Is he delusional? "Actually, I wanted to talk to you about my phone. Austin got some texts from me that I definitely didn't send."

He freezes in the middle of picking up his backpack, then sets it back down on the desk. "Uh, okay."

"Do you know anything about it?"

His gaze darts away briefly. "Why would I?"

Wow, he's really going to make me spell it out? "I had lost my phone at about the time the messages were sent. And you were the one who found it."

His lips twist to the side. "What are you suggesting?"

I sigh, tired of beating around the bush. "Did you send those texts to Austin telling him I only want to be friends?"

His expression is carefully neutral. "I thought you *were* only friends with him."

"I was the last time you and I talked. But things have changed since then. And you didn't actually answer my question."

He makes a scoffing sound. "I don't know how you could even accuse me of something like that."

So that's how he's going to play it? Straight up denial? "You were the only one with access to my phone. And since you've made it obvious from the beginning that you don't like him, the motive's pretty clear, too."

He shakes his head. "Did he put this idea in your head? The guy's brainwashed you."

"It's not brainwashing when there's physical evidence on his phone."

"How long have you known me? A year? And you met him a month ago. How can you believe him over me?"

"You still haven't answered the question," I grit out.

He chuckles, but there's no humor in it. "Sounds like you've made up your mind. Why bother asking me, then?"

"Because I want to know why. What would possess you to steal my phone out of my bag and tell lies?"

His gaze flashes with defiance. "Why are you sexting him asking him to lick your pussy?"

The air between us hangs heavy, thick with tension as my cheeks redden. Well, that was a confirmation, at least.

"That was a private conversation. Our relationship is none of your business."

"You made it my business when you got involved with someone from the study."

"I told you before, it has no impact—"

"What, because he's got fucking muscles you lose your mind over him? He's not good enough for you, Tessa."

Okay, now we're getting somewhere, even if he's acting crazy. "And you think you are?" That's what it boils down to, right?

He stands taller, his chest puffing out the slightest bit. "Yeah, I know I am. I've been waiting in the wings for you all this time and you haven't looked twice in my direction."

I stare at him in disbelief. "Well, for starters, you never told me. How am I supposed to read your mind? And you've got some image of yourself as the nice guy, but you're not."

His brows narrow. "Yes, I am."

"You talk over me, you don't listen to me, you're negative and critical." I tick each point off on my fingers, growing angrier the more I go on. "My God, you've brought me coffee for a year when I've said so many times I don't drink it. And then somehow guilt me into thanking you for it."

His mouth opens and shuts as he formulates a response. "If you had an issue with me about those things, you should have told me. I can fix them. I can change. I deserve a chance."

Is he serious? "Joel, I can never trust you again. You sabotaged the best thing that's ever happened to me."

He laughs, a dark sound I've never heard from him that sends a rush of uneasiness through me. "*He's* the best thing that's happened to you? Look, I get that your brain's full of endorphins from all the sex you've been having, but once that wears off, you'll see he's some dumb jock you shouldn't have looked twice at. And you'll be lucky if I give you another chance after that."

I stare at him, dumbfounded. Okay, there's no reasoning with crazy. We're just yelling at each other and name calling now.

I move past him, but he's quick, grabbing my arm to spin me back toward him. "I'm not done talking to you."

A frisson of fear tingles down my spine before I shake it off.

"Seriously, why would you sleep with him?" he demands. "Is it because you stayed with him after the break-in?"

I take a step back, the anger in his voice concerning. "We grew closer after that, yes, but—"

"Fuck." He slams a hand down on the desk, startling me. "I knew I should have made you stay with me. You were supposed to stay with me."

There's that word again. *Supposed.* He said it the night of the break-in, too.

An inkling forms in my mind, incredibly outlandish, but it gains traction, spinning over and over until I can't let go of the thought. "Did you have something to do with the break-in?" I whisper before I can stop myself.

Guilt crosses over his face, so clear I can't explain it away as anything else.

My hand covers my mouth to contain my gasp. "Oh my God, how could you?"

His jaw firms. "It's not what you think."

"Oh my God, oh my God," I mutter on repeat, retreating towards the door.

He says something about how it was only a way for me to see him in a different light, that it was for us, that he didn't actually rob me so it was okay, but I can barely focus, trying to make it to the door without it seeming obvious I'm running away. My hand reaches the knob, fumbling to grip it, and then his palm is there, applying pressure to keep it closed.

"Let's talk about this, okay?" he asks, nervousness seeping into his voice.

I turn and kick backward, connecting with his leg, and open the door, screaming Austin's name. Can he hear me from this far down the hallway?

The door slams shut again as Joel recovers and locks it, then he drags me by the arm over to the far side of the room.

"Stop screaming. You're going to get us in trouble."

"You mean get *you* in trouble. You're crazy." I'm trembling, hardly able to get the words out.

"Just keep your mouth shut, okay? I can still fix this."

"Austin," I scream at the top of my lungs, hoping he hears me.

"Shut up." Joel slams me against the wall, rattling me, and presses his palm over my mouth to silence me.

Oh God, oh God. I squeeze my eyes shut, trying to remember what Austin taught me during our self-defense lessons, but it's all a blur. I never thought I'd actually have to do any of those things.

I stomp my foot as hard as I can on Joel's, and though he makes a noise of pain, he doesn't let go of me. If anything, it only seems to piss him off more. He presses into me so I have no room to move, my arms awkwardly caught between our stomachs, his legs holding mine in place against the wall so I can't maneuver enough to knee him. I had no idea Joel was this strong. Or maybe I'm just that weak.

I struggle to breathe, my head dizzy from that slam, anxiety overtaking me until Austin's deep voice sounds from the hallway, calling my name. Relief crashes over me, my thoughts more in focus now. I'm not alone. He'll save me.

"Don't do anything stupid," Joel whispers through gritted teeth. "Or you'll regret it."

I try to yell again, but it's muffled against his palm. How is Austin going to get in with the door locked?

"If you tell anyone about this, I'll make sure no one believes you," he hisses in my ear. "I'll discredit you. Tell them you've been sleeping with the participants. Say I found you making up data. It'll invalidate the whole study. Is that what you want?"

The doorknob jiggles, my already racing heart somehow going faster. I need to unlock that door.

Austin pounds on it, like a real-life death knell. "Joel, you better open this fucking door right now."

Both of us freeze at the fury in his voice, and it takes me a moment to remember it's not directed at me. I don't have to be scared.

"If you touched a hair on her head, I swear to God…"

Joel's hold on me loosens slightly, his gaze darting wildly, and I use the opportunity to get my arm out from its awkward position and pinch him as hard as I can on the underside of his upper arm. He flinches back, creating more room between us, and I knee him in the groin.

I slip out from between him and the wall as he stumbles back, startling again as there's a slam against the door, the whole frame rattling. Is Austin trying to bust through?

I rush forward, afraid to look back and see if Joel's right behind me.

"Hold on a second," I call out, and unlock the door for him.

Austin rushes in, giving me a quick once over. "Did he hurt you?"

"My head," I tell him, touching the tender spot on my skull.

He turns, violence in his gaze, and I place a staying hand on his wrist, holding him back. If he goes over there, there's no telling what he might do. It would be all I need for Joel to somehow blame Austin for any of this.

There's a murmuring from outside the door and I peek over, realizing a crowd has formed. I guess my screams attracted more than just Austin's attention.

"What's going on in here?" an authoritative voice booms. Dr. Price strides into the room a moment later, stopping when he spots Joel kneeling on the ground, clutching at his crotch.

"She's crazy," Joel says, pain in his voice. Good. I hope his balls hurt like hell. "Don't believe anything she says."

Dr. Price turns to me. "What's he talking about?"

"Joel attacked me. He was trying to cover up a bunch of stuff he's done to me recently, including breaking into my apartment and stealing my phone."

"I didn't steal anything," Joel shouts. "She's lying."

Oh God, what if Dr. Price believes him? "Can you call the police?" I ask, my voice trembling. "I want to file a restraining order against him."

Dr. Price swivels back and forth between us, alarm on his face. "I… Let's call the campus police and see if we can get to the bottom of this." He calls out to the hallway, "Kelly, can you do that?"

"I want the actual police, too," I tell him. I'm pretty sure the campus police's main job is to protect the university more than individual people.

"I'm leaving," Joel says, gingerly standing. "This is bullshit."

Austin steps in front of the door as Dr. Price says, "You stay."

Joel eyes Austin warily. "But I've done nothing wrong."

Dr. Price crosses his arms over his rumpled lab coat. "Then why could I hear Tessa screaming from my office? Why couldn't anyone get in this room? Why is Tessa shaking?"

Oh God, am I?

Joel's lips set mulishly. "I'm not the one at fault here. She's sleeping with one of the participants."

Dr. Price's gaze flicks toward me.

"He's my boyfriend," I explain, gesturing toward Austin.

"I'll pay back any of the money I earned if it's an issue," Austin adds.

Dr. Price turns to Joel. "You're upset that her boyfriend's in the study? Researchers recruit friends and family for their studies all the time."

"I…" Joel stutters.

"And it's an independent six-week study," Dr. Price continues. "As the administrators, you and Tessa don't hold a position of authority or control over the participants." He turns to me next. "As long as nothing… untoward happened in the Stress Lab?"

I clear my throat hastily. "No. Absolutely not."

He focuses on Joel again. "Now, what do you have to say about Tessa's accusations against you?"

Joel looks from person to person and out into the hallway to the crowd. "The whole thing is a misunderstanding."

Oh, no. There's no chance he's going to weasel his way out of this. "What part did I misunderstand?" I ask, my voice not as strong as I'd like, but it'll have to do. "The part where you've been harassing me for weeks about Austin because you're jealous? The part where you staged a break-in at my apartment and tried to force me to stay with you after? Or the part where you stole my phone and sent messages to Austin claiming I didn't want to be with him?"

Joel's jaw goes hard, grinding his teeth, but I'm not giving him a chance for rebuttal yet.

"Or did I misunderstand today," I continue, "when I confronted you about it and you slammed me against the wall and wouldn't let me escape? When you threatened me that I'd regret saying anything. That you'd discredit me and invalidate the study. As if I care about that when it turns out you're a psycho."

He stares at me, nostrils flared, murder in his gaze. "I don't know what I ever saw in a slut like you. You'll open your legs for anyone, won't you?"

Austin tenses, his fists clenching, and I move beside him, whispering, "He's trying to get a rise out of you. Don't give him a reason to press charges." That would be all this situation needs.

He nods once, vibrating with pent-up aggression, but doesn't leave my side.

Dr. Price makes a noise of disbelief. "That's disgusting, Joel. You can't speak to your colleague like that. And you're not helping your case any." He turns toward the door, shouting, "Kelly, how long until the police get here?"

"Um, she's still on the phone with them," another voice pops up. It's Nathan, one of the guys from the study after ours. "Will we be able to use this room today? My first participant is already here."

Dr. Price sighs. "Tessa, you wait in the lobby for the police. Joel, come with me to my office."

Joel shoots daggers at me with his gaze as he exits the room without further comment, and I grip Austin's hand tightly, all the fight leaving me once we're alone.

"Come on," Austin murmurs after a moment, leading me out to the lobby. I ignore the crowd of spectators in the hall, thankful no one has their phones out filming.

"I should have let you come with me to talk to him," I murmur, regret filling me. "I had no idea it would turn out like that."

He tugs me into his chest, kissing the top of my head. "How could you? He's insane. You said he was the one who broke into your apartment?"

"Yeah. I still can't believe it."

"Jesus." He soothes a hand down my back. "How's your head? Do you want me to take you to urgent care to get it checked out?"

"I'm okay. It shocked me more than anything. Everything happened so fast."

"You had me scared out of my mind when I heard you scream." His hand moves to my neck, massaging out the tension there. "I've never felt that kind of… terror."

A swooping sensation settles in my stomach. "What about all the guys you've faced in the ring?" Willingly putting myself in a situation where I'm guaranteed to get punched in the face sounds pretty terrifying to me.

"That's nothing. But if something happened to you…" His fingers brush lightly over my cheek. "I couldn't live with myself."

I swallow heavily, trying not to let emotion get the better of me before I have to give my statement to the police. "When I heard you out in the hall, I knew I'd be okay. That you'd save me."

"I didn't do anything."

"You did. He loosened his hold on me when you showed up. Enough so that I could escape."

"Tessa." He shakes his head, wonder in his voice. "That was all you. You saved yourself. You did everything you were supposed to do."

"No, I got trapped—"

"And you got out. I'm guessing you kneed him in the balls based on how he looked when I came in?"

I nod and he hugs me tighter. "I'm so proud of you."

I smile into his chest. It's been well over a decade since anyone's said that to me. The words are nicer to hear than I thought they'd be. "Thank you."

"Seriously, you did amazing. I hate that you had to use that self-defense training we did, but I'm so glad we did it now. Maybe I should train you in boxing too…"

"Whoa. One thing at a time."

"Right. Police first, boxing later."

I bite my lip, snuggling further into his embrace. Thank God I have him. There's time later to talk about everything that went down and decide on next steps, but for now, I soak up the comfort he gives me, simply wanting a moment of quiet with him.

There's no one else I'd rather have with me right now, no one else who makes me feel so safe. So loved. So worthy. "I love you," I murmur.

He makes a soft sighing sound. "I'll never get tired of hearing you say that. I love you, too."

It's the same for me. And now that I have him, I'm never letting him go.

EPILOGUE
AUSTIN

Six Months Later

BOOTS WINDS herself around my legs as I enter the apartment, meowing up at me. I bend down and pick her up, kissing the top of her head. "What? Tessa didn't pay attention to you all night?"

I glance over at the couch where Tessa's hunched over, staring at something on her computer screen while biting at her thumbnail.

"Everything okay?" I ask, locking the door behind me.

She looks up, blinking a few times before she focuses on me. "When did you come home?"

"Just now." I sit beside her, placing Boots on the cushion next to me. "What are you so absorbed in?"

She sighs, pinching the bridge of her nose, and gestures to her laptop. "The psychology journal I submitted to didn't accept my paper. They said my study is too similar to something they published this month."

"Ah, shit. I'm sorry." She was so stressed out about that, especially since she had to do it by herself. "Can you resubmit it in a few months?" She's explained the process to me before, but sometimes her explanations are a little… technical.

"I could. But I want it all squared away before I apply to grad schools so I can put it on my applications. And that was the same journal Mia got published in, so I always had this idea that I would, too."

I stroke a hand down her arm in comfort. "Are there other journals you can submit to?"

"Yeah, there are. Probably better ones, actually."

"Well, there you go. And let them know it was your part of the study that won. That should help you get in."

Her lips quirk to the side. "Just because the relaxation group outperformed the meditation group doesn't mean I won."

"Well, I was part of that group, so I consider it winning."

She laughs lightly, but the tension doesn't ease from her.

"What else is going on?" I ask, wrapping an arm around her shoulders.

She leans toward me, resting her head against the side of my chest. "I have to finalize my list soon of which grad programs I'm applying for, but I also still have to figure out what my study for this semester should be. I'm supposed to pitch it to Dr. Price in two weeks. I haven't even decided on a topic yet."

"Why are you worried about that? Weren't you telling me last week about all the ideas you have?"

"Yeah, but if I choose one, then I can't do any of the others."

I keep my grin to myself, loving how ambitious she is. "You have a lifetime to do all those studies. Save them for grad school."

She blows out a breath. "Yeah. You're right."

I tug her further into my side. "You want to talk about grad school? You're applying in a few months, right?"

She nods. "There are three good schools within a thirty-minute drive of here I'm considering. But I need to cast a wider net in case they reject me."

Why does she always assume the worst? "Any school would be lucky to have you."

A small smile escapes her before she sobers again. "That's nice of you to say, but I also have to think realistically. I'm worried... Well, what if I have to relocate? We just moved in together a month ago, and your job at Marty's is going so well."

Her hands twist in front of her and I lay a hand on them to stop her from freaking out. "If you have to move, I'm right there with you. Apply wherever you want."

She bites at her bottom lip. "But what about taking over for your uncle in a couple of years? And your family here—"

"Tessa." I release her and turn on the couch to face her, giving her a long, slow kiss until some of the tension leaves her. "You're my family, too. I'll go wherever you do, no questions asked." Yeah, things have been going great working for Uncle Marty, but he'd understand if I had to leave. "Let's cross that bridge when we come to it once you know where you got in."

She gives me a relieved smile. "I know. I shouldn't freak out about it until it actually happens."

Even so, that tension doesn't fully leave her. "What is it?"

She glances up at me and away. "What do you mean?"

"You're still upset about something."

Her hands reach for mine, tracing a finger over my knuckles. "How do you read me so well?"

I wait her out, knowing she'll tell me whatever she has on her mind in due time.

"Joel's getting released next weekend."

I suck in a breath, not expecting her to say that. "But his sentence was for eight months." It's only been six.

She shrugs, still focused on brushing the tip of her index finger over my hand. "I guess they're letting him out early for good behavior."

I keep to myself my comment about what kind of behavior he's capable of. "Is there anything you have to do? In the courts or something?"

She shakes her head.

"And your restraining order is still good?"

"Yeah, there's two and a half years left on it."

"Any chance of them getting those burglary charges to stick?"

"No. They said there wasn't enough evidence and he wouldn't confess to it. Only the assault charge."

I pull her onto my lap, wrapping her in a bear hug. My mind's going a mile a minute, but I need to keep calm for her. "You never have to see him again. He was expelled from your school and he can't get close to you without getting arrested. You're safe."

She clings to me, burrowing into my chest. "God, I'm so glad you're here all the time now." She stiffens, then leans back. "Not that I asked you to move in for safety reasons."

I smile, tugging her close again. "It's just a perk, right?"

She chuckles. "There are a lot of perks to living with you. This last month has been amazing."

"You act like you never saw me before." We pretty much traded off apartments every other night.

"No, but it's different. Like you said, we're a family now. You, me, and Boots."

The cat in question yawns sleepily next to us on the couch.

"Oh, shit. I just remembered something." This is awful timing.

She sits up, alarmed. "What is it?"

"I'm supposed to go out of town next weekend for a tournament. Lawrence told me about it today."

Fear flashes in her eyes. "When Joel's released?"

"I'll tell them I can't do it."

"No. You're about to transition to lead trainer. You can't miss a tournament. I… I'll be fine here."

She's right that I really can't miss it. My guys rely on me and I've got a great winning streak going. But I can't leave her here by herself, anxious with worry. "Come with me, then." I can switch things around and get my own hotel room for just the two of us.

"You're traveling for work. Besides, I have to work next weekend, too. I can't leave town."

"Stay with Danielle, then. Maybe it's best to be out of the apartment completely."

"That's a good idea." She relaxes against me, hugging me tight. "How do you always manage to talk me off the ledge?"

"That's my job."

She smiles into my chest. "Okay, enough about me. Tell me how your day was."

I stroke her back, telling her how Johnson's improving in the ring, how Uncle Marty and I reconciled inventory today, how the Intro to Business class I took over the summer paid off because I understood what he was talking about when he kept going on about distributors and overhead and supply chain issues that I never would have known about previously.

"Mmm," she says, snuggling further into me as I scratch between her shoulder blades, reacting the same way Boots does when I pet her. "My college boy is so smart."

I laugh, trying not to tip her off my lap. "I've taken one class."

"And you got an A. That's a four-point-oh GPA. Higher than mine."

My cheeks flush the slightest bit, even knowing the whole thing's a joke. "Well, I could bomb these next classes coming up. I still can't believe you talked me into taking two this semester." I think I can handle Small Business Management, but Business Law? I don't know anything about law.

"I'll be here to help you every step of the way. And I promise what you learn will pay off one day if you take over for Marty."

I nod, knowing she's right, and stroke my palms down her arms, intertwining our fingers. I rub my thumb over her left ring finger, already anticipating the day I can put a ring on it. Once I make lead trainer at work, I'm putting anything extra I earn with my pay raise into a special savings account for her ring.

"I love you," I whisper. The need to tell her that often still hasn't abated, even six months in.

She doesn't seem to mind, though, leaning back to smile at me. "Love you," she murmurs, kissing me deliciously.

Things have come a long way since those first days of hiding how we felt, convinced the other didn't feel the same. Sometimes it still doesn't seem real that this amazing girl is mine, and I do my best to show her every day how much she means to me.

I deepen the kiss, enjoying her surprise as I pick her up and carry her into our bedroom to lay her on the bed. Her dark eyes gleam with anticipation, desire evident as her gaze rakes me up and down. She's not at all subtle about what she wants anymore.

And I wouldn't have it any other way.

ACKNOWLEDGMENTS

Thank you to my husband for your love and faith in me. And of course for your fanatic-level knowledge of boxing.

Thank you to the bloggers, reviewers, bookstagrammers, and anyone spreading the word about this book. Your time and efforts are invaluable. If you enjoyed the book (or even if you didn't!) please consider writing a review. I love to hear your thoughts.

And a huge thank you to my readers for loving these characters in the Lessons Learned series as much as I do. I'll be making the jump over to the Green Valley world next!

ABOUT THE AUTHOR

Allie is also the author of the Crescent Pass series, the Bishop Brothers series, and the Suncoast University series. She lives in sunny Florida with her husband, daughter, and two cats. A librarian by day, she spends her nights writing happily ever afters. She enjoys reading, playing video games, and all things Disney.

Follow for all the latest book info and news:
Website: alliewinters.com
Newsletter and bonus epilogues: alliewinters.com/extras
Instagram: instagram.com/alliewintersauthor
Facebook: facebook.com/alliewintersauthor

Find Smartypants Romance online:
Website: www.smartypantsromance.com
Facebook: www.facebook.com/smartypantsromance/
Goodreads: www.goodreads.com/smartypantsromance
Twitter: @smartypantsrom
Instagram: @smartypantsromance
Newsletter: https://smartypantsromance.com/newsletter/

ALSO BY ALLIE WINTERS

Want more Austin and Tessa? Get a free sweet and sexy bonus epilogue when you sign up for Allie's newsletter at alliewinters.com/extras.

***

Also in the Lessons Learned series:

Under Pressure (Lessons Learned #1)

Mia knows stress. She's dealt with it her whole life. So when she gets an opportunity to run a psychology study to help her get into grad school, it should be no problem dealing with the prickly guy she suddenly finds herself paired with.

The one she had a secret crush on last year. The one who refuses to let anyone close. The one she's discovering by the day may have a softer side than he lets anyone else see…

Tyler knows stress. He's grappled with it for as long as he can remember. And just because he has to share credit with this girl on his new psychology study doesn't mean he has to be friends with her. Except she somehow keeps worming her way into his life. In school. In the boxing gym.

In his bed.

But everyone knows it's safer to keep to yourself. You can't hurt anyone that way. Even if it means giving up the best thing that's ever happened to him.

As things heat up in the Stress Lab, will this match be able to work together without disruption, or will this growing attraction between them eventually… combust?

Not Fooling Anyone (Lessons Learned #2)

The deal is simple—pretend to be Ethan's girlfriend for a psych study and we each get a nice payday. Despite him being a dumb jock who willingly gets punched for fun at my dad's boxing gym, I can handle it. I've mastered the art of keeping others at a distance. Especially after… Well, never mind that.

Except, I didn't count on him not understanding the definition of boundaries. Suddenly, we're having to fake being in love all over campus to keep up the ruse. And when he tries to slip under the barriers I've worked so hard to create? Yeah, that's not happening. Even if it turns out he's surprisingly understanding… and funny… and charming… and smarter than I ever would have given him credit for. Not to mention that muscled body from all that boxing…

No, that's irrelevant. I may have misjudged him, but that doesn't mean I'm interested. He has no idea what kind of baggage I'm carrying. A relationship is the last thing on my mind.

Even if I'm not fooling anyone.

***

The Crescent Pass series is a contemporary small-town romance trilogy that follows the Taylor family siblings as they find love in the Pacific Northwest.

<u>A Forest Between Us (Crescent Pass #1)</u>

- Owen -

Harper Calloway is the one who got away.

Gorgeous. Vivacious. Witty. Everything my introverted self could never be. And though that single night five years ago is all I had with her, there's no forgetting the girl who steals your heart.

So when the woman in question shows up on my doorstep demanding an annulment for a drunken Vegas wedding I don't fully remember, it seems like a sign. A second chance to make good on that connection I've never felt with anyone else.

Except she doesn't have any interest in reconnecting, even as things between us heat up the longer she stays in town. What will it take to convince her I want forever?

- Harper -

Owen Taylor is not who I expected.

Protective. Thoughtful. Humble. And the sexy lumberjack vibe he's got going on? Who knew I was such a sucker for that?

I didn't come to Crescent Pass to start anything up. My life is in Chicago, not the forests of the Pacific Northwest. But the longer I stay here waiting for an annulment, the harder it is to resist this rugged mountain man who shows me for the first time what it's like to be understood. Cherished. Worshipped.

We both knew from the beginning this couldn't last. So why has he gone and stolen my heart?

<u>A Mountain Divides Us (Crescent Pass #2)</u>

- Kristen -

Eli Andrews wasn't supposed to be anything other than a temporary roommate.

On paper, it all makes sense. I rent out a room to him to earn some much-needed cash when my work hours get cut. I'll stay on my side of the house and he'll stay on his. Away from me and my kids.

But he wasn't supposed to be tall and gorgeous and make butterflies flutter in my stomach. He wasn't supposed to be helpful and charming and supportive in a way I didn't know I needed. He wasn't supposed to waken that part of me that's laid dormant for so long, an attraction building between us the longer he stays. I wasn't supposed to fall under his spell.

Or into his bed.

For years, I've made sensible choices. Ones that are best for me and my kids. Ones that don't involve sexy blue-eyed strangers who are only in town for a month.

Eli Andrews isn't staying in Crescent Pass. But tell that to my heart.

\- Eli -

Kristen Taylor wasn't supposed to be the woman of my dreams.

On paper, it doesn't make sense. She's a widow with two kids, while I'm the guy who avoids relationships. Only, when plans fall through and I'm stuck on a job with nowhere to stay, she's the one who comes through for me.

But she wasn't supposed to be so easy to get along with. She wasn't supposed to show me what a family could really be like. She wasn't supposed to make my heart pound.

Or tempt me beyond belief.

For years, I've kept to myself. It's safer that way. No one to disappoint or hurt you in return. Besides, I'm not staying in Crescent Pass.

So why can't I get her out of my head… or my heart?

<u>A Fire Within Us</u> (<u>Crescent Pass #3</u>) releases Fall 2023.

***

The Bishop Brothers series is a contemporary romance trilogy featuring three sexy billionaire brothers who find love in Manhattan.

<u>Resisting the Billionaire</u> (<u>Bishop Brothers #1</u>)

\- Gabriel – When I'm forced to make a deal with my father to marry the woman of his choosing for a business deal, I never expected to find someone I connect with. Someone who doesn't fawn all over me because I'm the heir to a billion dollar fortune. Someone who sees the real me. And someone I can't get enough of in turn.

There's only one problem—I can't have her. She's the wedding planner.

- Mackenzie - It's the chance of a lifetime—plan the wedding of a billionaire's son that'll put my event planning business on the map and get me out of debt. A no brainer, right?

Except the bride wants nothing to do with this arranged marriage. And as the groom and I get closer, the professional lines between us keep blurring until there's something there neither of us can deny. With my business on the line and our chemistry off the charts, I'm torn whether I should keep resisting the one person I never expected to fall for.

Marrying the Billionaire (Bishop Brothers #2)

- Serena - Marrying the man of your dreams after crushing on him for the last decade should be cause for celebration. So why am I crying alone in the honeymoon suite on my wedding night? Because there's just one problem—it's a fake marriage. Purely for appearances as part of a business deal between our fathers' companies.

But I can't sit idly by pretending this is only a platonic relationship, especially as sparks begin to fly between us. So what will I have to do to convince my stoic Prince Charming I want him for real? And what will I risk along the way?

- Archer - The plan is simple—act like a husband in love publicly after I foolishly got myself involved in this fake marriage, and behind closed doors keep things separate. But the longer we continue this charade attending events and staging selfies, the more I'm unsure what's fake and what's not, especially when things start to heat up in private.

As the successor to my father's billion dollar company, work has been my life. Focusing on my job has never been harder, though, when there's a temptress living in my guest bedroom. What are the chances this business deal of a marriage could turn into the real thing? The last person I ever expected to fall for is… my wife.

Seducing the Billionaire (Bishop Brothers #3)

- Connor - It's all on me now. The billion-dollar company I just inherited from my late father. The public eye waiting for me to slip up. The pressure of keeping it all together.

At least there's one bright spot in my life—my new assistant, Emma. My dream woman come to life if I didn't know better.

It's too bad the paparazzi would have a field day if they discovered something going on between us. I can't afford for anything to jeopardize my new role as CEO of Bishop Industries.

Even if she is temptation personified.

- Emma - It was supposed to be a simple assignment. Become Connor Bishop's new assistant and convince him to buy my father's company, Montague Media. So how do I do that? By any means necessary, according to my dad—including seduction. Otherwise, I lose everything.

But no one told me how hard it would be to seduce a billionaire who insists on acting like a perfect gentleman, especially when real feelings begin to emerge. At what point do I stop the charade and tell him who I really am? Before or after I fall in love with him?

***

Check out the Suncoast University series – Four steamy new adult romances that will have you swooning.

Let Go (Suncoast University #1)

- Charlotte - Putting yourself out there? Getting close to others? No, thanks, I'll pass. It's safer to keep to yourself. I've learned that lesson the hard way. So when I accidentally tell the muscled hunk I've been secretly drooling over all semester how I really feel about him, it's not like I meant for him to take an interest in me. I don't want a boyfriend. Not even when it turns out he's so much more than just brawn.

My goal for so long has been simple—get into grad school. And when I get a dream TA position at the beginning of the new semester that will help me achieve just that, I'll have to forget about him now that he's my student. Easy, right?

- Luke - I can't get her out of my head—the shy, sexy brunette that's trying so hard to keep me at a distance. I can be patient, though. Anything to break through that reserve and get under her shields. But just when I thought I've succeeded, she's off-limits. Say hello to my new TA. Even though I'm hot for teacher, there's no way she would risk this opportunity. Right?

Watch Me (Suncoast University #2)

- Samantha - I need a place to stay ASAP when my living arrangements fall through before college starts. And I shouldn't have any trouble resisting my new roommate… despite how much I find myself connecting with him.

- Levi - I have absolutely no interest in the beautiful blonde living in the room next door. She's not my type. Not even when it turns out she's nothing like I expected.

She's only here for the summer, so it shouldn't be a big deal to act on this attraction before she leaves. It doesn't have to mean anything, right?

No One Else (Suncoast University #3)

- Evan - I messed up. I admitted to the girl of my dreams I'm in love with her, only to have her run away. Why don't they ever warn you things like that happen?

Now that we're paired up for a class project, I have to figure out a way to keep things from being weird between us. I can't lose her again.

- Natalie - We shared a kiss the night after I broke up with my boyfriend of three years. A heart-stopping, panty-melting kiss I still dream about. But I wasn't ready then for anything more.

Now that I am, he's unavailable. What will it take to get us both on the same page - and stay there?

First and Only (Suncoast University #4)

- Jake - When my dreams of going pro are crushed by a career-ending knee injury, I have to figure out how to use brains over brawn for the first time to graduate college. Enter Eden, my new Biology tutor. Except she doesn't want to be paid in the usual way. She wants me to give her relationship tutoring to attract a guy she likes. But this shy, awkward brainiac is turning out to be so much more than I expected. In the words of a scientist, will this equal exchange turn out to be more than the sum of its parts?

- Eden - Hot guys don't fall for nerds like me. It's just a fact of life—one I've come to accept like gravity or thermodynamics. So even though others think Jake's interested in me, I know it's just this tutoring deal we have going on. I show him the electron transport system and he shows me how to kiss. Simple as that. There's no sense in getting my hopes up, even as I realize this ex-jock and I fit together in a way I never thought possible. Rarely does an equal exchange turn out to be more than the sum of its parts. Even when I desperately want it to.

ALSO BY SMARTYPANTS ROMANCE

<u>Green Valley Chronicles</u>

<u>The Love at First Sight Series</u>

<u>Baking Me Crazy by Karla Sorensen (#1)</u>

<u>Batter of Wits by Karla Sorensen (#2)</u>

<u>Steal My Magnolia by Karla Sorensen (#3)</u>

<u>Worth the Wait by Karla Sorensen (#4)</u>

<u>Fighting For Love Series</u>

<u>Stud Muffin by Jiffy Kate (#1)</u>

<u>Beef Cake by Jiffy Kate (#2)</u>

<u>Eye Candy by Jiffy Kate (#3)</u>

<u>Knock Out by Jiffy Kate (#4)</u>

<u>The Donner Bakery Series</u>

<u>No Whisk, No Reward by Ellie Kay (#1)</u>

<u>Dough You Love Me? By Stacy Travis (#2)</u>

<u>Tough Cookie by Talia Hunter (#3)</u>

<u>The Green Valley Library Series</u>

<u>Love in Due Time by L.B. Dunbar (#1)</u>

<u>Crime and Periodicals by Nora Everly (#2)</u>

<u>Prose Before Bros by Cathy Yardley (#3)</u>

<u>Shelf Awareness by Katie Ashley (#4)</u>

<u>Carpentry and Cocktails by Nora Everly (#5)</u>

<u>Love in Deed by L.B. Dunbar (#6)</u>

Dewey Belong Together by Ann Whynot (#7)

Hotshot and Hospitality by Nora Everly (#8)

Love in a Pickle by L.B. Dunbar (#9)

Checking You Out by Ann Whynot (#10)

Architecture and Artistry by Nora Everly (#11)

<u>Scorned Women's Society Series</u>

<u>My Bare Lady by Piper Sheldon (#1)</u>

<u>The Treble with Men by Piper Sheldon (#2)</u>

<u>The One That I Want by Piper Sheldon (#3)</u>

<u>Hopelessly Devoted by Piper Sheldon (#3.5)</u>

<u>It Takes a Woman by Piper Sheldon (#4)</u>

<u>Park Ranger Series</u>

<u>Happy Trail by Daisy Prescott (#1)</u>

<u>Stranger Ranger by Daisy Prescott (#2)</u>

<u>The Leffersbee Series</u>

<u>Been There Done That by Hope Ellis (#1)</u>

<u>Before and After You by Hope Ellis (#2)</u>

<u>The Higher Learning Series</u>

<u>Upsy Daisy by Chelsie Edwards (#1)</u>

<u>Green Valley Heroes Series</u>

Forrest for the Trees by Kilby Blades (#1)

Parks and Provocation by Juliette Cross (#2)

Letter Late Than Never by Lauren Connolly (#3)

<u>Story of Us Collection</u>

My Story of Us: Zach by Chris Brinkley (#1)

My Story of Us: Thomas by Chris Brinkley (#2)

<u>Seduction in the City</u>

<u>Cipher Security Series</u>

<u>Code of Conduct by April White (#1)</u>

<u>Code of Honor by April White (#2)</u>

Code of Matrimony by April White (#2.5)

Code of Ethics by April White (#3)

Cipher Office Series

Weight Expectations by M.E. Carter (#1)

Sticking to the Script by Stella Weaver (#2)

Cutie and the Beast by M.E. Carter (#3)

Weights of Wrath by M.E. Carter (#4)

Common Threads Series

Mad About Ewe by Susannah Nix (#1)

Give Love a Chai by Nanxi Wen (#2)

Key Change by Heidi Hutchinson (#3)

Not Since Ewe by Susannah Nix (#4)

Lost Track by Heidi Hutchinson (#5)

Educated Romance

Work For It Series

Street Smart by Aly Stiles (#1)

Heart Smart by Emma Lee Jayne (#2)

Book Smart by Amanda Pennington (#3)

Smart Mouth by Emma Lee Jayne (#4)

Play Smart by Aly Stiles (#5)

Look Smart by Aly Stiles (#6)

Smart Move by Amanda Pennington (#7)

Lessons Learned Series

Under Pressure by Allie Winters (#1)

Not Fooling Anyone by Allie Winters (#2)

Can't Fight It by Allie Winters (#3)

The Vinyl Frontier by Lola West (#4)

Out of this World